"Erin Stalcup has written a collection of stories and a novella that shows us what metaphor and magic can do and why both are so vital to our human reality. The collection manages to be both sexy and scientific and pushes us to rethink easy aesthetic values. In *And Yet It Moves* even a wake of feeding vultures is transcendent in its beauty."

TIPHANIE YANIQUE, author of *Land of Love and Drowning*

"*And Yet It Moves* is an exquisite collection, a breath of new air, fresh and sparkling. What pleasure in seeing our world as Erin Stalcup does, the magic revealed in among the mundane, in accepted laws of nature, in the weary human heart—which in these stories is repeatedly revived. A gift to us all, this is a lyrical winning argument for adoring the 'gleaming and grotesque' beauty of our fragile, surprising lives. Bravo!"

ROBIN BLACK, author of *Life Drawing*

"Erin Stalcup's intelligent, provocative stories grow inside your mind and body long after you have absorbed their marvelous inward and outward views of the individual heart and the human community. These stories cast you into the darkest dreams, and they startle you awake. Like all mystical experiences, *And Yet It Moves* opens your heart by breaking it."

KEVIN MCILVOY, author of *Hyssop*

"Brace yourself for Erin Stalcup's uncanny access to heretofore unknown forces, strange particles, and hidden dimensions. Mourners and exotic dancers, elevator operators and scientists— Stalcup explores each of her characters with remarkable compassion, depth, and insight. These virtuosic stories defy gravity and genre with equal aplomb, utterly transforming our sense of the world we thought we knew."

TIM HORVATH, author of *Understories*

"Stalcup offers readers a world viewed through a filter—one in which the forces of love can counteract the forces of gravity, and where even the most hardened ghostwriters are eventually haunted by their own words. Part parable, part cautionary tale, these stories are sure to stun the heart, steal the breath, and leave readers in that wondrously uncharted terrain between the grotesque and the sublime."

B. J. HOLLARS, author of *This Is Only a Test*

"Simply put: these stories defy gravity. Step aside Newton, *And Yet it Moves* assigns Stalcupian laws of motion and movement, and is sure to pull its readers in."

ZACHARY TYLER VICKERS, author of *Congratulations on Your Martyrdom!*

"Erin Stalcup is a writer new to me, and I am happy to make her literary acquaintance in this strong collection of stories suggesting an important new literary innovator. These stories are original in concept and execution, clearly informed but not constrained by contemporary trends in fiction. The narrative sensibility is intelligent and highly personal, attuned to all that is askew in contemporary culture but nonetheless especially interested in acts of generosity and kindness. Stalcup is a writer who manages to suggest the possibility of goodness without sacrificing a tough-minded insistence on reporting foibles and follies, often of the comic variety."

VALERIE SAYERS, author of *The Powers: A Novel*

And Yet It Moves

break away books

Michael Martone, series editor

And
Yet
It
Moves

Erin Stalcup

INDIANA UNIVERSITY PRESS

Bloomington & Indianapolis

This book is a publication of

INDIANA UNIVERSITY PRESS
Office of Scholarly Publishing
Herman B Wells Library 350
1320 East 10th Street
Bloomington, Indiana 47405 USA

iupress.indiana.edu

The paper used in this publication
meets the minimum requirements of
the American National Standard for
Information Sciences—Permanence
of Paper for Printed Library Materials,
ANSI Z39.48-1992.

*Manufactured in the
United States of America*

*Cataloging information is available
from the Library of Congress*

ISBN 978-0-253-02203-5 (paperback)
ISBN 978-0-253-02213-4 (ebook)

1 2 3 4 5   21 20 19 18 17 16

for
JUSTIN,
my favorite.

Contents

Acknowledgments

Thank you to everyone who helped these stories become a book. Michael Martone, for showing me the tradition of "nontraditional" writing, for reading this book (along with Valerie Sayers) the way I hoped it could be read, and for being a champion of innovative writing—here at Break Away Books, and elsewhere. Sarah Jacobi, for finessing these stories into their final form. Robin Black, for your constant loving guidance. Mom and Dad, for the love and encouragement, and for agreeing that this is a thing worth doing with my life. Seth and Carla, for the love and support. Kathryn Wiens, Erika McDonald, and Rebecca Bush, for the companionship. Thank you to all these educators and writers who told me something I needed to hear: Dave Thompson, Sylvia Cox, Kevin McIlvoy, CJ Hribal, Rick Reiken, Judy Doenges, Susan Neville, Moustafa Bayoumi, Miro Penkov, Kelly Wisecup, Tiphanie Yanique, Jynne Dilling Martin, Anna Clark, Amy Minton, Allison Paige, Cyndi Reeves, Dave Peterson, Gary Hawkins, Landon Godfrey, Jonathn Yukich, Jessica Seessel, Jamie Poissant, Tim Horvath, Jason Robinson, Zach VandeZande, Andy Briseño, Sidney Thompson, Elise Matthews, Kyle McCord, and most of all, Courtney Craggett. Thank you to my colleagues at Northern Arizona University and throughout Flagstaff, some of whom were my first teachers: Ann Cummins, Jane Armstrong, Allen Woodman, Barbara Anderson, Monica Brown, Nicole Walker, Angie

Hansen, Jeff Berglund, Steve Rosendale, Karen Renner, James Jay, Jesse Sensibar, and Stacy Murison. Jim Simmerman, thank you for making me think of myself as a poet, even when I write prose. Thank you to every magazine editor who believed these stories were worth reading, and every author and scientist who made me think they might be worth writing. Thank you to my students, who teach me every day. Thank you to my fellow editors at *Waxwing*, and everyone I've published there, for the inspiration. Thank you, everyone listed, for your friendship, and for creating such a vibrant community. Thank you to the nun who inspired Sister Violet. And Justin Bigos, thank you for being the best possible partner—in art, education, editing, and life; I am enamored, ravenously in love, so glad to be by your side.

And Yet It Moves

Gravity

"We are suspenders of disbelief, easily enchanted by possibility, addicted to wonder. So whatever measure of faith we harbor in the fallibility of gravity may, like our faith in so many things, be sustained not by facts or lack of facts as much as by the sheer strength of our longing for it to be so."

—JON MOOALLEM

I longed to fall in love in the way of the cinema, fairy tales, tall tales and great novels of all time—I had faith it would happen to me someday, any day now.

He dressed like a banker but didn't stand like one. I wore skirts every day. We didn't always ride the elevator together, but often. If we were waiting for it side by side, when it arrived he would hold the door, let me walk in first as if he'd opened that door, as if he had drawn aside a velvet curtain to a box seat at the opera. I'd walk to the corner and he'd stand in front of me, let me see his back. He wore well-cut suits I could sense the texture of just by looking—I didn't touch, for a long time. The elevator floor pushed against our feet and our feet pushed downward, driven by a force that felt like it was coming from above, but wasn't, instead drawn down from the center of the earth that wanted us to return to where we came from, ashes to ashes, dust to dust. Our feet were pulled downward and the floor of the elevator pushed upward and it pushed harder so we rose.

And then one day as we lifted through the levels of a building he looked up, into the mirrored ceiling, and I did too, and we saw each other, our faces framed by the tops of many heads, the ceiling a goldenish metal so that our faces were lit, glazed. We smiled. I got off the elevator first, as I always did, and as I stepped around him I drew my hand across his back. We were both wearing heavy golden rings, then.

* * *

I always said the number for my floor, seventeen please, and one day he didn't push the button. We sailed up while the others exited, and then we were on the top floor. The doors slid open, he walked out and into the corner office. I followed. He shut the rich mahogany door without windows so no one from the office could see inside. Two walls were glass overlooking the city, we could be seen by others in the other towers if they picked this window to look into out of all the hundreds of windows. He lifted me onto his desk, lifted my skirt around my waist, ran his thumb inside the top of my thigh-high hose, said, "Nice," knelt before me. And before he knew my name I was moaning. Before I opened my eyes he was standing and inside of me, and when I wrapped my legs around him I felt like I was tumbling, like we were spiraling up and away. He yelled himself into me and when we opened our eyes we were up against the ceiling. His papers, pens, phone, computer, briefcase, briefs, printer, chair, desk, staplers, post-it notes, paper clips, thumbtacks, books, bookends, newspapers were spinning slowly around us, as if in a decelerated tornado. Everyone everywhere was screaming. We looked into the windows of the other towers and it was as if someone had shaken all the seventy-eight-story

And Yet It Moves

compartmentalized snow globes, people and their objects hovered in the air, slowly swooned and swayed and lifted and lowered as if on the moon.

"I always knew I could do this," I said—break a bond, be released upward, change the world—and he dipped me into a back-bending kiss that tipped us upside down, though down was now just a concept.

We spun and flitted and delighted, moved around the room touching things, we took off our rings and let them float and one time they clanged against each other, making a barely audible tinging sound, then drifted away.

* * *

At his place we took our clothes off and they floated next to us, the puddle of a dress, his trousers on their own walk. No fetters, we were everywhere and right there at once. We bounced around the room, my legs wrapped around his waist to keep us together, then we tried to stay suspended in the middle. "Stay with me, stay in the air with me," he said, and I thought we could just hover, still and balanced, but we couldn't, not for long—every tiny move propelled us: a shift in the bend of my hip made us scoot backward a touch, a roll of my shoulder made us spin—the body was much more responsive to the body without the weight of gravity pulling down, tying us to a center.

We rose to the ceiling and touched it simultaneously, both of us reaching out as it approached, both stretching fingertips to have that feeling as soon as we could, both with the same awed, child-like expression of amazement and desire to feel it fully, and I knew we'd done the right thing. Our fingers hit the roof of the room, our palms were against it, and then we were flying away, the contact enough without friction to send us orbiting back down toward the floor. Falling felt like flying, felt like the rising we'd just done, and as we spiraled and cascaded and tumbled without speed, without fear of landing, we touched the rug and bounded back upward.

Soon I'd lost my direction, didn't know up with eyes closed. The entire room became our bed, we covered most of it, the furniture so mixed, lifted, and jumbled that opening my eyes didn't immediately tell me which direction I was headed. Only the fastened light fixture and stapled-in carpet were left as signs.

When it was all over we thought to swim to the bathroom and bathe together, but of course water no longer fell. We toweled each other off, went to collect our clothes.

* * *

He called his wife, who was traveling on business. She was safe, but scared, because it had happened there too, gravity had gone away everywhere, and of course she didn't know why. He didn't tell her then what she would be arriving home to—him gone, and me too, moved into a new place together—but he did speak to her soon after she arrived; he never told me how she reacted, but I presumed there was screaming and attempts at slapping, that drab, matte, heavy woman's palm flying toward his face, though it's difficult to hit someone hard these days.

* * *

I went to my house, packed my things by snatching them from the air. I swam through the halls, my husband following me, and he couldn't exactly grab me and yank me to face him because any pull on me yanked him too. There was still air to carry sound, air to swim through, but his yelling felt muffled by all the objects floating through every room. I packed two suitcases as full as I could and they never felt weighted. I told him the truth, that I'd been slowly suffocating for years, that I'd never loved him the way

And Yet It Moves

I wanted to love someone, I just married him because I didn't have a good enough reason to say no but finally realized I hadn't had a good enough reason to say yes, either. "Now?" he asked. "You're leaving me now, when everything's crazy and up in the air?"

"I can't think of a better time," I said, and swam away.

＊ ＊ ＊

Once you cut the chain and leap, there are no chains, all is leaping. When gravity goes you see all the chains are our own invention. It was never a force, it was something we postulated and then lived by. We felt the pull downward because we'd been told we were supposed to feel it. When you decide that obligation isn't really there, it isn't.

＊ ＊ ＊

He brought me flowers in vases weekly, and as they twirled around the rooms often the water stayed inside. He bought me jewels, looped them around my neck, slid them through holes in my ears, twined them around my wrists, left them on my body when my clothing was removed.

After our lovemaking, puddles would sometimes slip from me and stay suspended, glimmering, moonlight turned liquid. He liked to take my clothes off and arrange them in the air into my shape, so that he could watch the clothed me while he touched the naked me. I watched too.

＊ ＊ ＊

All the doors were removed from the elevator shaft, the elevator itself taken away, the inside refurbished, tiled, so that it was a long pleasant column of air, lit, no longer dark and frightening. To get to another floor we boosted ourselves up through the huge tube: some flutter-kicked their feet, some pulled themselves up with the cord left running through the middle, some bought little propellers that blew them up and along. No longer the ritual of waiting, of pressing bodies together in a box, pushing buttons, being lifted.

❀ ❀ ❀

Sleep was so different—there was no need for a mattress, something to cushion from the pressing down, no hard surface to ever be trapped against, again. We drifted, and to stay warm and feel coddled we began by carrying our blankets with us, wrapped and tangled around limbs. But in the night they would slip away, end up across the room, blown in their own limp trajectory.

Some people laced themselves to their beds so they stayed there all night as it floated, with purchased lashes or whatever rope or silk they had lying around the house. I presumed with all these straps more and more people were going S&M, loving being tied up, reenacting a former form of being ensnared; for comfort, maybe. One bound, one free, the pinioned one relieved. Your fate is not up to you to decide. Like the laws of physics, once. There used to be certain things determined as true. You jump, you fall. Now no.

Once, for old times' sake, we locked ourselves in a closet, to fuck without flying around. I pressed my hands on the ceiling and pressed him against a wall. He gripped me and the wall next to us and we remembered what it felt like to have leverage. For a moment I missed the friction I used to fight against.

❀ ❀ ❀

It seemed that the earth was still orbiting like before. There was still night and day, seasons. We still had our moon. Still dawn and dusk, twilight and noon still came at the same hours. Though, gravity used to hold the air around the earth, drew an atmosphere down around the globe like a down comforter, feathers to sustain us, keep us warm, alive. But it was floating away, no longer held here; we wondered when it would become harder to catch our breath. People dreaded sunburn and asphyxiation, plans were being made for SPF 212 and portable oxygen tanks. We didn't want the weight of a tank to make us feel bound all over again—the tank would float like we did, of course, but carry the memory of weight. I said we could think of it like we were underwater explorers, swimming in our new world. He said he'd rather be flying through the air.

He said, "This is all starting to feel like real life."

*　*　*

He and I, we didn't feel guilty, knew the planet agreed to what we had done. The loosening of bonds, lifting of laws, the planet reconfigured itself around us, and without the planet's grip it was him I was laced to. Threads of what we had done wove us together, stitching my skin to his. The string could stretch, however far we moved apart we were still tied, filaments through our flesh, taut, always lenient, our bond a bind as we bounded around this new world.

*　*　*

At work we'd meet in his office, spy on the people in the buildings across the way. Sometimes it was bosses and secretaries, sometimes custodians and CEOs, sometimes it was higher-ups in their corner offices with their wives, then mistresses. We were the ones who broke the chain, we were the first to fall into love upward, but of course other lovers got to benefit. We watched them in all their positions, all their inventions, we marveled at their acrobatics and their passions. The lovemaking of those who didn't have much time.

And then I'd want him so badly it would be a bodily force, and time after time I'd make him duplicate our beginning. "Pretend it just happened, pretend we just made it happen," I'd beg, and he'd tip me backward, wheel me upward to the ceiling, kiss me with the zeal of the first day, but it was always playacting, a memory enacted, he never kissed me with that passion when we weren't performing.

*　*　*

No longer any separation between all of us and space, nothing dividing our orb from the universe any longer, I could swim to the moon. The air around me was sky, the sky was space, and my will moved me through it. I told myself I could go anywhere I wanted.

*　*　*

When my mother died—no surprise, but something that still felt sudden—I had her cremated. Burials were problematic. Gravediggers had to toss the earth in a bolted-down lidded box, then bury the coffin by covering each shovelful with a sheet to keep it there, then plant grass on top and nail it down until the roots knitted the soil back together. My lover didn't know how to comfort me in grief so I alone took off the lid of the urn in the forest, shook it, loosened the cinders upward, what had been burnt in an electric kiln in these days after fire, ashes to air, dust to sky. Some collected in a cloud around me—I intuitively held my breath until I remembered I breathed packaged air, no danger of inhaling ash—but some seemed to rise.

When I got home I wanted the comfort a body can give so I went to him, not talking, took off his clothes, wrapped my legs around his waist to keep us locked, and the floating around the room didn't make me feel jubilant, I felt uncentered, homeless. My internal gyroscope was tired of keeping up, and it wasn't the dizziness of passion or desire, but of fatigue. I clung to him to remember where I was, I felt like I was sinking and only he could keep me

And Yet It Moves

afloat, I looked at him to try to remember why we were both here, in this weightless world, and he was looking right through me, as if I weren't there, as if I were air.

* * *

As a child I'd been comforted that the air wasn't empty, that there were invisible particles between me and every object, touching me, containing me but leaving me free to move, encircling and cradling me, carrying messages from my surface to the surfaces of everyone else. I felt less alone when I thought the air encased me, entered me, came into my lungs and then back into what everyone else breathed. But then there were no particles, no invisible atoms, there was nothing there, and it was impossible to feel free, or held, or comforted, when making love to someone in a gas mask.

* * *

I thought he would stay unbound with me, bound to only me, our immorality would bring immortality, we would always feel as giddy and as unfettered as when we made the snap happen. But it couldn't remain free-falling always, freedom, the same elation from the beginning. He and I weren't enticed to pinwheel through rooms, didn't throw the things we had thrown just to see them fly newly across space. I thought we would love the sensation always—no longer beholden we were emboldened, assented to ascent, gave in to the vertiginous spin. People used to think the stone fell to earth because it was made of earth, we fell to sky because we were sky. The gravity which bent starlight, made them appear to be in places they weren't, no longer bent us to its will.

But even that broken taboo became tedious.

We waited for other conventions to crack, for a breaking of another prohibition to splinter a law. We wondered if it was still only our responsibility, if we were still the ones who had to do it.

I imagined electricity and magnetism breaking apart, becoming two phenomena. Light would no longer exist. No x-rays, no ultraviolet, no cancerous radiation—but no light to see by. The bulbs all failing, the sun no longer sending forth rays. I imagined entropy reversing, so that broken glasses mended, tangled sheets made themselves into a tidy bed, mussed hair styled itself. Clothes would fly onto my body, and the furniture coasting around our rooms would right itself, find a sustainable pattern that didn't require gravity to hold it. Given a day the dishes would be done, the floor swept, the books tallied, the cracks on the sidewalk vanished, all surfaces varnished. The law of thermodynamics would no longer apply, heat not moving by contact, warmth not draining predictably from the hotter body to the cooler. We would flush for no reason, freeze without cause. Two touching bodies could be flaming and chilled, not affecting the other at all, not bringing the other into balance. If E doesn't equal mc^2 then energy could create itself without destroying matter, sparks could fly from my fingertips, light from my eyes, without singeing flesh, without sacrifice.

Light would hit us like sand, like water. The speed of light might shift, so that a flipped switch took days to react, light flooding a room before we thought to pull the cord. Sunsets and sunrises would happen instantly, or take days to take place, so that we'd exist in a constant state of dusk or dawn, like cars colliding, the light always coming, always going, never staying.

✽ ✽ ✽

He and I wanted to feel we were in a new world again. We thought of all the bans we could disobey to smash laws. We brought home homosexual lovers, we had threesomes and orgies, we made love with children, with our siblings and parents, animals. In our hysterical desire not to be trapped again in a world like the one we always knew, we had sex with strangers and paid some for it. Fucked willing and unwilling partners.

And all we managed to accomplish was forgetting why we had done this first thing, why we had made love in an office, in a tower up in the sky, windows all around, exposing us to whatever strangers wanted to see. Because we'd been so drawn to each other that we couldn't do anything else. We flung ourselves into each other's arms and everyone got flung upward, and we couldn't make it happen again, and we couldn't remember why we'd leapt in the first place.

* * *

And so today I just don't want to do it anymore. I've stepped out of our house, I look at all the people burdened by silver reservoirs and even the stylish small ones look vulgar, and all they want is normalcy, all they want is to feel the same safe way they've always felt, feel it again if it gets disturbed. They want to go back to before, pretend none of this happened. I want to go back to after, pretend it just happened, pretend it happens every day—enthralled the only standard, the world always reflecting the euphoria my lover and I feel.

My faith was wrong. And even though all these people are just like me, wanting something they can never have, I don't feel drawn to any of them. A woman walks her dog in its own mini-mask, a man in a suit gets in a modified jet-propelled car to go to work, a woman unloads groceries from her tiny helicopter hovering by her door. Two people float by, holding hands, and they have an oxygen-filled dome around both of their heads so that they can talk, and kiss. Before, you had to remove the mouthpiece from your air tank, kiss while holding your breath—I hadn't seen this solution before. They twirl, hold hands, I can hear their laughter even though it's impossible for it to travel to me.

Today, I've stepped outside of my house without my air tank. I don't want that weight, even in a weightless world. I look into the windows of the house I moved into, I see my lover, his gas mask obscuring the face I fell for. He doesn't look up, he doesn't see me, his eyes don't connect to mine one last time. He doesn't know how to keep me, he hasn't realized he just let me go, and so I slacken, I let myself lift and float away. The air has all been released, and I am breathless again.

In the Heart of the Heart of the Empire

After William H. Gass

A PLACE

An island next to the richest island in the world, connected by cabled bridges and aerated tunnels. Rain brings the smell of the sea that surrounds it, men and women clean it daily, and it is filthy. Buildings of low brick and stone, some towers of glass, and the sky goes silk moiré behind these lineations, the lit shifting blur blocked by places where people live and work and eat and sleep and fuck and run. Clouds leap through loops of razor ribbon and you can count the stars on any given night: twelve, seventeen, three, eight. Pigeons, rats, and roaches outnumber people; more languages are spoken here than any place in the world. A cluster of discrete villages clinging to a homogenous metropolis, a tangle of immigrants across the river from suits and banks and postcards and skyscrapers that sometimes crumble, it is not named a stolen native name like its neighbor. It is layered: we all live on top of each other, and under.

*　*　*

I came here, to B, from Indiana, from a small town fastened to a field, years ago now.

Now I am here, still, in recovery from love.

WEATHER

The time of year when humidity stops clinging and the air releases us to appreciate the bright dome above, the coming crispness. Each tree flings itself into color, brittleness, death at its own pace, each a different shade—green, veined with umber, aflame in orange, bare—as if they can't concur on the proximity of winter, the appropriate response.

A man's body can't pace time like a woman's.

I pace your absence: I bled the day you left, so I know when it's been twenty-eight days after, twenty-eight days after, twenty-eight days.

MY HOUSE

Whoever lived here died or was pushed out, so workers fixed cracks in the walls, painted, tore up the kitchen and bathroom floors and retiled, replaced cabinets and stove and refrigerator, but left the wood floors, other people's dirt in the cracks, generations of what couldn't be swept away. Parquet, shined from varnish and burnished by feet. Management negotiated so I pay twice what the family before paid (I asked to see old leases) but rent-controlled; the longer I stay the more reasonable it becomes. If the neighborhood continues to fill and if I stay for decades I could end up with one of those legendary apartments, a steal, a deal no one can believe. It takes commitment. I've put in four years so far.

I filled the rooms with the newest appliances, and the roaches that had hidden during construction came back through the pipes and filled them.

A PERSON

She invented the term Patrician Portion—the percentage of tax dollars acquired through luxury purchases (defined as any

And Yet It Moves

nonnecessity: HDTV to a Lexus, espresso machine to a mansion in Forest Highlands) allocated to the military. It is determined by the amount of sales tax a government channels to the army and the quantity of luxury purchases the people of that country make. Not only the patrician class makes these purchases, of course—the most impoverished class is known to spend money on brand-name sneakers and iPods, and most people own a gadget they don't really need: garlic press, different glasses for different kinds of wine, books. Most of these purchases contribute just a few cents to the Patrician Portion. Under a dollar.

Her dissertation was on how taxation funds neocolonialism, how Americans' desire for material goods explicitly funds our military aggression and gives implicit permission because we so willingly pay for it. Almost as long as the United States of America has existed, our Patrician Portion has been the highest of all the nations, while some countries have a Patrician Portion approaching zero: little military, little luxuries available, little spending, a phenomenon we can't fathom.

She teaches at a college. She's famous in certain circles, studies shit no one knows about, shit that keeps her up at night. Though, she'd be awake anyway.

WIRES

Electrical wires parcel the sky, carry currents, voices, television images, words and scenes stretched thin. Birds perch on the wires, outside what used to be our window. I never should have stayed here.

The birds are starlings.

You drew birds on my skin, in ink.

I drew birds on your skin. I told you orgasm was like that, like a flock of swerving birds. I could predict when they would veer but I would always be wrong. They'd cut a moment before or after.

You drew birds on my skin, in flight; waves that tumbled an instant before or after you thought they would, throwing back light at the summit; bars and musical notes, symphonies at crescendo. You used a quill, metal-nibbed, and sometimes it scratched. I thought you might tattoo me, run ink into the wound, and I didn't mind.

But you never drew birds resting on a wire, the birds that gather outside my window, the swarm that accumulates to jaw and snarl at me.

They keep me awake. They mimic car alarms. You didn't predict them.

You drew brackets on my sternum. This is us, you said. Everything else is outside.

THE CHURCH

Where men sleep on steps, under roosting pigeons.

MY HOUSE

When I wake I know if it's raining by the slinging on the street three stories down. At evening the tops of the buildings light gold like the sun does to trees in a forest. I have five rooms—bedroom, guestroom/office, kitchen, living room, bathroom. I live in all five, if that is what you call this. Luxurious, more than I need. More than most do. Clotheslines connect my kitchen to the kitchen across, the courtyard a mosaic of shiny granny panties, towels, patched quilts, old-lady dresses, primary-colored children's clothing, socks, T-shirts, saris, waving in and out of sunshine like flags. A line full of sheets, each lifting in the wind, the shapes of the air made visible.

The entryway is low and dim, ceiling dropped to make room for storage above, and one day you met me at my door, lifted my skirt above my hips, thumbed aside my panties, lifted me, wrapped my legs around you.

And Yet It Moves

You said, Put your hands on the ceiling.

You told me, Press down hard.

POLITICS

I have a spoon to stir or scoop sauce. A spoon to scoop food, but let the sauce fall through its slats. A ladle, which is different from a spoon. A spoon with teeth around the edge, and slats, meant for scooping pasta. A metal spoon with teeth around the edge, meant for scooping grapefruit. Soup spoon, coffee spoon, dessert spoon. Wooden spoons of many sizes. Some corresponding wooden forks, for clasping and lifting. Salad fork, entrée fork, dessert fork. Utensils that cut: some serrated, some dull, some meant for meat, others for bread, others for butter, some for cleaving, some for slicing, some for chopping, some for spreading. Flat square spatulas for cake, lasagna, pizza, all with slats. Measuring spoons. Measuring cups. Cups for coffee and tea. Glasses for water, juice, whiskey on the rocks, red wine, white wine, martinis, champagne, cognac, schnapps, beer, cordials.

I have a device that slices boiled eggs or kiwis into perfect discs. Put the object in an indentation, then lower a lever of parallel wires which cut the soft flesh. I have a rubber cylinder that scrapes skin off garlic. I have a garlic press. I have a potato peeler. Potato masher. Lemon zester. Lemon juicer. Bottle opener. Cocktail shaker. Cocktail strainer. Long spoon to stir cocktails. Corkscrew. Wine key. Jigger. Pouring spout. Basting brush. Basting syringe. Crêpe ladle. Double boiler. Thermometer. Can opener. Cookie cutter. Mortar and pestle. Chopsticks. Handheld cheese grater. Kitchen shears. String to slice dough. Tongs. Whisk. Nutcracker. Rolling pin. Fish scaler.

The old utensils are still around—pliers to pull out fingernails, knives, drills, hammers.

Bought with tax dollars generated through buying things.

Polyurethane nonstick stirring spoons, silver serving spoons, full-tang knives sharpened to blades that could sharpen a sword.

PEOPLE

The girl at my grocery store, molded into designer jeans, Baby Phat satin jacket in hot pink and black, flaming magenta hijab safety-pinned neatly, hiding her neck, a black headscarf underneath straight across her forehead, rhinestones. Makeup, severe and impeccable. A middle-aged woman with a bindi, speaking in Hindi to her daughter who wears jeans, flowing shirt, and a nose ring. The daughter answers in English. Tall, slim, dark boy in a purple hoodie, purple Jordans, purple Yankees hat cocked to the side, jeans slung low. A burka, all black, eyes and hands exposed. Dark pinstriped suit, light striped shirt, pastel striped tie. The girl at the local dive bar with orange hair, black bleached as close to blonde as it'll go, Japanese rock star orange, cut into an impossible shag which would look like a mullet on anyone other than her. Her frame is lithe and wiry, her face expressive as anime. She dresses so funky even the hipsters are impressed—track suits and flip-tongued Adidas, boxing shoes laced up to the calf, one pants leg pulled up to the knee, ripped T-shirts, acid-washed jeans. She tells a newbie the drink specials (the Joyce—shot of Jameson and a Guinness for eight bucks, the Whitetrash—shot of Jack and a PBR for five), and he says, Man, you talk black. From East New York, she says. Waddya expect? Men wearing starched white shirts, black pants with white strings hanging from the sides, black yarmulkes, black hats, hair clipped close except for two long ringlets down the sides of their faces. Men in heavy fur coats, cylindrical fur hats, whatever the weather. Women in calf-length skirts or longer, forearm-length shirts or longer, all with the same haircut, the same color hair: brown, shiny, shoulder-length bowls, because they're wigs. Only their husbands see their hair, elbows, collarbones, knees, just like the Muslims down the block. Businesswomen in prim skirted suits—Nikes on the trains, slingbacks on the sidewalks. Teenaged girls with thick hips in tight jeans, tight shirts, hair slicked up into a tight ponytail, left to frizz and curl after the elastic. Their names in gold script on rings, necklaces, across the loops of large gold earrings. Yessenia. Yahaira. Precious. Cherish. Quanesha. Julisha. Kadijah. Maria. Wrinkled women carrying produce home in plastic orange Chinatown bags. The guy in the navy Armani, Republican red tie, flicks his wrist like a fist, just checking the time.

VITAL DATA

One of us became a militant Muslim. Changed her name.
One of us became a male feminist.
One of us donated to a cause.
One of us learned all she could.
One of us took to the streets.
One of us remembered the good old days.
One of us turned a corner.
One of us danced all night.
One of us was tortured.
One of us was silenced.
One of us really changed.
One of us got raped.
One of us earned less money than a man.
One of us couldn't marry her wife.
One of us emigrated.
One of us stopped paying taxes.
One of us watched the birds.
One of us joined a third party.
One of us pretended it wasn't happening.
One of us turned up the air conditioning.

One of us never ate anything but American food.

One of us couldn't bear to bring children into this world.

One of us charted the temperature, recorded the weather.

One of us started walking.

One of us raped.

One of us voted. One of us voted, but it wasn't counted.
      One of us didn't vote.

One of us joined the service.

One of us taught.

One of us believed a different world was possible.

One of us opened doors for others.

One of us slit her wrists.

One of us jumped off a bridge.

One of us bought the penthouse, worked in the penthouse.
      Read *Penthouse*.

One of us wasn't impeached.

One of us got reelected.

One of us came on too strong.

One of us fell in love and stopped caring.

One of us fell out of love and had to care again.

One of us got left behind but didn't fall out of love.

One of us wrote it all down.

EDUCATION

I only see up to her knees, occasionally other pieces of her. Across the courtyard, one story down, her window faces mine. She cooks late, only our two windows lit. Borscht, I presume, because she slices beets, onions, leeks, her hands stained the same red as her burgundy-laced linoleum lit by a single hanging bulb, the same that lights my tiled floor. Sometimes her hands pick up steaming tea, I see the bodice of her housecoat, the slippers on her feet, but her half-pulled window shade obscures her face so I wouldn't know her on the street. I'm up after abandonment, autumnal body loss. Why's she awake?

BUSINESS

You and I made pesto. We made caprese: towers of mozzarella, heirloom tomatoes, basil leaves clipped from my window box. We made mozzarella. We bought premade hors d'oeuvres—pâté on toast points, smoked salmon wrapped around capers, tiny truffled quiches—we warmed them in the oven and had two-person cocktail parties. We drank Pouilly-Fuissé and Pouilly-Fumé and Barolo and Brunello and Super Tuscans, wines I'd never heard of but learned to discern. We used every utensil and appliance I own. They each had their purpose. I bought a decanter.

For moments I allowed myself the illusion everyone has—that what matters most is my own enjoyment of the world, whatever I can have, the things I can touch.

MY HOUSE, THIS PLACE AND BODY

The flock is a hypnotic event. It gathered after you left—a tree full of trash and one starling out my window became dozens of birds that lifted and lowered lightly from the wires, condensing and expanding, sometimes specks, sometimes a mass, sometimes dark, sometimes dissipated. The photonegative of stars in the sky, dark asterisks, tightly winding across a slash like the Milky Way. Their shrill voices battle. Their shit streaks everything, white and acidic, eventually it will eat away stone. Iridescent like gasoline on water, their sheen shifts shades. Soon white stars will appear—dark all year, in winter their feathers collectively speckle.

I wanted what the starlings knew, that every moment matters, that being one with another body is possible. They sense movement, sense the shift, predict the way another will swerve and swerve a moment before in the same perfect arc the other body wanted. Prophesy the swirl about to happen all around them. The tilt of a feather in flight tells them the desires of the shapes next to them, shapes they can't even see, separated by many bodies. I wanted this but I wanted it with just one, not a constellation. I wanted to be one with one. I wanted to know what you were thinking as you thought it, hand you the food you craved before you spoke, undress you as you desired, discover the way to open your doors to me. I dug my thumbs into the place right below your hipbones, trying to connect directly with your current. If I spent hours on your ribs, clavicle, belly edge, I would know your every thought, create an electricity that would tell me everything.

THE SAME PERSON

She—an expert in her field, who has written many books on the subject—will give this lecture, tomorrow, to her Postcolonial Literature and Theory class, made up mostly of English majors taking EN 3201 to fill their theory requirement, not because they are outraged by the continuation of colonization in the "postcolonial" era:

"Imperialism—as we've discussed in previous weeks—is a process where raw materials are taken from the colony, manufactured in the mother country, and the finished products are sold back at high prices to the colony. In the essay you all read for today, Juan Bosch argues that, in contrast, pentagonism is a process by which the United States colonizes its own people. Imagine an SAT word problem—capitalism is to imperialism as overdeveloped capitalism is to pentagonism. Pentagonism is not different from imperialism, it's just a much more extreme variety with a different purpose, and so it merits a new name. The new colonial endeavor still involves oppressing people overseas, but not in order to take their raw materials. Instead, the government takes our own resources through taxation—since 1951 more than half our tax dollars have gone to the military—and oppresses people overseas by existing in perpetual war with them, because wars generate incredibly quick profits." All quotes and paraphrases are from Juan Bosch's "Pentagonism: A Substitute for Imperialism," which only about half the students probably read, which is why it is necessary for her to summarize this argument with which they should already be familiar. The brightest students will see this as an extension of the military-industrial complex, and will write that phrase in their notes at this moment in the lecture. She has stopped trying to notice who does, to avoid the disappointment that always comes with her expectations not being met.

"It isn't easy to convince the American people to spend over half their tax dollars on just one thing. The public must not think that these are colonial wars. The public and the soldiers who fight them are, as Bosch says, 'led to believe that they are going to their deaths to help the attacked country, to save it from an evil.' In Vietnam we protected the South from the North. In the first Iraq war we protected the attacked Kuwaitis. Before the second Iraq war we described ourselves as the 'attacked country'—even though Iraq did not attack us, we warned that they would attack soon. (When wmds were not found we easily changed the justification to protecting the Iraqi people from the evil of Saddam Hussein.)" Many of her students believe the media's insinuation of a connection between the 9/11 terrorists and Iraq, so she'll often throw in this: "But conveniently, terrorists from a similar-enough country that also has brown people *did* attack us, and so we could conveniently say Iraq had something to do with it, and certainly would also attack us soon, and we could conveniently invade a country we'd wanted to invade for years." This is usually met with puzzled looks.

"According to Bosch, 'Only a state of war—which the pentagonized people accept as an emergency situation—permits fabulous expenditures and the quick signing of contracts with firms.' In order to bring his 1968 argument into the two thousands, add the fact that now American companies not only produce, as Bosch says, the 'bullets, bombs, medicine, clothes, cement, equipment to build barracks and roads and bridges,' and 'food and drink for the soldiers,' but we also rebuild the barracks and roads and bridges that our bombs destroy. In the 'old' imperialism, colonized countries had no roads or schools, so the mother country went in and built them. The twenty-first-century twist is this: we now go into countries that do have roads and schools, and museums and mosques, and we destroy them. Then we hire American companies to go in and rebuild. The CEOs of these companies are paid the highest salaries in the world, they spend more money inside their home country, and we all become more prosperous." What she thinks at this moment, every semester, but never says: *How's that for trickle-down economics?*

"Most people assume we are in Iraq for their oil, for their raw materials, which would be an 'old' imperialist reason to go in. I cannot discount that that is why we are there. But an extension of Bosch's pentagonism would say that we are there for the military contracts, and, we invaded Iraq also for the civilian contracts to rebuild the country."

What she wants to say now, but doesn't: "The main thing most people talk about after reading 'Pentagonism' is whether it is really different from imperialism, or not. I think that's a valid discussion and I'm sure that we will have it. But I don't think that's the *most* important question posed by the book. Bosch asks, 'Is a worker in South Dakota guilty of the death of a Vietnamese child burned with napalm?' Unfortunately, over forty years after his argument, I have to ask, 'Are students in a New York City classroom guilty of the death of an Iraqi child burned with napalm?' Because our troops are using napalm in Iraq. (The government denies it— they prefer to call them 'firebombs,' which aren't napalm, because

And Yet It Moves

napalm uses gasoline and benzene, and firebombs use kerosene-based jet fuel.) Bosch makes the argument that the American people are being exploited through pentagonism. But I think the most important question he asks is this: How responsible are we for what the Pentagon does with our money?" She doesn't say this because she has tired of the blank stares, the looks that tell her all the nineteen- to twenty-one-year-olds in the room don't really want to be bothered.

"Questions?" They usually don't ask questions. And she knows it's her fault. She knows she hasn't inspired them to want to know more, she knows she hasn't shown them the right questions to ask, she knows she's given this same exact lecture verbatim for years, and if she doesn't care anymore why should they? She knows it's her fault and she knows they know it so no one says anything.

WEATHER

Our first night, after we slept awhile, a storm blew in. Bolts streaked above brick apartment buildings, pulse-lightning igniting the clouds arrhythmically, paparazzi bulbs. Currents of rain blew across the street, across teenagers out late, yelling and feeling alive, across a car alarm set off by the thunder. The sky couldn't rest, couldn't catch its breath, a jagged tear cracking the dark— nothing but light beyond the dome capped over us. I could see the color of lightning: pink, nearly purple, ultraviolet, sort of orange, the color the Brooklyn Bridge's lights turn the river below them at night, the color I loved as a child. The sky rumbled, shots ringing across the low growl.

We watched, didn't fully wake, and you were inside me again, all of it starting over. The rain flung itself against my window like pebbles, like a jealous lover trying to get in. I had no one who would be jealous. The tree outside my window shook and shuddered, I feared it would shatter. Branches dug their fingernails across my window, and I thought the wind would bring the storm inside. I shook and shuddered. I want to scream, I said. So scream, you told me. I screamed louder than I ever have. No one in my building of parchment walls heard me.

We lay there, sheets thrown off and drenched, as if we'd walked in the rain. We listened to the storm and didn't talk.

I didn't know what you were thinking. I never did.

PLACE

We went to a game, ate hot dogs, drank beer (I explained that Budweiser's right-wing family donates money to the Republican Party and the Coors family funds anti-affirmative-action politicians and legislation, but those were the only two options so we drank both), ate peanuts and Cracker Jack. The green of the infield made me believe I could win bets; it sparkled, bathed my eyes. The seats arced up and away and filled with people who spoke in one voice, clapped simultaneously, shouted and roared and rejoiced. When the count's three and two; when it's the bottom of the ninth; when the pitcher looks nasty, dropping in balls that soar high then click right into the right place; when the other guy takes a huge cut and swings through only air; when our guy flies horizontally and snatches the ball before skidding on his belly; when we connect and know by the clack that that ball is far, it is long, it is gone; when we pull a textbook double play; when we slide in under the throw; when we strike them out looking; when we catch one at the wall; everyone's attention is on that one moment, time stretches, we hold our breath, we all think one thought, please let it happen, please let it be, please make it be, please please let it, and it's the closest thing to prayer most of us have known, then we leap to our feet and raise our arms into the air all at the same time.

It's as if—if I clap the right way, yell loudly enough, believe enough, think the right thoughts, really believe them, I can make it

And Yet It Moves

happen: I can control the swing of the bat, conduct the ball, make everything be where we need it all.

I said to you, there, the "World" Series is only between American teams, because clearly the world wants to wear Levi's, drink Coke, eat hot dogs, sing the national anthem. The one Canadian team just highlights the absence of any other part of the planet, and isn't it ironic that the other Canadian team moved to Washington, DC?

I said, the Indians' mascot is a red, smiling Indian with a feather in his headband. Fans pound on drums at the games. They call themselves the Tribe. I insisted, the Cleveland Indians will never win the "World" Series until they change their racist name. They haven't won since 1948—in 2007 they beat the Yankees in the ALDS on Columbus Day, you gotta love that, but they'll never go all the way. And then there's the Braves!

I tried to explain all of this to you.

It's just baseball, you said.

I don't stand for the national anthem, here in the heart of the heart of the empire.

PEOPLE

We put ourselves in the spaces others leave. We try to move through a whole day without bumping anyone, stream down concrete and across subway stations and in and out of subway cars, trying not to touch. Some exit the train, so a person shifts left and I cross my legs, putting my foot where he just was. An elaborate Tetris of bodies. Eyes shouldn't meet in the same space. We should look only where everyone else isn't, the beam of gazes should never connect.

MY HOUSE, MY CAT, MY COMPANY

I listen to the walls, the liquid circuitry of water through pipes, steam through radiators, the gurgle and hiss and clank. The sky breaks open its ozone capsules and though it's still blue I smell rain, the kind that will slick the roads by night, glint green, amber-orange, ember-red in the streetlight, by morning the bare branches gleaming fragile as glass, crystalline chandeliers. The wires will freeze, too, become thick, white, a thrown can could shatter them, arcing shards. I wonder where the starlings go on a night like the one that is coming.

I got a cat, picked the one least likely to get picked by anybody else: a brown cat going gray, fur full of snarls. Sometimes I put him outside to explore his instincts; when he wants to come back, someone lets him in downstairs and he climbs the three flights to claw at my door. I hope to never find star-filled feathers clinging to his mouth, but I let him out anyway.

My company, besides the cat, who has no name because naming him seems too personal? Memories. Theories. Theses. Antitheses. Syntheses. I invite no one in.

POLITICS

In my bathroom: eyeliner brush, eyeshadow brush, eyebrow brush, mascara brush, lipstick brush, foundation brush, concealer brush, powder brush, blush brush, hairbrush, comb, toothbrush, tweezers.

Coco Fusco, who watched detainees clean the ground with a toothbrush, said, "I learned about how easy it is to make another human being break psychologically without having to use overt physical violence."

Everything makes me think of everything.

When I smear makeup over my skin in streaks, before I blend it, I think of war paint.

I come from a place with few native people left. I come from the middle of this nation; I moved to this periphery which is the center.

And Yet It Moves

We say they are heathens.

They dress their men in skirts, women in pants.

They worship the devil.

They worship false idols.

They watch *American Idol* and *Fear Factor* and *Who Wants to Be a Millionaire*, they wear jeans and bling and miniskirts, they sing "Baby Got Back" and "Fresh Pair of Panties" and "The Thong Song," they buy Clorox and Ziploc and Tide and Joy.

They dye their hair blonde.

They starve themselves thin.

They sicken.

They worsen.

They upgrade, they update, they take our jobs, they become obsolete.

They should thank us.

They owe us money.

They live on two dollars a day.

They pray three times a day.

They pray five times a day.

They share a holy land.

They wear orange hoods, they are connected to electrodes, they are not allowed to sleep, they are not being charged with a crime.

They should be ashamed.

They feel superior.

They smell bad.

They are going to hell.

They buy a car.

They buy a house.

They buy a gun.
They work together.
They fall apart.
They pray.
They sacrifice.
We hold their breath. They hold ours.

EDUCATION

I can tell by fragments I see between frame and window shade that she has one of the old apartments in the building—paint darkened by cooking fumes, a stove from the forties, cracks in her wall, buckled yellowing linoleum, everything sticky. It will not be renovated until she leaves or dies.

Cooking is her one work. I wonder if she sells her borscht; she couldn't possibly eat all she makes. No family comes to visit. No friends come for dinner. I can't know if she's content, full with the necessity, completion, satisfaction of her task. I can't know if her cutting and stirring is meditation, each action a repetition approaching perfection. I can't know how empty she may be, bereft, left grieving the leaving of all she ever loved. She may be lonely, her legs don't tell me. She may be her own little economy, thousands stored in socks. Who will come for her if she dies? Will I be the only one to notice?

BUSINESS

is good.

THAT SAME PERSON

She fucked like her survival depended on it. She was not herself with him. She was stunned and roiled, the fantasy she'd always wanted to be. Every time she thought she went too far he met her there, pushed her further. They did everything. They were everyone.

She was happy. He was the source of it.

She would have said she loved him. She did say it. Still would.

He bought sheets when he started staying over often. Fine Egyptian cotton. She thought to herself as he tucked them in, sheathed the pillows, that it is called Egyptian cotton because workers there used to pick it, turn it to thread, then send it to Great Britain—the mother country—where it was woven and made into clothing and linens on industrial machines then sold back to the colony at high prices. Then, he lay her down on the sheets, and she stopped thinking. Stained the fine thing he bought her.

She threw the sheets away, couldn't keep the memory of their fuck froth and loss. She sleeps on the same bed, though all that passed between them seeped down and boils right below.

WIRES

Wires string up the bridges. Wires wound with wires wound with wires make cables.

Wires rush light through them, bring power to the bulb, illuminate the filament. Magnetism coils around the wire, vibrating the air. Wires carry sound, lengthen a voice to travel the miles. Electrons bring images, a talking person I see on my television, speaking of debt, death, elections. I hear nothing from you, see nothing of you that is real.

Within each wire is a wave, a current, a surge. Sometimes I unplug all the appliances, pull wires from the walls, fearing fire.

WEATHER

The morning after our first night we woke, showered, dressed, prepared to present ourselves to the world. The day was full of sunlight and steam, ninety degrees, no remnants of the storm before.

We didn't hold hands while walking to work. I didn't ask when I'd see you again. When we got to the gate the security guard asked, Well how'd you two get here?

What?

Haven't you heard? Tornado in Brooklyn last night. Tore up a coupla neighborhoods.

Trains aren't running, you aren't going to have any students today. Might as well go on home.

You took my hand. We turned around and walked back. Took off our clothes, crawled under comforters with the air conditioner on, turned on the television.

It started in Staten Island. Tornados can't move over water, so to get to Brooklyn it tightrope-walked across the Verrazano-Narrows Bridge, a top on a string. Churned up a block in Bay Ridge, then a neighborhood in Sunset Park. Threw trees in the air, tore off roofs, smashed cars, the whole deal you expect only in Kansas.

You said, We made that happen, you know.

PLACE

Razor ribbon cuts and tangles, always stray plastic ripped into it in this city, dangling, blown in the wind. You stepped toward me, holding our shared cigarette, a habit I'd picked up for the chance to touch your fingers, and you kissed me on the mouth, then stepped away. You stumble-laughed backward a little, just laughing, and the sky was spread out behind you, shifting colors, all lit up, razor ribbon and factories with glass broken out framing the sides of your body, the glass still in the frames rich with a layer of grime and age and grit gathered into a gloss, blurring and blending until it was gasoline on water, oil on a puddle, a thick

And Yet It Moves

smear of color we couldn't see through anymore so the filthy windows reflected the sky. Thin tall angular machinery silhouetted against the stolid buildings, the equipment that was used to build them, fill and empty them of their wares, apparatuses unused for years still standing around, watching, wanting a cigarette to pass the time, and I knew I'd never come to a place like this again, with you. I knew I'd never again see this particular industrial beauty of the city, this corner, I'd never see a man laughing with delight like that, I'd never again feel the way I felt. That image of you, flaming, as streaked with light as the sky was, I think of it at least once a day.

PEOPLE

I go to the top of the Empire State Building. No one else is laughing.

Up here—you can barely see them below, all motes. I look down and can't tell color, race, gender. I can't discern creed, religion, orientation, politics, profession, immigrant status, nationality, loyalty, ambition. They all move in a pattern and I know each makes a distinct thread within the larger grid, but from up here all I can see is the lattice and everyone in unison with it. I can't hear the honks and screams and curses which reveal that people disagree about who should be where, when. They look aligned up here, off to go to jobs they love, to be industrious, build a better world, invent, create, do good for the planet, help old ladies cross the street and kiss children along the way.

I'm sickened, want to go back down.

HOUSE, MY BREATH AND WINDOW

On the best days my breath fogs the glass, and I don't think about who's on the other side. I sit here and don't forget to breathe. I forget how many vertebrae we have, and when the private company of King Leopold was founded in the Congo, when Rhodesia became Zimbabwe, and I forget that most mornings I don't want to wake, and I forget about poverty and war and loss and hunger, and I forget that I have five rooms in my apartment and just one me, and I forget what I'm reading, what I'm writing about for that journal that's going to publish my essay so I can keep my job, and I forget it's about to be winter, but I don't forget to breathe as the moist sheet disappears and reappears and reminds me.

My one chance at happiness on the other side of glass, fused sand, my breath a furnace blast, ash.

POLITICS

In my online shopping cart:

Oxo Silicone Utensils. These kitchen gadgets are designed for superior comfort and durability. The ergonomic handles are not only easy to hold, but they also provide an excellent gripping surface, even when wet, so less effort on your part provides better results.

Prep Boards by Copco. The durable, nonabrasive surface will not dull knives, while the curved edges keep food and liquids contained. The slated board design allows liquids to run away from the cutting area.

All-Clad Lame. This double-sided blade is used to slash the tops of bread loaves in artisan baking. The slight curve allows you to cut flaps considerably thinner than would be possible with a traditional straight razor, so that bread can properly expand in the oven without tearing the skin or crust. Scoring allows you to control exactly where your breads will bloom, bringing your artistic talent to your baking.

Cuisinart Professional Stainless Steel Mandoline Slicer. Stainless steel straight and wavy blades can be set to any thickness with the easy-turn dial, and allow for smooth or fluted edges. The slicer stays stable with nonslip feet that sit wide apart, and the body is curved to leave plenty of space below for food to accumulate. You may want to order our coordinating metal glove to wear on your pushing hand in order to avoid accidents.

FINAL VITAL DATA

I would predict the weather.
I would reduce my carbon footprint.
I would feed the hungry.
I would undo history.
I would not pay taxes.
I would read it all.
I would reach out.
I would bend over backwards.
I would let it go.
I would show him the door.
I would turn a corner.
I would run for the hills.
I would ride into the sunset.
I would ride the rails.
I would sail the seven seas.
I would shoot the breeze.
I would walk on the wild side.
I would tie one on.
I would sing along.
I would shape up.
I would ship out.
I would shake things up.
I would simmer down.
I would fire it up.
I would jump for joy.

I would take a leap of faith.
I would fall from grace.
I would face the music.
I would see the light.
I would be a light unto the nations.
I would stick it to the man.
I would hit the nail on the head.
I would blow them away.

EDUCATION

Across the courtyard from my window lives an old man. He uses the clotheslines connecting our windows, but I don't—I hooked up a washer and dryer in the guestroom/office, hidden behind a vintage Chinese screen. He always looks dirty, his clothes faded to the same slate gray. I wonder who lived in my apartment before I moved in, hope it wasn't his best friend. He has the same boxers I bought for you, from the little store down the block that sells clothing and appliances and utensils and hardware and tools and all the things one might need. The mom-and-pop equivalent of a Home Depot and a JC Penney and a Sears. All we need. The boxers are varied patterns in blue: stripes, squares, plaid, circles, other stripes. So when the old man washes them in the sink and hangs them on the line between our windows, I sometimes think you did laundry.

Below him lives the lonely old woman. In no universe do I believe they meet and fall in love.

ANOTHER PERSON

He teaches Modern Physics, Quantum Mechanics, and Chaos Theory at Brooklyn College, where she teaches Postcolonial Literature and Theory. They work in different buildings.

He taught her things, obviously drawn from lectures he's given:

"When electricity runs through a power line, it creates a magnetic field around it, circling the current. If you run an empty wire through a magnetic field, it will create an electric current through the wire. Electricity and magnetism are the same thing, each field running perpendicular to the other, moving through space as an orthogonal sine wave. Light is an electromagnetic wave. Ultraviolet and visible, microwaves, x-rays, the light emerging from stars, the sun, a bulb, and all the light we can't see are variations of the same phenomenon."

Under his blazer he often wore a physicist's idea of a funny T-shirt:

God Said Let There Be Light—

$$\oint \mathbf{E} \cdot d\mathbf{A} = q \,/\, \varepsilon_0$$

$$\oint \mathbf{B} \cdot d\mathbf{A} = 0$$

$$\oint \mathbf{E} \cdot d\mathbf{S} = -d\Phi_B \,/\, dt$$

$$\oint \mathbf{B} \cdot d\mathbf{S} = \mu_0 i + \mu_0 \varepsilon_0 d\Phi_E \,/\, dt$$

(Maxwell's equations of electromagnetism).

"The thoughts we think are electricity. Firing synapses create a current between them, and we move, reminisce, fuck, eat, draw, cook, run.

"Physics tells us that reality is participatory. Light is both a particle and a wave. When an experiment is run to test whether light is a particle, it is. It manifests itself as a particle, if that's what we want it to be. If we run an experiment to test whether light is a wave, it is. It appears as a wave, if that is what we are measuring for. The act of observing alters that which is being observed. We create our own realities."

She wanted him to arrive, and he did. His leaving was not her choice. Apparently quantum physics does not have a one-to-one correlation with the macroscopic world.

THE FIRST PERSON

She is only known for her work.

I don't want to be remembered only for that.

HOUSEHOLD APPLIANCES

I don't understand the kind of living they want to do, close and tight and heated. I open my recipe box and roaches shuffle out from between cards, from folded papers with my notations and drippings of whatever I cooked. They leave behind brown dots, roach shit, I presume, though it looks nothing like shit. It looks like they excrete brown syrup that dries into flecks. They like to live in tangled things, where objects crisscross and condense the available space—the newspaper pile; the bowl of sundries where I keep chopsticks, spouts, openers, dice, peelers, etc.; the sink full of undone dishes.

They like the appliances most, as if electricity warms the circuit even when not flowing. They weave along the wires, dig into the plastic and metal and walk along the channels. When I press the lever of my toaster they swarm out, the red filament glowing inside. I toast the air to scatter them, when it pops back up I drop in bread, run it again, make more crumbs for them to feast on once it cools.

When I leave this place, I'll abandon microwave, blender, toaster, coffee maker, espresso maker, juicer, margarita maker, rice cooker, bread maker, dehydrator, Cuisinart, waffle maker, iron, steamer, hair dryer, hair straightener, hair curler, vacuum. I could tie each in a plastic bag for weeks, suffocate them and trust I wouldn't be taking a live horde with me to the next place. But I can't. I use the machines for now, close my mind to the slight stench, know I'll be gone from them someday. I drown them when I can, wash them down the sink, flush them away with water from my cupped palms, knowing all the while it's a waste of time. They live in the pipes.

THE CHURCH

Razor ribbon wound a helix behind you, cutting and tangling whatever came near, the metal as thin as the plastic shredded into it. Wire diamonds of a fence framed bits of brick, metal, gravel, cloud, bird, sea. You stepped toward me, holding our shared cigarette, a habit I'd picked up for the chance to touch your fingers, then you stepped backward, facing me, your eyes on mine. You laughed and stumbled a step back, just laughing, and the sky was spread out behind you, every color, all lit up, the pollutants cracking the sunlight into colors off the spectrum. Barbed wire and factories framed the sides of your body, glass broken out of the windows shattered into a sparkle below, breathable glitter, and the glass still in the frames was rich with grime and age and grit gathered into a gloss, blurring and blending until it was gasoline on water, oil on a puddle, a thick smear of color I couldn't see through, so the filthy windows reflected the sky, shone with the light shining off you. Machinery leaned against the buildings, silhouetted, the equipment that was used to build them, fill and empty them of their wares, angular apparatuses unused for years that still stood around, watching us, wondering what would happen next, and you were laughing with gladness, and I thought I could hold it all. The top of a chain-link fence lined the horizon like a row of steeples, and that image of you, flaming, as streaked with light as the sky was, laughing with delight, surrounded on all sides by such beautiful destruction, you—on the day I thought you were going to ask me, but you didn't, you didn't, you never did, that image, I still think of it at least once every day.

Sunday I go to Coney Island in the snow.

Everything bleached and dirty, the tenements on fire, steam from hundreds of radiators drifting from roofs, it is one of those winter days in New York, the kind where you look outside the window and the sky is white so you wear gloves, a hoodie and a jacket, a scarf and two pairs of socks. You step outside, expecting the ammonia stab in the back of your throat, but the air slips into your lungs easily, it isn't as cold as you thought it was going to be.

You walk past where you can buy clams, beer, corn on the cob, hot dogs, and cotton candy in the summer, past where they have fireworks every Friday night, the place so packed with bodies and color you can't tell that everything is peeling, old and unreplaced. You walk past the Cyclone, the oldest wooden roller coaster in the world; it bangs you up, rattles, five bucks a ride, but when it's over the carnies inside will let you give them three for another. You walk past the Circus Sideshow building where the sword swallowers, glass eaters, the Fat Lady of the Circus named Helen Melon, the Bearded Lady, and the bed-of-nails walkers work. Ravi, the Bendable Boy from Bombay, claims he was stung by scorpions as a child and instead of killing him the poison made his bones flexible. Insectivora's feet were toughened by volcanic rocks when she was a hermit on Fiji, now she climbs a ladder of swords and swallows fire, her face tattooed and pierced, a stabbed canvas. Heather, the former Mormon who kept her normal name, was struck by lightning as a child and can now endure deadly amounts of electricity zapped through her body that's so sexy it's clear she was never going to stay a Mormon, was bound to run away from the Midwest plains— like you—and join the circus. You walk past the Sideshow School, where they will teach anyone how to suppress the gag reflex, where every year new students learn to pound nails up their noses.

You walk past the Parachute Tower, the tall, red, Brooklyn-style Eiffel-scaffold, and want to climb it, see out to the horizon on all sides, look out over a flat landscape with inflated children's toys rising up out of it, bleached and broken, the things that make memorabilia—pale carnival rides without their lights, a pier trailing out into the ocean. You want to see people with metal detectors scanning the snowy beach, old men fishing, the haunted house, water slide, arcade, batting cage, bumper cars, miniature golf course, flick-a-ring-onto-a-bottle-and-win-a-teddy-bear-or-a-goldfish game, kiddie roller coaster, tilt-a-whirl, pirate ship, all the rides that lie locked up in a lot, behind chain-link fences, in winter.

Hushed and incubated, the clouds, sky, sun, all different shades of white. The sound of sand crunching under your feet, waves rolling, melting the snow, and you a little too warm in your layers. You can see the sky out here, watch the clouds change throughout the day.

They're going to tear it down. They'll leave some of the relics—the Wonder Wheel, Cyclone, minor-league baseball park. They'll keep none of the businesses down the boardwalk. Instead, luxury condos, "amusements," fancy restaurants, turn it into the Disneyland they've made of Times Square, no more pimps and peep shows.

Baudrillard says Disneyland exists to allow us all to believe the rest is real.

People won't creak-step down the salt-saturated boards, grease staining paper containers of onion rings and mozzarella sticks, butter on boiled corn, cartoon signs of everything you're eating on the front of the tiny stand selling it, corn dogs and clams, breaded and fried, bad draft beer so cold it's worth the bathroom you have to pee in.

It will all be gone, this place where bulbs from a starlet's dressing-room mirror adorn every corner, where decades-old rides are lit with every color of neon and singing, where the sideshow runs all day, the rows of worn bleachers filling from stage right, emptying from stage left, once you've seen the same act twice, you've seen the whole show. It will all be gone, this place made to maintain our idea that joy is sustainable, only some people are miserable, not anyone here.

I don't hear calliope.

The merry-go-round will run next summer, one last season as a grand finale before they disassemble it. Children will sit astride its wood-carved creatures, claim a Pegasus, elephant, zebra, rhinoceros, dragon, hippopotamus, giraffe, hippogriff, tiger, or beautiful mare as their own, squeal as the gears speed up and they spin faster. Parents will watch and wave, some will ride for old times' sake, teenagers on dates will climb on trying to be suave in their tight or loose clothing and they will giddily laugh and dare each other to reach for the golden ring, one of the few remaining carousels in the world still with a golden ring, and they'll grab for it. Every time they pass they'll stretch for it, hold the bars and reach their arms out as far as they will go; they'll stand on their dolphins or lions but they still can't touch it. You can't get it, it's impossible, no one has ever gotten it but everyone wants to try, everyone longs to stretch beyond what they're able, all of us whirling around think about leaping off our fading and peeling stallions or unicorns and grabbing it in the air everyone wants to try, and some still do.

And Yet It Moves

Keen

"... because there is hardly one of us who has not been moved at some time to do just what she has done, and every time, it has taken all our strength, and even the strength of our friends and families too, to quiet us."
—LYDIA DAVIS, "Fear"

My first keen was for my brother. I hadn't seen it done, my mother hadn't yet taught me, but when all the neighbors came to the house, when my mother took my hand and led me to look at his rigid, relaxed body on top of the dining room table, when she started the wailing it felt like the exact thing I wanted to do and when she looked at me I knew I could. I expected the whole room to join in, everyone would want the release I felt, but they just listened, let us do it for them.

My mother used language, listed the lineage of our family going back further than I knew, but I hadn't yet been taught what to say so I just made sounds. Then my brothers filled and shouldered the small box my father had built and we followed it to the graveyard. As we walked down city blocks everyone we passed turned and walked with our funeral three steps, then turned back and went along their way.

At the edge of the hole my mother threatened to throw herself in, I pulled out a hunk of my own hair. There was a spot of blood at the root, the brightest bit of the red lock, and that hadn't been something I'd known I could do. It hurt in a way I didn't mind.

We didn't stop our cries until each family member had turned three shovels of soil onto the top of the box, not until the sod that had been sent over the ocean was laid on top of the packed surface, a darker shade and scent than the bright grass that had been disturbed. A neighbor said to my da, "She's got some lungs, for a five-year-old." He pressed a coin into my father's palm, and my father handed it to me back at the house, as everyone ate soda bread from the oven and soup.

* * *

Today, a man calls to schedule a keen for the Lucero family. Cormac Lucero. His daughter is dead. And her two children, his young grandchildren. Three drowned together in the Massachusetts Bay. Sailing accident. In my twenty years of practicing this art I've never keened more than one at a time. I ask for the lineage and scribble in the section of our appointment book meant for this. He says he was adopted from Ireland by a Mexican American family. He married a Mexican American woman, and his daughter married a Mexican American man. "They're all dark but me," he says. "I stand out like a sore thumb in this family, you'll know me." He has the faintest trace of the lilt that has always sounded to me like family, though it's mostly covered with a stronger Chicano accent. My voice is all Southie, but his reminds me of a home I've never known. "Tell me more," I say. The lineage lets us pay respect, honor the ancestors and the living and the descendants. All keening women before me have asked and all after me will ask for the lineage because that makes it make sense—What is this the end of? What is left?

And Yet It Moves

"We're Mexican seven generations back," he says, "but there was one Irish ancestor, before me. He was a San Patricio, Irish American who defected during the US-Mexico War and fought for Mexico. He'd come over because of the Famine," he says. "Irish were hated in the Army. Many went to the Mexican side, since they were Catholic too. After the war he stayed in Mexico and was never caught, not hanged or lashed or branded on his face with a D for deserter like the others. He married my great-grandmother, if you add five greats. A few generations back the family emigrated to the US, and my parents adopted me in his honor. Contraceptives were illegal to buy in Ireland until 1980, there are plenty like me. That's the story. But I was raised Mexican. So were my daughter and her children. Is that all you need?"

"What is the condition of the bodies?" I ask.

"They weren't in the water long," he answers.

I tell him we'll be there in three hours. I tell him to gather his people.

* * *

When I started we were only hired by our block of families from Éire. Big families out of habit, not because anyone here believes birth control is a sin anymore, so plenty of work. Most neighborhoods are still homogenous, but for the past decade or so we've been employed throughout Boston. We don't advertise, but word of mouth explains it well enough. Asian Americans, African Americans, Hispanic Americans, they all hire us now. Even people from the Middle East. People live near their own, but they all invite us in.

My mother and I take the T to the apartment and even though I'd been told the lineage I'm surprised when I see the deceased mother. She looks like a darker version of me, like my burgundy hair has been stained russet, like my green eyes were painted with a layer of lacquer. She has freckles, but on skin not nearly as pale as mine. Her hair is more wiry than my curls, more wild. The children are darker, flashes of red buried in their hair, green hidden in their eyes. Everyone in the room is dark except me and my mother and the dead woman, and one man in the corner of the room, with hair a brighter crimson than even my father's. I nod in Cormac's direction and he seems to know not to speak to me yet.

Candles are everywhere, Jesus and Mary and saints whose names I don't know and creatures painted on glass that look more pagan than saintly. Green and red and blue and yellow flames, little lit gems on every surface. I walk through the room and people clad in black cloth move out of my way. The kitchen has yellow walls and lace curtains. I heat water in the kettle we brought, the same one that will soon make tea, and I fill my basin and walk back into the living room. I feel my forearms heat while my mother dips a clean white cloth into the bowl and washes the bodies. She changes them into white linen in her practiced, efficient way, never showing skin that shouldn't be shown as she removes what they wore when they died, still slightly wet to the touch, and piles it in a heap in the center of the room. We do all the things others don't want to do. They know not to cry yet, not to distract the souls as they travel. If we keep from sobbing while touching them, everyone else can too. The skin is cold. The children's limbs are stiff. The mother's arms and legs are pliant. I don't touch them, but I can tell these things through my mother's hands. She ties each body's two largest toes together with twine.

Then we make tea, our own blend, and lay out the filled clay pipes. We no longer explain that tea is good for the spirits that are still in bodies, and that even those who don't regularly smoke should do so after a death, in our tradition. Word spreads ahead

And Yet It Moves

of us. The room fills with wisps and it is a barrier between them and our wails once we begin. The souls are talking to God now, we can't call them back. Everyone can cry now, but they usually don't. We do it for them.

"Daughter descended from Hibernia and Aztlán," my mother begins. "Daughter to honor a warrior, kin of a soldier who fought for the freedom of your motherland. You lived your life north and west of the lands of your ancestors. Why are we now alone?"

"Why were you taken?" I sing. "Did we not love you enough for you to stay?" Love isn't enough to keep anyone here, but it feels like it should be. I say, "Why is your beauty now gone?" I feel a heat behind me. Someone is upset by my words. That is why I say them, to take the sadness out of all our bodies and put it in the air. But what I feel behind me isn't just grief.

There's guilt in this room. "Why will we not see these children grow?" I moan.

My mother cries, "We curse the boat that capsized. May its boards splinter. We damn the water that filled your lungs. May it boil away to oblivion. May the objects of your destruction suffer as we suffer."

The heat behind me intensifies, begins to feel like fury, so I shift to just sounds, and my mother follows my lead. The expectations of how we should sound are different throughout the counties, so my mother and I have mastered each, since people here are from throughout our island. In Leinster in the east, our wails are said to be so piercing they can shatter glass. In Kerry in the west, we're said to be a low, pleasant singing. In Tyrone in the north, in the part that is not our country anymore, we make the sound of two boards being struck together. In the farthest north, Rathlin Island, they say we sound like barn owls. We scream, screech, and shriek, and no one covers their ears.

* * *

My father's father came over from the Aran Islands. Gaelic was his, and my father's, first language. Once it was clear I was entering this profession, my grandfather told me, "There are no more merry wakes because there are no more good deaths. No more old people at the end of a life well lived, no children young enough to be easily replaced." He said he was the leader of the fine boys back home, the one to rig the body to sit up in the middle of the night, the one to toss sod and broken pipe pieces at anyone who dared sleep. "The rougher the games, the better," he said. "You always wanted to almost topple the body off the table, but not quite. My brother, your great-uncle, lost himself an eye at a merry wake. After I'd come to this country he got caught by a hungry ghost, stepped on the place of a famine death and had no bread in his pocket to feed the spirit fixed to that spot. They waked him without me." Grandfather told me of mock marriages, said, "That was what the priests hated most about our wakes, the way we pretended to have their power. Performed their rites. They said it was all the poitín we drank, the uisce beatha, but that wasn't it." He told me, "The village waked us when we decided to come to America. Maggie and myself laid out on the same table, madness and merriment around. They knew they'd never see us again."

Merrymaking resisted desolation, resisted colonization, resisted Catholicism. My people only brought part of their tradition here.

* * *

At the graveyard we move into hysterics appropriate for a triple death. All the others stay dry-eyed. The boxes are closed. It's amazing to me still, after two decades, how much dead people still look like people. This town knows if they want to do things our way, with no chemicals, they have to call us quickly. So the faces still

And Yet It Moves

look like faces. Now it's usually me who threatens to throw myself over the edge, into the gap where the soil's been dug out. We never said anything about it, but we seem to agree a younger woman has a stronger effect. My mother is still a beauty, dark Irish, with black hair and blue eyes, but the white streaks in her long locks make the threat to bury herself with the bodies more pitiful than tragic. Me, I'm in the prime of life.

I lean over the edge and I hear Cormac gasp.

I don't know the people I keen, at least not to make me sorrowful enough to show. So while I bawl and weep, I mourn other things. The rainforest birds that will be extinct before we know they exist. Children who die from hunger. Shot children. People who die by bombs my country built. My grandfather, who worked as an electrician his entire life and never earned enough money to return to Ireland, his first love. That he didn't teach me Gaelic, didn't want me marked by accent. That I cannot remember my dead brother's face. That baby elephant, separated from its mother in a dust storm, following the footsteps of the herd, but the wrong way, out into the desert alone, which I watched late one night on television, sipping Irish by myself, and have been haunted by since. The camera people filmed it, and didn't turn him around. The melting of once-permanent ice. That whale, who sings in an octave so low others can't hear her, so she's alone. There's plenty of loss to recognize.

And if we all mourned these things, all of the time, in what ways would that open us to each other? What might that let us reach across?

One man behind me is clenching his jaw so tightly he might break his teeth, and there's a thin woman next to him not touching him. I feel my skin connected to Cormac, the only other redhead amongst all these Mexicans, I feel myself pulled toward him even as I holler over a grave.

"Daughter of Saint Patrick's Battalion, children of Éire and the Aztec Empire, why did you leave us?" I wail. I've learned not to actually tear my hair out, I don't have enough to yank a hunk every day I work, but I pretend to, and miss that sharp sensation.

*   *   *

Back at the house Cormac hands me tequila. We're paid in cash, but also in food and drink, as is the custom. It's enough so I don't have to have another job, and I've eaten food from every nation. The Africans newly here feed us stews and rice, spices I can't name, and they say how much we remind them of their ancestors, our keening like what they used to hear in their homelands. The African Americans who've been here for generations feed us ham and collards and okra, fried chicken, southern food even here in Boston. The Asians give us noodles and transparent packets of shrimp and vegetables and say they've never heard anything like us, they thank us for easing their pain, for taking it on for them, from them. Italians give us pasta and glasses that are never empty of wine. We are offered too much food, too much booze, but my mother taught me how to drink, and I can put a lot away and never show it. My body burns whatever I eat. We work separate parts of the room—people want to feed the keeners, want to watch us take shots, people want to speak to the wailing women now that we just talk. I click Cormac's glass and throw back the shot and of course I don't ask for lime or salt.

"Thank you," he says.

"You're welcome," I say.

"Where are your people from?" he asks, and I say the Aran Islands. He says he was born in Galway, but he's not certain his unwed mother was from there.

"We can consider ourselves neighbors anyway," I say, though we're thousands of miles from that place.

And Yet It Moves

"You look just like her," he says. His daughter, he means. He is thinking of me as kin.

I think of her frizzy hair, her spooky eyes, brown ringed green. Her strangely tinged skin, freckles the color of milky tea. "I look like half of her," I say. "The half that comes from you."

"It's more than that. You have her sense. Her way of being." He leads me to the food, and we pile plates with stews seasoned deep red, rice, beans. "That's spicy," he says while pointing to a salsa that looks like confetti, and I say it's fine as I scoop some on top of chips. "That's tongue," he says, and I put some on my plate and say that's fine, too. I find myself saying, "I like intensity." With his middle finger he hooks a bottle by the neck and carries it to our table.

"The man who was clenching his jaw isn't here," I say.

"Her husband," he answers.

"Oh," I say. "The father." I picture the woman next to him, refusing to touch him in public.

Something must cross my face because Cormac says, "Thank you for doing this, despite the circumstances."

"Wait," I say. I think. "You didn't tell me the full lineage?"

"You said you only needed the histories of the dead."

"The father, the husband, was leaving. . . . You had us keen a suicide? A *suicide*?" A self-killing couldn't have been buried in the graveyard in the old country, there would have been no wailing. Just silence. "And a murderer? She killed herself and her kids because he was leaving her. Christ. Why was he at the funeral then? Why was she?" My voice is rising and I lower it. My mother catches my eye from across the room and I barely shake my head. I'll handle this. Someone fills her glass and then Cormac fills mine. She takes her shot and I take mine. "You're Catholic," I say. "You know what this means. The one unforgivable sin."

"We're not really Catholic. More like leftover Catholic."

"Us too," I say. "But still. It's the one taboo we have." I fill my mouth with meat.

"The family was afraid she'd become La Llorona, the wailing woman, and I told them if I hired wailing women you could stop it. I said the Irish custom could cancel out the Mexican myth. No one believes in her, La Llorona. But we've been told of her since we were children. Every one of us thinks we've heard her at least one time. The idea that you can do something to bind yourself to this world, something that won't let you into the next, we might not believe it, but it's true enough to worry about. I told them you'd wail and Gloria wouldn't have to. Just in case there's any truth in an old legend."

"Shit," I say. I keep my voice low. "Just in case?"

"Maeve, I'm sorry."

"No. You don't choose when you go. That's the rule. You stay until you're taken. You stay here, you suffer, just like the rest of us. That's the deal we all made—find a way to make it worth it. Find a way to love it all, even the bad. You fucking stay here and you fucking find a way to rejoice and that is how it works. What she did goes against everything we believe," I say, wrapping a strand of hair so tightly around my finger it's turning the tip purple. I don't unwind it yet. I need to catch my breath.

"I'm sorry," he says again. And then I can breathe a bit better because he looks deflated and about to scream. "When my wife died, I thought it couldn't get any worse. Now I have no real family. The parents who adopted me are gone. I will never see that puto madre chingaso cabron who married my daughter ever again. The rest of the family will invite me to birthdays and quinceañaras because I kept their cousin, their niece, from becoming a ghost. And I'll go. But I have no more real ties here. Thank you for helping me say goodbye." Grief makes some people numb. It has sharpened

And Yet It Moves

me. I see it hasn't dulled Cormac—it has made him ferocious. My mouth is spiced, full of the taste of tongue. "Do you think she's in hell?" he asks me.

I consider it. It's possible. "Definitely not," I say.

Cormac shakes salt onto a chip, a glittering layer of crystals, and I must raise a brow at the amount because he says, "It makes them taste sweet," then chews.

I shake on as much salt as he did, and he's right. They're the thick kind of chips, rolled out, cut, and fried by hand in the tortillaria down the block. Then I bite a pickled jalapeño, the tang of brine intensified by the sweetness that had been there.

"You're not going to hell now, right?" he asks.

"What we do, it's not really religious." I think of having sex at fourteen, using birth control then and since, fantasizing about our handsome priest, getting confirmed but knowingly sinning the next day, having sex with myself. I haven't confessed in over a year. I go for the pageantry, I don't go because I believe. Not in that. "The worst that will happen is word will get around to the Irish and they won't hire us anymore." The salsa is hot, he was right about that. Cormac pours me another, another for him, and we each take our shot. It makes my mouth hotter. I add, "Well, the worst that will happen is we pissed off the ancestors."

"I'm sorry," he says for the third time. "I said you'd end it all," he says.

"Did I?"

"For them. Mi familia. Yes. With the help of your mother, of course."

"She's got some lungs."

"Nothing like yours, though."

"That's what they say." I think, *I haven't ended it for him, yet.* I don't know if it can ever be over for him.

I've only wanted to offer comfort the way I'm about to once before, when I was a teenager and a teenager had been killed by a gun, and at that funeral all the women joined me and my mother. They keened right alongside us. The way we helped was by showing them how, not doing it for them. The kid's best friend was the most forlorn person I'd ever seen. I could tell he'd lost the only person who'd ever really loved him, ever seen him. I went home with my mother but I wanted to come back. I imagined seeing him on the stoop, smoking. His name was Nelson. He was tall and skinny. He had a long nose and big eyes and dark skin that went indigo in the creases. I imagined him taking me up to his small room. I didn't go back because I was afraid of the look the mother's eyes might show, the keener back in her house, the person who's meant to leave and take it with her. But whatever tenderness and toughness we might have shown each other that night, had I gone back, I think it would have done us both some good.

"We're still here," I say. I say, "When you leave, I will go with you. If you want." Maybe my grandfather is right, maybe there are no more good deaths. But maybe Cormac and I can find a joy together, even for a night, to resist this that seeks to ruin us. I dimly register that he doesn't look like my father. My father does not attend wakes with me and my mother. My father is a joyful man. Yet there's something thrilling about how sorrow tears people open. "Don't worry," I say. "I don't actually look like your daughter. This isn't about that." And then I say, "Don't worry. This isn't part of the services of a keening woman. This isn't part of how we soothe grief, it's not included in our pay. Not something I typically do. I just think you could use some company." Comfort.

Cormac looks like he's not sure if he wants to step toward me, or away from me. It's all on his face.

And Yet It Moves

I waked a suicide. Someone who couldn't feel all there is to feel. But I can.

I broke that taboo. Maybe there's no taboo not worth breaking. I think Cormac and I should find out.

"You aren't like other people, are you?" he says.

"No," I say, "I'm not. Not anymore."

With Strangers

I.

One puts fingers and instruments into her body, nonsexually smells the smell between her legs. One scrapes plaque off her teeth, scrapes below her gums, makes her bleed, makes her drool down her chin. One shines beams into her eyes, contracts the irises, then puts in drops that leave her sensitive to light pouring in. One flexes and points her ankles, runs electricity through her skin to heal deep tissue wounds; one pierces her skin with long, thin needles; one cracks her spine. One slides metal into her veins, fills a vial with what keeps her alive, with what can pass on sickness. One listens to her heart, tells her if the pulsing of blood through her veins is strong enough to keep her alive a little longer. One sends radiation through her body, examines reflection and absorption, white shapes that indicate bones, tendons, muscles, absence, her frame. One helps with athlete's foot and bunions, pain when walking; one examines her urinary tract; one presses her breasts between metal plates, reads the lumps, tells her if she's malignant.

Some doctors know daily that they are hated.

Lacey's glad someone's willing to do it.

Because they tell her things she can't know herself, Lacey loves paying visits to doctors. She loves that they have to see what others don't want to see.

Lacey doesn't read a magazine while she waits in the gynecologist's lobby. She knows what they say. She knows what they show. Lustrous pages of women who look just like her. Lacey is the kind of woman the magazines say anyone can be if she just tries hard enough, but Lacey doesn't have to try at all—no surgery, her only exercise is her work, and she eats whatever she wants. Lacey knows she's just a bag of bones, just a container filled with lots of fat in some places, very little fat in other places, and she doesn't understand why other people think there is something marvelous about her dimensions, something miraculous, something that matters beyond pure coincidence.

A youngish girl, maybe fifteen, in jeans and a tight baby tee, big sneakers, sits next to her mother, an older, more formally clad version of the girl. Maybe the girl is here for her first appointment, she has that nervous way of sitting, not sure whether to cross her arms over her breasts or her belly. Lacey smiles, and is not surprised when each woman only half-smiles back.

Her name is called. She stands, taller than most women, offers her hand to the new medical technician she hasn't met yet, says, "I'm Lacey"—after that ringing, *Beautiful and full of holes*. Lacey thinks that phrase every time anyone says her name. She shakes hands like a man, walks toward the examination room in remarkably high heels, and everyone in the waiting room watches her go.

※　※　※

"Everything looks good in there," Dr. Wilson tells her. He pulls off his gloves, washes his hands. Lacey has been seeing him since before his hair was gray. "I'll call you if there's anything abnormal, like always, but it looks like you're healthy. See you next month, Lacey," he says, tapping the box of Kleenex as he walks out the door. Lacey wipes herself clean, dresses, drops the gown in the laundry hamper. Hearing that there's nothing wrong with her should be thrilling, but she's disappointed every time. If there were something wrong with her she would know why she always feels like there's something wrong with her.

11.

After her appointment Lacey goes to work. She uses her real name onstage, didn't have to start calling herself Fantasia or Eurasia, and she works the moniker, wears only lace bras and lace-topped stockings, wonders if anyone gets the joke.

Tonight after her set she doesn't have to walk around in boots and a thong talking to the men, asking if they're having fun, seeming interested in showing them more of herself, because tonight when she's onstage a man watches inches from the edge, his face as close to her as possible, and when she's done dancing he takes her elbow and escorts her to his table.

When dancing for this man calling himself Harold, Lacey makes sure he knows exactly what is up against the cloth of his fine suit, covered with a thin film of lace. Harold says he wants to see more of her. Lacey has never served him before, but he knows how it works—he walks to one of the rooms in the back meant for private dances, tells the bodyguard what he wants, Lacey nods agreement, the bodyguard names a price, and Harold pays. Skin is the only club in the state with no cameras, the only club that offers immediate gratification. Most bodyguards watch, but this one, Louis, always turns his back. "Tell me if you need me," he says.

Lacey pushes Harold's shoulders so he sits in the chair in the middle of the room, then sits in a chair across from him, legs spread wide. Harold wastes no time, quickly starts doing what he's paid to be allowed to do. He tells Lacey how beautiful she is. Mirrors ring the room.

Lacey lists all the places she wants him to put himself, one by one. He's not paid for that tonight, but when new clients are feeling Lacey out they want to hear it anyway, want to know what she's willing to do, what they can come back for. She gives the same inventory to each man, but each item gets altered depending on his reaction, cut and tailored into the perfect shape to slip over his body, cover him in exactly what he wants. When Lacey gets to the last item on her list, "My hands," Harold's grimace tells her what she needs to know.

She talks about her hands, how dirty they are, how public, how everyone touches them and anyone can see them. She tells Harold, "Let me catch it. Harold, let me hold it in my hands." She kneels in front of this man in a suit leaning back in a chair, cups her hands in front of him, looks him straight in the eye, and she's found the exact right thing. After his mask of concentration breaks into a revelation of release, he smiles, says, "Thank you," and for the first time, he looks human. Lacey rubs her palms together, rubs her fingers between each other, tells Harold to visit her again, slips through a door to wash up.

When she takes the money from Louis she gives him fifty bucks back: the thing that makes it worth it for him, to break the law by letting her break it. Sometimes they accidentally let a cop back there, and then they both pay a fine, both spend a night or two in jail, but most of their clients are regulars, have proven by now they aren't undercover. Lacey never leaves the premises with men. They often want her to, but then there's no bodyguard. No cut— she'd be an independent businesswoman—but she never takes that risk.

The rest of the night goes quickly. The man paying for "anything goes" spanks Lacey with a hairbrush and calls her Marsha, and Lacey hopes his daughter's best friend or his secretary or his daughter is freed through his play. She trusts he knows that isn't the kind of thing he can do in real life. That's why he needs her. Someone to agree to it all. Someone who has different rules. Samuel, the slim, dark-haired man with near-translucent skin, blue veins, thick lashes, he comes to her weekly with slashes along his thighs. It's clear he uses a blade on his shoulders, sometimes there are burn marks in places clothes will cover. Tonight she pulls his hair, runs her nails down his back leaving a scratch. She spanks him and when he dresses he is astonished by her handprint, the smack of five fingers, a palm, the look on his face telling Lacey he knows the mark will fade and wishes it would not. "You make me feel normal," Samuel says after they're done. "When I'm an old man," he says as he puts back on his clothes, "too old to want to do this anymore, I'll buy you stiletto heels with stiletto blades. I'll come to you one last time, and we'll do what we just did, or as much as I'm able. Then I'll lie on this couch and you'll stand on my chest, crouching, all your weight balanced on the balls of your feet. And when I say the word, you'll stand, one foot over each lung, and pierce through with your heels. My last vision will be the pillars of your legs, between them."

Lacey wonders how many times Samuel will want to tell her about his new fantasy in the coming weeks. "I'd have to be put in the will to do something like that," Lacey says with a smile.

"That seems fair."

"By the time you're old enough to want to check out, I'll be an old lady too."

"You'll never change," he says. "You'll always be as you are."

Because Lacey's clients have her to come to, because she meets their sick, twisted, needy, inventive, creative, far-ranging desires, because she's not afraid, she knows her clients hit their wives less, curse their sons less, fondle their daughters' friends less, shoot into buildings less often. She allows her clients to let go of something, allows them to let something else in. But they always come back.

By then Lacey's made enough money that she doesn't have to take any more clients, can sit in the dressing room with some of the other girls, wait for closing time. There's Exotica, a girl twice as wide as Lacey, whose following of men worship her bulging curves, her bounty, though none know she's really named Beth; there's Chynna, actually Japanese, actually named Jane, here while she gets her master's in social work so she can graduate without debt, accept a low-paying job, serve those no one else wants to serve; there's Majestik, real name Selma, whose look was all the rage in the eighties, dark eye circles that seem to be smudged makeup but stay after she has washed her face, jutting hipbones, cheeks hollowed out to reveal the skull beneath—because she always makes enough to score all the horse she desires she never seems as desperate as she seems detached, unsuffering in the way of zazen monks setting themselves aflame. Out of all these women, Lacey always earns the most.

The manager, Pete, asks Lacey to watch the new girl's last set, stage name Eros, to see if she needs any pointers. She was working at another club in town so she should be well trained, but he wants to make sure she's top notch.

Pete doesn't warn Lacey that this new woman looks uncannily like her. Her body seems identical, illuminated from every angle by bright beams; her face seems shaped the same as Lacey's, though her hair is not as pale as her own. And her dance isn't the same—Lacey's routine is athletic, frenetic, set to Joy Division or Tool, but Eros's striptease is slow, sultry, relies on the agony of waiting. Lacey makes it hard for men to catch their breath; when watching this woman dance, all the men hold theirs. Eros leaves the stage and a man at a table near Lacey asks for a lap dance. Eros is all pro: she doesn't let him touch her, she only touches his shoulders and arms, she doesn't release the tension her dance has built, she implies what can happen outside the public eye. He doesn't take her to a private back room, Eros says, "Maybe next time," and the bartender yells last call.

Lacey meets her in the dressing room, and Eros's handshake is as firm as her own. She introduces herself as Kate. Lacey says she did a fabulous job and Pete claps a hand on each of their shoulders.

"Eerie, isn't it?" he asks. All of the dancers nod. "You two could be twins."

Jane says they should do a routine together, a duet, and Lacey smiles, says sure. Why not? She thinks of all the stage names she could take on: Eros and Thanatos. Or Eros and Narcissus, the cursed demigod who was told if he came to know himself, he would die, but who found himself anyway. Or Eros and Nymph, a creature who mated with men or women as she willed, outside the control of men or gods, the basis for Freud's name for a psychosexual disorder—nymphomaniacs, women who enjoy sex too much. Lacey has always loved mythology, what people once thought was real.

Kate looks at Lacey's face, and says, "It's like looking at an improved version of me. Higher cheekbones. Bigger lips. Smaller nose." She spins Lacey around, to see her from every angle. "Smaller waist. Bigger, higher breasts. Slimmer arms. Firmer thighs. Tighter ass."

"Thank you," Lacey says. "But to me, we look the same."

"Almost. But not quite."

"We're lucky to have her," Pete says. "Lucky to have you both, now."

Lacey imagines having one leg, a cane, a hearing aid, a limp, a port wine stain across her face, a slash of a scar along her cheek. She imagines feeling Kate's body with her hands, pressing against something outside herself to know her own dimensions. "It will be nice having you around," Lacey says instead. "She's a real professional," she says, turning to Pete.

III.

Lacey has been having dizzy spells, and though the easy explanation is that they're often after she dances a set, after she spins and slides upside-down down a pole and lights flash at her from every direction—anyone would be dizzy—she schedules an MRI just to be sure. Her general practitioner asks if she's certain: she pays out of pocket, and the chances of a brain tumor are slim, but she says better safe than sorry.

The technician tells her to take off all her jewelry, leave it in a locker, asks if she has any metal under her skin. She lies down on a thick plastic plank. The technician explains she should not move. The machine slides her inside and the top is closer to her face than she thought it would be. She was told there would be three series and each would be fifteen minutes long and she already wants it to stop. The clanks are a claustrophobic metallic symphony, polyphonic and three-dimensional, the levels of tones resounding in her body, reverberating through her bones. The magnets circle to bounce waves off of her from every angle, and it is suddenly clear she is being tested. The air pulses with a hammer ringing on a tin roof, a hammer thudding on a railroad tie. She wants to scream, but she knows she can endure anything, so she quiets her breath, stays still even in the panic that makes her want to thrash.

A voice asks, "How you doing in there?"

"I don't like it."

"Do you need it to stop?"

"No, I can keep going."

She feels each joint, each tendon, each notch and curve of her surface. She feels straitjacketed. When the voice leaves the space she thinks, *Well isn't that what we ask ourselves daily.* Sometimes it is so lonely to know exactly how your body feels—*I want this to stop happening. I want to stop feeling this way*—what is done to us by grief, sickness, desire.

For consolation, to invent solace, find a focus, Lacey imagines hiring Kate like people hire her. Kate would already be in the back room, waiting, legs crossed, fully dressed. As Lacey walked in Kate would stand and take off her clothes. White shirt, black skirt, black heels, garter belt, stockings, bra, panties. She'd lead Lacey in front of the full-length mirror on the wall, stand behind her and take Lacey's clothes off, the same outfit, slowly, in the same order. Then she'd put her palms on Lacey's ribs, rub up and around her breasts, run her hands along Lacey's shoulders, across her throat, inside her thighs, as if Lacey were watching her own hands touch herself, unable to guide them.

Kate would walk in front of Lacey, let her watch her hands roam over a body so like her own, without feeling the sensation caused by her palms.

Lacey would touch Kate between her legs, watch her face change. Kate would bend forward, press her palms against the mirror, let Lacey see her back, keep her face lifted so Lacey could watch her expression chronicle everything. Their images would reflect in the mirrors behind them, back and forth, a tunnel to look into. As if Lacey could finally see herself the way she is seen. Lacey would use both hands, then reach down and lift Kate, press this woman's body against her own, hold her in front of herself like a shield, watch Kate's body in the mirror, watch her responding to Lacey's body, Lacey's touch.

"You're done," the technician says, and the machine slides her body back into the open air. "We'll have your results in a few days." He doesn't say he hopes she'll be just fine, he doesn't say he hopes it's not a brain tumor, he doesn't offer her any company or comfort at all.

And Yet It Moves

Lacey decides to give some of her body away. She is paid to take what people want to give her; now she chooses to give freely what other people want. She wants to help. On her day off, she donates blood, signs up to donate plasma twice a week—Lacey figures if she donates the payment to a fund for people who can't afford to buy plasma-based medical products, that doesn't count as getting paid. She gets the inside of her cheek swabbed to see if she's anyone's bone marrow match; she gets her finger pricked to get on a kidney matching list—she wouldn't mind the scar, thinks the wound will be sexy when she dances.

She volunteers for two drug studies. She can't participate in the heavy-duty tests because there's nothing wrong with her— she can't do the fish oil versus placebo study because she's not depressed, she can't do the new miracle-drug trials because she doesn't have cancer, she can't sample the new finger-prick method and newest variety of insulin because she doesn't have diabetes. It's not that Lacey wants cancer, but if she ever gets it she hopes a drug trial will accept her so that she can go to the doctor weekly, get monitored, feel like something miraculous is being done for her—for others. She participates in a study of a new cold and flu remedy, a new variety of Midol. They ask her pages full of questions, take her vitals, give her a bottle of syrup that may or may not contain a placebo, another bottle of pills, tell her to take one dose every two hours the next time she gets sniffly, the next time she's feeling cramped and bloated, then come back for more measurements. They'll send her blood and urine off to a lab, and the people who examine her before-and-after fluids won't know who they came from. Just a number. Atoms from her body, the people in white gloves who figure out the messages those cells contain will have no idea what the body is like that enclosed them.

To become an organ donor Lacey changes her preferences at the DMV. The man in the uniform tests her perfect vision, tells her to stand against a white screen. While she waits for her picture to be taken she imagines her corpse laid out on a table, examined by first-year med students, or by oncology experts or endocrinologists high-ranking in their field. She pictures the cuts on her body, the Y slice through her torso, heart removed, other kidney gone, liver given to someone with yellow skin. Her eyelids sewn shut, two people given the gift of sight, one of their brown eyes paired with her bright blue—freakish, but at least a freak who can see.

She hopes whatever isn't harvested or put into jars of formaldehyde for future study will be burned, the preserving chemicals evaporating with the smoke. She imagines her ashes left stored in the place where all unclaimed remains stay, her cardboard box touching other boxes, her last intimacy with strangers. The man says, "Smile!" and the flash is an explosion. For a moment, she can't see a thing.

v.

Her second night at the club Kate almost makes as much as Lacey, and everyone in the dressing room is impressed. As all the women clean up, get ready to go home or go out, Kate tells them that her husband runs a fancy hair salon where she used to also work, so if they ever want their hair cut for cheap, she'd be happy to. She walks to Lacey and lifts a lock. "Split ends. You need a trim."

"You're right. I'll make an appointment."

"If you aren't too tired I can do it now. Then you can tell all the other girls how incredible I am."

Selma asks if she can get pink streaks put in next week and Kate says sure; Beth musses Jane's hair and tells her she's never had a split end in her life, says she'll give her a ride home. As the women leave Lacey asks what Kate drinks, gets them neat bourbons from the bar. The room settles into silence as Kate washes Lacey's hair in the sink, surrounded by sequins and feathers, the showgirl attire some of the girls wear. She rubs Lacey's scalp and temples through the suds, each finger pad circling and circling, then her nails scratching the skin in small loops. She rinses her hands and brings her wet fingertips down to Lacey's shoulders, kneading deep with her thumbs. Lacey knows Kate does what she used to have to do for the clients in the shop in order to hear her sigh of satisfaction.

It's five in the morning, near dawn, and then even the bartender goes home, but the women can't see the sky because there are no windows in the building where they work. Lacey pours them each another and Kate leads her to the empty stage, the place where there's the most space, where the hair will make the least mess. She clicks on one overhead light, pulls up a chair. She combs out Lacey's long locks, rhythmically parting and untangling, stretching out a length of hair and trimming, little cuttings sprinkling the floor, longer pieces curling as they hit the stage. She rhythmically runs a humming blow-dryer down each section and curls the ends under neatly. The repetition is soothing, and then she turns off the little machine.

"I'm going to take a little more off, neaten you up, make it messier in some places," Kate says. "Just sit still." Lacey nods. In a salon she'd be facing a mirror, see each strand sliced away. Lacey stares into the black offstage, where there's usually an audience. She wonders what kinds of men and women would be aroused by watching this simple intimacy. She can hear tresses being sheared, can feel her head lighten and lift from her shoulders as each miniscule weight drops away. "When I was little," Kate says, "my mom used to cut my hair at home. We'd sweep up the trimmings every time and carry them outside, let the wind blow the wisps away so birds could use them to make their nests. Little bits of myself blown away in the wind. I searched the woods, found a nest only one time, and there were threads of my hair woven through sticks and twigs. The eggs were bright blue. In the crook of a branch of a maple. I thought it was so beautiful. Though no robins or maples here. Just squawking grackles, oaks infected with mistletoe. Now all we see are these bright green parasitic plants stuck to bare gray branches. Nests abandoned for winter. But I guess the trees will bloom soon, cover them up. I'm not from Texas. Where I'm from we have real winter, and the trees make a forest, aren't just trees. My kids don't know what they're missing. They were born here. We carry their hair outside, though. Let it be blown away in the wind. Do grackles build nests? Are those grackles' nests we see? When the trees are full of leaves, we can't see who's in the nests. You don't know, do you? The Spanish word for them is much more beautiful: *urraca*." She stops cutting. Lacey wonders what it would be like to live somewhere else, be someone else. Then Kate says, "Well, I'm not sure what you're going to think about this. I took a lot off. It seems I've given you the haircut I actually want, but haven't yet been brave enough to get. Fabulous. But different. Do you want to see it?"

Lacey looks at the face everyone says is so like her own. She doesn't know what she looks like. "No thank you," Lacey says. "But thank you."

Kate sweeps the stage and fills Lacey's cupped palms with a tangle of pale hair. She picks up Lacey's purse for her, opens the door. They walk into the parking lot, a black slab with bright painted lines, only two cars left. The horizon is pastel. Lacey stretches out her hands, releases a part of herself to unknown places, unknown uses. What might help make a home. And while Kate watches Lacey's hands lift and empty, she thinks how astonishing beauty can be, how gleaming and grotesque.

Ghost Writer

"How do I tell them?"

I'm trying to give this client my full attention, she's saying something about not wanting her parents to think this is their fault, it isn't, and I'm listening but not. A letter from Joseph arrived this morning. It's in my desk drawer, underneath my elbows. Joseph is gone, obviously he's gone—but the letter tells me why, what kind of gone. I finally touched him, and haven't seen him since.

"How do I tell them?" she asks again. This one's name is Kristen. I remind myself so I don't have to ask her again. "So that they'll understand why I have to do this?"

"One way to help people understand, Kristen, people who don't feel the same way you do, is to tell them about the weight." Maxwell Jackson, Ghost Writer. I compose suicide notes for other people for a price.

"What?"

"Heaviness. Most of my clients feel it, and specifically describing it can help other people comprehend." I have files filled with these descriptions, but pulling one out feels a little formal right now. I tell her some from memory: "Nails fell from the sky, and one client had a board he carried over his head. The nails didn't stab him but they pierced the wood. If he didn't hold the plank high the tips would gouge his face and arms. The board got more and more weighted, and finally he was too tired to keep holding it. Another, she was walking through waist-deep water, had felt it ever since she was a child, but then drops of tar were being added so the level was rising, the mix thickening, becoming harder and harder to drag her legs through. Another had a net over his body, creatures in burrows pulling it tightly down. The worst part was that sometimes his head, or an arm, or a shoulder, would poke through the mesh, and he would feel what it was like to move part of himself freely. Then another net would always be thrown over, again."

"It's how you say how hard everything is," she says. "How you tell them something you feel, but they don't."

"That's right. A metaphor can help you do that, bridge that gap." For Joseph—the letter postmarked from here, from this town, telling me that when he left he didn't go far but what would it matter where he went, he went—for Joseph the air felt like lead dust falling from the sky. The particles stuck to his damp skin, melded, solidified into slick layers, a blanket heavier than the one the dentist uses to protect us from x-rays.

"I like the one where she's walking through thick water," Kristen says. "That one seems most right—it's like it isn't coming from overhead, it's coming from all around. Or below. Can I use that one?"

I look up from staring at the desktop. "I want each person's letter to be original, a distinct description to your friends and family. It seems the right way to do things, to me. So let's try to come up with your own unique metaphor."

This is when she bursts into tears. "I just don't know how . . . ," she starts, and then I'm on the other side of the desk, holding her, handing her tissues, telling her yes, I know, it is hard to explain, but it's important to explain, and that's what I'm here for. To help. They will appreciate her trying to explain. It will help them. The letter from Joseph, the letter that is either a copy of the suicide note he and I wrote together, or a different letter, telling me something else, it is far away now and though I don't want to touch it yet I do want to be near it.

"The worst part . . . ," she says, looking up, directly at me. People look so horrid when they cry. "The worst part is, I just don't know."

"Don't know what?"

"I don't know why I have to do this. I just know I have to. I don't know how to tell them."

"That's what I'm here for," I say. Again.

In the last half hour of her session we agree that life has felt like walking through shin-deep particles of fine sand, glittering but exhausting. We write the paragraph together, her talking, me taking notation and editing as we go. We don't finish, but we get one solid paragraph, and she agrees to come back tomorrow. I usually don't like letting clients leave without a complete product, but she's in no shape to keep working today. She says she'll see me soon. I don't ask if she'll be okay until then.

Tall. A brunette with a beautiful body. Plump in all the right places. Her shoulders are thin, her arms are thin, but her breasts are weighty globes, and as she walks out the door I'm amazed such an ass can widen from such a small waist. I could wrap my hands around her middle, touch my fingertips, squeeze. Her serious, curious face, effort sheening her skin, her white arm reaching out to point to a word, her arm not marked by freckles or scars or hair, just a long, pale, lustrous arm.

* * *

I take the letter out of the drawer. Joseph's handwriting. *Maxwell Jackson, Ghost Writer. 9 Shallot Street.* Just what my advertisements and business cards say. I run my finger across the loops. He used an ink pen, not ballpoint, so the nib didn't bite in, but if I licked the paper the ink would run.

Instead I read the letter I've read every day since he left, the one saved on my computer.

The sky is made of lead particles. They melded on my skin, solidified, encased me in graphite, layers thickening to armor. Bulletproof chainmail. There is too much between me and everything else. I can't move.

I had to be destructive—demolish what was caging me, locking me in a coffin. I spent my life in a sarcophagus. Don't light candles, don't put my name on any crypt. I know it was gruesome. Grisly, ghastly. I carried my driver's license in a plastic bag in my pocket; I hope they didn't ask you to ID the body. I wanted none of you to ever see me again.

There can be no open casket.

I lasted, I lasted, I stayed as long as I could, for you.

Now, it has happened. Now you don't have to wait for it anymore.

Thank you for loving me as much as you did,
Joseph

My eleven o'clock appointment rings the bell.

I close the document on my computer, slip the letter back into the drawer. I check the appointment book.

"Come in, Tracy," I say.

"Hello, Mr. Jackson."

"You can call me Max," I tell her. She is skeletal.

She shakes my hand, sits, pulls out a notepad with jottings all over it.

"You need help writing a letter?"

"I pretty much know what I want to say, but I need help organizing my thoughts." She looks up from the pad. "That's what they always told me in college, that I had interesting thoughts, but I needed help structuring them."

And Yet It Moves

I don't ask her if she dropped out, if she graduated. That kind of information won't help us. "Why don't you just start talking, and I'll type, to get a very rough draft. Then we can edit together. Start with whom you want to address this letter to. Whom do you want to read it?"

She bites her lip. For some, this is the hardest part. But if they really want me to help, be in on this, then they have to be able to say it in front of me.

"Dear Mom, Dad, Sasha, and Kyle."

"The last two—sister and brother?"

"Sister and boyfriend. Fiancé."

I don't know who else mourns Joseph. I should have known that we shouldn't go forward, when he wouldn't tell me names.

"Okay. Tell me what's on your notepad."

She talks about pleasure and pain, about the ability to feel intense joy, but those happy moments aren't worth the dark times in between. The good days are coming less and less often. And in the bad times she feels nothing, not even sad, just numb now, and that she cannot stand. The cutting doesn't let it out anymore, doesn't let her feel. She's not wanted to keep going through this since she was fifteen, at least then, maybe before, but she held on for their sake. But it keeps getting worse. "Kyle, when I met you," she says, "you thought you could make it not so hard. Save me. I'm so sorry I let you try. Imagine," she says, and she looks up at me, not at her handwriting, "imagine if you'd wanted something more than you wanted anything else, you wanted it for over half your life, but everyone who knew tried to stop you from having it. Tried to tell you that you're wrong, that such desires are crazy, deviant, must be medicated and trained out of your brain. Everyone, everyone thinks they can help, change it, save you. But it never changes. They ask you to continue suffering, keep lasting, because they don't want to let you go. For them, not for you."

She looks back down. "I took all the medicine," she says. "It didn't work." She takes a deep breath. "I was convinced love could save me," she says. "It didn't work."

I try to explain in every letter I write, in each client's voice, that love isn't enough to keep anyone here. It can be. For a long time. But that's not love, truly. Shame. Guilt. A desire to not hurt the people who will be most hurt—and yes, that is a form of love, but not the kind that adds joy to a life. Just the kind that adds obligation, another kind of weight.

I do wonder how many of my clients believe, or did—though they never say it out loud—that a great love could save them. That a person does have the power to make the world a place worth being in. They never tell me what would have saved them, they only have me help them tell others why they were impossible to save.

I wonder what makes them finally stop looking.

I wonder how many people I never meet, because a great love saved them.

"I understand," I say. "We have a lot to work with. Your thoughts are pretty clear and precise, I'm just trying to shape them for you." I turn the computer screen so she can see my draft of the opening few paragraphs, but she doesn't look, she goes on, not looking at her notes. She has whatever she's about to tell me memorized. "I don't think my plan is inventive," she says, "but I think it will work. I'll stand on top of my desk with the noose around my neck. Then I'll slit my wrists and step off the edge. When I spin, my blood will fall and trace patterns on the ground. I hope whoever finds me will think it's beautiful."

"I can't know this."

"I already have the rope and the blade. I'm just waiting for the right time."

"I don't think you understand. This is something I cannot know."

And Yet It Moves

"I think writing this letter will tell me when the time is right. I want the letter to be underneath. I want to aim for it when I step. I want to decorate it with my blood."

Who will touch it? "Stop," I say. "It's part of the deal of working with me. I can't know the method or the date."

"Why?" She's startled—as if of course this would be something we could discuss.

There are about seven ways most people kill themselves: hanging, slitting wrists, swallowing pills, shooting themselves in the head or the heart, jumping off a bridge or building, lying on train tracks or stepping in front of a car or train, car exhaust in a garage, so none of the methods really surprise me anymore. When I hear the technique—the commitment of stepping over a cliff edge, of staying still while freight hollers toward—I know most of the ways will work. Except pills. When someone says pills, I think he or she isn't serious. Pills, the body wants to reject them, will vomit them up. Most people don't know how to take a lethal dose correctly. Eliah knew how. She didn't tell me her method in advance.

"This is not a sick, twisted game I play," I say. "I'm not morbid. The details, I can't carry that for you." Tracy, that's her name. "I respect your choice, Tracy. I hope I've shown that I do. We both know things aren't going to get better. But if I know the day and time and way, I'll wish for you to get through just that one moment, which isn't fair."

"Okay," she says with a deep breath. I can tell she's disappointed.

"I do want you to live. But I won't try to make you live, like everyone else."

"Okay," she says again.

I wish I could post my rules so clients would know what to expect. But I don't advertise exactly what I do. It's not illegal—I don't think, though I've never looked it up—since I don't do the killing or even help people arrange it. I just write. Maybe if I knew the manner and date I'd be considered negligent, or complicit, I'm not sure. I don't post details because I don't want the right-wing and religious folk picketing, calling my number, but anyone reading my ad in the right mindset will see what I'm really offering. *Is there a letter you know you must write, but you don't know how? Do you know what you want to say, but you can't find the right words? That's what a Ghost Writer is for. Appointments Monday through Friday, 10 to 6, walk-ins accepted whenever possible.* My address, my number, my e-mail. I advertise in the phone book, on the internet. I get some teenagers calling, asking if I can write their girls smokin' hot love letters, sexy poems that will get them laid. Most of them just call, though, aren't brave enough to come down to my office, and I tell them I don't do work over the phone. Some mothers who are estranged from their children show up. Husbands who want to know how to ask for a divorce. I do that work. I don't mind it. I help at a moment of crisis, do what I can to give them the life they want. That's what my job is, at best. I'm considering sending my business card to hospitals in Oregon, where they legalized doctor-assisted suicide. I'd do that work over the phone.

Six years. I've been doing this six years. I used to be an accountant. But when I found Eliah, and found her letter—well, I wanted her letter to be better. I wanted her note to tell me something I didn't already know.

She did it in the tub, warm water, the drain left slightly open, hot water dripping in to wash the blood away, to save the person who found her from seeing it. Slit wrists, the long way. We learn this is the right way to do it, most of us in junior high. But she didn't trust just that, she also took pills with wine, the bottle and glass resting on the edge away from the floor so she wouldn't drip on the tiles. A few pills every fifteen minutes, with alcohol, lets it sink into the body slowly, so that it will enter the bloodstream too slowly for the body to react, so that the body won't save itself, so

And Yet It Moves

that even medics can't save it. For Eliah, this was no cry for help. She always had an intuitive sense about her body, but I bet she did her research too. At the end, the wine bottle fell out of her hand, into the water, so whatever wine was left, her second bottle, was washed down the drain, so there was nothing that looked like blood in the room, nothing red at all, when I found her.

Tracy has been talking, and I haven't been listening. I switch my attention back on and she says, ". . . watching films lately. There are films of people jumping off bridges. In California, San Francisco, off the Golden Gate Bridge. People see them getting ready, stepping up on the ledge, or even just pacing near the edge, and they film them from their cars. Sometimes other people notice, and get out and try to stop them. Try to talk them out of it. But there are these other people who never enter the frame, they just record it. There are dozens. They're all so beautiful."

She goes on. "And the people jumping out of the Twin Towers. I watch on repeat, so it seems like hundreds of people leap out of those buildings."

She's making me breathe funny, like I can't catch a full lung. I interrupt. "That's different. Those people were choosing between fire and falling. That's murder, not suicide."

"It's different. But it's so beautiful."

"How can you say that?" Very little shocks me, and then . . .

"Who can explain beauty?" she says, firm her in her desires, her aesthetic.

Eliah was wearing a white dress, not naked, when I found her. Nothing underneath. The dress didn't move in the still water, it only moved when the paramedics lifted her out. Then, it fell heavy against her body. In the water, it floated away from her skin. I thought it might be tinted pink with blood or wine, but it was only tinged with the color of her skin below, which wasn't yet blue—the water was warm because of the hot water circulating in, so her skin wasn't yet cold. Her face, which had stayed out of the water, was cold, lips blue, the rest of her, all of her, still a little pink. The gauze over it made her body more beautiful. I'm certain that's why she didn't do it naked—not out of modesty, but to make her body more stunning.

I didn't want to do this in our home, but I had no other place to go. Thank you for being the only place I ever had to go. I did it where it wouldn't stain, where you wouldn't have to clean.

I want your last vision of me to not be ugly. I want you to see me as you saw me in life—beautiful, but aware of my drama, and utterly hopeless. Don't remember me alive. Remember me dead. That's how I always was, I just finally gave in. I couldn't take it anymore, my love. I hope seeing me dead as you saw me in life will help you know I was always dead. Don't be sorry. You did all you could. This is not your fault. I'm not sorry. I did all I could.

She didn't see how images stain the eyes, didn't think of our stained bed. Her study is now my office. Her letter told me only what her white dress already had.

I do remember her dead, but that doesn't stop my longing for her. If she'd done something more horrific, if she'd shot herself in the face or stabbed herself in the heart, and I'd found her like that, then remembering that would be the primary memory I'd have, would push away images of her under our sheets, her over a cup of coffee, her cooking quiche and greens for dinner, walking around our apartment in her underwear, reading every book with a pen in her hand, her not talking to anyone but me for days. The image of her being lifted from water, water streaming off her body, her body not yet stiff, her body just starting to lighten pink to blue, that doesn't undo all the other images. Better to find her bloated, decaying. Not herself, not herself.

And Yet It Moves

I'm clutching Joseph's letter under the desk, where Tracy can't see. Another lover gone. And I've again lost track of what she's saying.

"This week! Jumping from buildings. But one, inside! In the library, he fell down the middle column, landed on the ground. In front of dozens of people. He made dozens, maybe hundreds, of people see it. Deal with it. It's so amazing."

"No. That's not amazing. He was forced into that. He didn't want to die, people just made his life unlivable. It's not beautiful. It's wrong. It's not right for you to be thrilled."

"We shouldn't live in a world where people are harassed for who they have sex with. Soon, I won't have to deal with a world that functions that way. But his style, it was so gorgeous."

My skin is pulsing at my collar. I feel heat emanating from the letter in my hands. I live in a city where it doesn't matter whose hand I hold in public, I don't have to worry about people caring whom I sleep with, whom I want to sleep with. But others die over it. And that's not the work I'm doing here. And the work I'm doing here isn't helping that. And sometimes this world doesn't seem like a place anyone can live in.

"I would step from the top of that staircase, spin over all that space, if I knew how to get in at night, fasten my rope. I don't want to fall. I want to spin. And drip. But I love watching people fall."

"Enough. Have you said what you need to say?"

"I have. I feel great. I haven't felt this good in a long time."

I look at her elated face.

"Give me a few minutes to revise, then I'll let you make sure it's what you were hoping for." I work for ten minutes, trying to concentrate, her body and her heat and my letter unnerving me. I print a copy and hand it to her.

She reads it and says, "Yes. That's right. That's exactly right. You took what I was trying to say, and you said it. Thank you so much."

I imagine her undoing my pants, me letting her. She hands me cash. We're off the clock. Her voice on the phone told me exactly what she'd look like. I think about the skull around her mouth. I imagine her body so pale it's blue, a strip of foil. Her skeleton, bones straining against skin, I think of touching her to feel her flesh because she's not a corpse yet. I'd be careful not to hurt her but I imagine being rough, and when it's over I would tell her, "You're still alive," neither of us able to tell if it's a good thing or not.

Better luck next time rings through my head as she walks out the door, the same Aitken Roshi quote I think of every time a client leaves my office. I don't believe in reincarnation. But I like the thought.

I hold the letter addressed to me. I finger the edges of the envelope, want to wear the seams ragged with my touching. If I handle it enough maybe I will break the borders and the letter will fall from inside, without having to open it. My twelve o'clock appointment, Kevin, doesn't show. That can mean anything—from forgetfulness, to deciding a letter isn't essential after all.

The day Joseph walked into my office, I had that shimmer behind the eyes of one too many cocktails the night before. He looked nothing like my love. He's one of the slimmest men I've known, loose bones, wrought tendons in his arms and his hands, huge eyes, too-big nose, an awkward laugh. He laughs often. He looks shy and hopeful by turns. Looking at him, you wouldn't know how miserable he is.

But he told me.

He looked like something could snap him awake. Salvageable. His flesh was as pale as Eliah's. I imagined his clavicle as rigid as hers, his hipbones poking from his surface like hers, the expanse of his stomach would reach to the corners of his body but his belly would be firm when I pressed it with my palm, hers gave way and received me. He'd be slim where Eliah was wide—her thick, marvelous curving outward, her bell, but he'd have hollows above the holes in his pelvic bone. His body looked to be a plane, hers was a pillar, one to press myself against, the other to wrap myself around.

He is much more beautiful than I have ever been, he is far less beautiful than she was.

I never touched him, until that last day. He met with me three times. Each time he stalled finishing, each time he came back. I reached out and pulled him to me and he knew everything I wanted. He unleashed everything I had been holding. He felt like rain inside my spine, flame in my arteries. It didn't last.

He made me feel desire for the first time since her. Now I feel desire for nearly everyone.

❋ ❋ ❋

Eddie says, "I see dying horses. Gut-slit or rotting."

Elaine says, "I see people eating glass. People walking with bare feet across glass."

Sharon tells me, "I see people getting their lips sewn shut. I see people getting electricity run through their faces." She looks at me, frightened by her own admission.

They say, I see fields of flowers. Walking through them, they slash me.

I see things that almost look human, but have flaps of skin where they shouldn't.

I see bees that eat meat. Pigs with human hands; humans with stilts on their hands and feet, running; raccoons with human faces.

I see toilets overflowing. I see basements full of curtainless showers, full of doorless stalls, the water rising from drains. I try to keep my feet from getting wet. There are people in the corners.

I see deserts, glimmers in the distance I know are not water.

I see people walking down the street, water pouring from the veins in their arms, water spilling onto sidewalks, running down their wrists, dripping from their fingers, soaking their feet.

I see strobe-lit knights in shining armor pierced to the wall with lances. I see sores being lanced from eyes, eyes being slit, julienned.

When I lie down to sleep, I feel worms crawl out my teeth.

I see a person in a box, a cord running through it, to be lit.

I see yolks broken open.

This is what they see before they sleep. They say, I hope death doesn't feel like falling asleep.

✻ ✻ ✻

But no one ever sees ghosts.

Most of my clients don't seem to believe in heaven or hell or an afterlife. They've stopped believing most of the things they were told.

When he was little, Joseph used to press on his eyes and make bright shapes appear. Red checkerboards whose lines moved, yellow bursts from a center, he could make blue concentric circles by putting the right pressure on his eyelids. He said it made the scary pictures go away, it covered up the other awful things he'd see, and some nights he'd do this until he fell asleep.

The first time he saw fireworks they frightened him—something from inside of him was being shown on the outside.

I use a letter opener, a dull blade.

Dear, Dear Max,

I'm sure you've figured out by now that I've done the thing I came to you to help me to do. If you need to remind yourself why, read the letter we wrote together. Address it to yourself.

I want to come to you right now, one last roll in the hay before I blow my brains out. The one person who understands me, and I have to let you go too. For how many people are you the one person who understands them? They all off themselves anyway. Have you ever thought about what that means? I'm writing you now because you made me feel something I hadn't felt in a long time. I had a good day. You gave me something to look back on fondly. Dare I say happy? I know it won't last. I've got to get this over with, stop delaying. How many of your clients do you fuck? How many send you rambling letters, like most people's suicide notes, off the top of the head and impassioned, after you help them write a sane, sustained, tidy letter? Much more appropriate for those left behind than this. Ha! Why are you always in a position to be the one left behind? Do you use protection when you fuck us? You didn't with me. As far as I know I'm not sick, but I might be. Trying to kill yourself slowly?

I'm writing to you on your own stationery, sheets of paper I stole the last time I was in your office. "Maxwell Jackson, Ghost Writer." Ghostwriter is actually one word. You clearly don't know that. But it makes sense. You don't write people into becoming ghosts, Max, but you are a ghost, writing. You are not substantial. You only interact with people who won't last, spirits, and that makes you one of us. I saw the hunger in your eyes. To touch you seemed cruel, we both knew I was leaving, but since you only spend your time around people who want to die, what other options do you have for contact?

What's wrong with you? Necrophiliac. Or savior complex? I know all the terms the psychoanalysts use to tell us why we don't want to live anymore, tell us why we do the things we do to try to spark the desire to live. Or do you love the thrill of the temporary—everything heightened, intensified, your version of hunting, or sleeping with married people?

If you wanted to live you'd do something besides help us all die more easily. What's wrong with you?

> You weakened my resolve.
> I'm off,
> Joseph

Last visit to the dry cleaner. Last time grocery shopping. Last time making love. Last time burning a hole in a thigh. Last time swallowing medicine. The last shower. The last time eating. The final sleep.

What do I see when I close my eyes? I see a body without a soul, lifted from the water. I see a white dress turned transparent by water. I see water streaming off a body, fabric trailing down off the body, I see water spilling off the surface of a body, water tracing the lines of the body. I see the water in the tub heal, smooth over the hole. I see clear water, not pink. I see a still-pink body lifted from water, in motion, making shapes with her body and her dress and the water, she is all curves and lines of falling water. I see them lay her flat on fabric, I see her fall flat, no longer floating, I see her curves and her falling disappear, I see them cover her face with white fabric. When I close my eyes I see arms with holes in them, I see a body I loved chopped to bits, I see Joseph's long, lovely thighs, I see ribs, I see blood pouring from bodies, I see bloodless bodies, I see green trees with kelp hanging from them, I see seawater with murky objects riding the waves, I see a smooth lake pierced by a falling body, I see flocks of birds splintering the sky, beehives exploding, stinging darts thrown into skin. I see myself pulling glass from my mouth, pulling viscous slime from my mouth. When I close my eyes I see myself turning into a sheet of falling water, I see myself collapsing on rain-tanged concrete, ricocheting into drops, rising as mist—evaporating, vanishing, I see myself paling to a shade, a ghost, and I don't know who to haunt.

Not Long for This World

After losing all that kept him rooted to this world—his congregation, then the man he left his vocation for—Pádraig Keane knows he is near his end, so he is about to describe his final desire to a stranger. He wants a Sky Burial, and needs her to perform the ceremony. Pádraig and Moira Miles climb the twenty-nine steps to his rooftop on one of those bright spring afternoons starting to shift to heat. Pádraig has to step up slowly in his fatigue, and though she walks ahead of him, Moira keeps his pace, his labored breath close at her back.

"This is lovely," she says when they arrive—plants and pigeon coops and a patio table with cushioned chairs and a view of Brooklyn all the way out to the water—and she has the kind of voice that makes her mean what she says. On the table are a bucket of ice holding longneck Brooklyn Lagers and a plate of cheese and crackers that Pádraig carried up earlier. Cheddar to seem simple, brie and manchego in case she likes fine things. Pádraig opens the screened doors of his four pigeon lofts before he sits, and when his one hundred birds swirl and swarm and swoop in the sunlight, she says, "No wonder you knew mine wasn't one of yours. Mine are so basic." One of Moira's pigeons had visited Pádraig's roof—a regular occurrence, many of Brooklyn's birds drawn to the ample sustenance and shelter—one week earlier, and the Tibetan amulet tied to its foot had led Pádraig to fasten a note to the other.

When she'd called she said the charm wasn't significant. "I know nothing about Buddhism. I grew up in a church," she'd said, "but I don't go anymore. I saw the symbol and liked it. All my birds wear anklets. Otherwise I can't tell them apart."

Pádraig opens beers and is glad to have something of an appetite, but drinks a long draught before eating for that wonderful feel of cold bubbles on an empty stomach. Moira loads her plate with crackers and slices of each kind of cheese and cuts the rind off her brie as if whittling wood. She wears jeans and a nice black shirt and comfortable shoes; she is wide with a plain face and plain brown hair, but something about her is tilted just enough to make her different, pretty. She says she had no idea there were so many kinds, his pigeons with their ruffs and colors and feathers cascading over their feet are so fancy.

"It's funny you call them fancy," Pádraig says, then tells her the story of his husband. "I met Francisco in confirmation class when we were teenagers. He didn't go through with it. He told his mother he didn't want to repent for what didn't feel wrong, so he shouldn't be confirmed in the faith, though he still believed most of it. His family started attending services elsewhere to save them explanation and shame. I didn't know this until I met him again thirty years later at a baseball game at Shea—tickets we both bought day-of led us to seats right next to each other. Francisco said, 'When we were kids I thought your name was Padre, so it makes sense you became a father.' We fell mostly in love that day. The friends we came with later said they knew exactly what was happening. My buddy, Sister Violet, she was trying to help, so she said to Francisco, 'Pádraig collects pigeons. It's called being a pigeon fancier.' I explained I don't breed or compete, just like to watch them fly and come home. I see no need to make them race. Francisco said, 'You fancy pigeons? That's so gay.' And the four of us laughed and laughed." Francisco has been gone nearly three years. Pádraig didn't know he could

And Yet It Moves

endure that kind of loneliness, so different from the loneliness he felt before him. He looks to Moira's hand and sees no ring. His is loose on his hand and he worries he will lose it.

"Sister Violet is a nun?" Moira asks. "And was okay with you being gay?"

"Still is. She knew nothing would stop what was about to happen from happening. Desires are fairly easy to deny when you aren't in love."

"That's why you aren't a priest anymore?"

"Defrocked. I could keep God if I left the church, but couldn't keep Francisco if I stayed." It's a line Pádraig has used many times, but it's true. He puts a chunk of cheddar on a salty cracker but he doesn't eat it because he thinks it's important to answer Moira's questions carefully. This will decide everything. "I got a job as a copyeditor," he says, "the colored pencils not the same but a similar sense, for me, of order, beauty. Francisco and I had twenty years together. I performed five of the seven sacraments for him. He was already baptized and had no desire to be ordained, but I confirmed him right after we started dating, gave confession and reconciliation weekly, communion every Sunday in our home chapel, and I performed our marriage, and then extreme unction, nearly three years ago." Pádraig chews.

"You think the ceremonies still count, even though you aren't a priest anymore?" Moira's voice isn't incredulous, rather curious, Pádraig thinks.

He swallows. "I think God honored the sacraments as legitimate."

"Even marriage?"

Now Pádraig can't read Moira's voice—curious or accusatory? He feels confronted with his own arrogance. "Marriage is the one I'm not certain about. You're right. I'm not sure God recognizes those vows. But I consider myself married," he says. "Widowed."

Moira uses her finger to spread brie onto a sweet cracker, puts her finger in her mouth. Her broad body moves in delicate ways.

Pádraig wants this woman to understand why he's done what he's done—he had to keep the sacraments in his life, outward and visible signs of an inward and spiritual grace, sanctioned or not, because he couldn't let it all go—because then maybe she will understand why he wants what he wants and then maybe she will do this thing for him. He is finally ready to let everything go.

He wonders if she knows what Sky Burial is.

Moira asks how Francisco died and Pádraig says he was a smoker for decades. He fought and got more years, but didn't want to fight until the bitter end. When it was nearly over Francisco accepted last rites from his husband's hands, the smears of oil, the bread for the journey. Pádraig doesn't mention the pills Francisco then swallowed, the pills Pádraig had gone to some trouble to find. Pádraig's mother told him when he was a child that suicide was the one unforgivable sin, the only, because you don't have time to ask for forgiveness. Since that moment Pádraig has focused more on God's mercy than on his prohibitions.

Moira makes a funny face at the words *fought* and *fight* and Pádraig wonders what her story is, what battles, wonders when he should ask.

Pádraig says, "I have cancer now, even though I ran and did yoga daily." In addition to daily prayer; Pádraig understands many kinds of devotion. "I ate well. Never smoked. But I'm not fighting. I don't want to stay here." Pádraig had been one of those slim, ropey men who looks like he'll live forever, but he knows he's shrunken lately, looks sick. He was never sexy like Francisco.

They sit in silence, watch the flock feed, drink, bathe, roost, strut and fly and coo. Pádraig understands that his carrier pigeons and rollers and trumpeters and highflyers are not mourning doves, though he finds in their reverberations of bereavement his own grief given voice. His pigeons are not Passenger Pigeons, he understands those birds existed in the millions but were hunted to extinction, and while his collection of every shape and size and shade should comfort him it doesn't. There is one kind he can never see. Some say Passenger Pigeons will be cloned, gone for a century but through the scales on the feet of stuffed specimens they will be made again. De-extinct. If loss can be undone then why lament? Await return. His birds know that's not how it works.

Pádraig will perform last rites for himself. Though that final sacrament feels crucial he wants a funeral from another tradition.

"Francisco got the exact burial he wanted," he says to Moira. "I couldn't eulogize him, of course. No Catholic would, but I got the next best thing, an Episcopalian in full raiment, all of her parishioners filling the pews, singing Francisco's favorite hymns with an organ and a choir—482, 'Lord of all hopefulness, Lord of all joy'; 208, 'The Strife is o'er'; and 657, 'Love divine, all loves excelling.' The bright Virgen de Guadalupe coffin and red roses were a bit garish, but it was all exactly as Francisco had hoped." Then the other ritual Francisco wanted, a party at the home they'd shared, their friends drinking Irish and añejo and smoking to help the soul on its journey, telling stories and jokes, not exactly an Irish wake since after the burial and not before, but their version of it. Pádraig thinks of Sister Violet in her black-skirted suit and pearls handing him a whiskey and saying, "It won't help, but it likely won't hurt." If they'd had a public wedding she would have been Pádraig's best man. They took their shots and she wrapped her arms around him and said, "I'm just so sorry." The only thing there ever is to say. She brought tequila and they clinked. To Francisco.

"I don't want any of that," Pádraig says. "I said in the note I sent you that I want a Sky Burial. I'm looking for a rogyapa, a body-breaker."

"I looked it up. It's usually only done by men," Moira says.

"I'm not attached to that."

"Me either. Women should be able to be priests."

"I agree."

"It seems violent, the ritual," Moira says. They both finish their beers and Pádraig opens them each another.

"Yes. But it's also considered compassionate. Alms for the birds. A final generosity, giving of my body so that others may live. Flesh as sustenance."

"Where would I take you? Where are vultures near here?"

"The vultures are here." Moira looks up, past the edge of the shade over their heads, squints in the sun. "Some days I see them, some days I don't," Pádraig says. "It's warm enough for them up here now. I did an experiment. I lost an Archangel a month ago. I left the body out in the open. I sat in the far corner of the roof and they weren't afraid of me. Three vultures came. The bones were picked clean in less than two hours." Moira shudders and that worries Pádraig. "Of course, I'm much larger than a pigeon." He laughs awkwardly. "There are different ways to do this. I'd appreciate the opportunity to be frank."

Moira's face is still, professional. She looks down, but she nods.

"One option is stripping my flesh from my bones and pounding them, or pounding the bones and flesh together into a paste. That's the most involvement. Or you could saw my body into bits and leave for a few days, then return to pound the clean bones. Or you can leave me whole and just come once to pound—"

"If I leave you whole," she interrupts, "I'm afraid people will notice the vulture swarm."

"They might. Faster is better."

"And if I'm not fast enough? If the cops find me with bloody hands?" Moira's voice is steady and calm. She has green eyes, like bottle glass.

"I will write a letter explaining the situation, so that if you should be disturbed there will be no legal trouble for you."

"You think that will hold up?"

They both take a drink.

"I would have it notarized. I know I'm asking a lot. I know you don't know me. I don't know you. Strangers. I asked Violet, I called a mortician, they both said they couldn't. Rogyapas usually use knives. I have tools you can choose from. A chainsaw, which will make some noise, which concerns me. Limb shears, for trees, which are very powerful, and quiet. I've bought a mallet, and I will make sure tea, butter, and flour are in the house, to mix with the pulverized bones. Make an edible paste. This custom started in a place where the ground is too rocky, often frozen, to dig. A place with no trees to burn. But here, it's the only thing that feels right to me."

He waits for her to speak. After silence Moira says, "It has been so long since I've known what feels right." Then she shakes her head with a quick flick, finishes her beer in one swallow. She looks as if she's readying to stand and Pádraig opens another beer and doesn't say anything, holds it out to her.

As his arm begins to tire she takes it. He's grateful his arm didn't start to shake.

Moira asks, "Can I ask you some questions?"

"Of course," Pádraig says. He feels he is being interviewed for an important position.

Moira asks, "Why did you become a priest?"

Pádraig answers truthfully. "I believed. When I was a child, I was good at following the guidelines, and they felt right. Confessing my few sins felt like announcing a mistake I wouldn't make again. I wanted to be the one to help others feel that sense of progress. Growing closer to goodness and rightness and God." Moira nods. Pádraig adds, "The way my father looked at me when I said

I wanted to become a priest, when I was sixteen, let me know my family knew everything. He said, 'Good, son. That's good.' My mother cried, tears of relief, I think, that I would be safe. By the time I left the church they were both dead, so I didn't have to tell them. Francisco's parents disowned him, but I don't think mine would have."

"Why do you want this ritual?" Moira asks. She bites into a thick cube of cheddar. She seems calmer now.

Pádraig senses he is meant to seduce her with his answers. His eloquence will make her decide. "It's the only way to transcend," he says. "I love the physics and the metaphysics of it. The vultures will digest me, I will become their muscles and their flight, my body in the sky, my soul above that. I will leave this earth completely. The birds will shit out what of me they don't need, sure, and when they die I will still be part of their rotting flesh, but part of me will become energy. It feels like the only way to truly be gone from the world."

Moira eats a briny cracker with evident pleasure on her face. She asks, "What will you miss?"

"Handing the sacred wine and wafer to someone. Eating the holy body and blood. Running at full speed, full strength. Doing a complete yoga class, every pose, with full attention, full extension. The intensity Francisco and I shared. The calm he gave me. Sex. Vivid wines, Brunellos and Barolos. Medium-rare steak with gorgonzola. Vegetables. Honey. All the spices. These birds who keep me company without knowing they do. Knowing my mother and father love me and want me to be happy. Coffee and tea. Singing in front of a room full of people. Vestments. Hearing confessions, helping people through the things they do." He pauses. "Most of the things I will miss I already miss. I'm not going longingly."

She nods. The way she puts another slice of cheese in her mouth before she's finished chewing the first reminds him suddenly,

And Yet It Moves

strangely, of how Francisco ate. It aroused Pádraig, that unselfcon-scious demonstration of daily desire, and seeing it here on Moira is bewildering and soothing. She wipes the corner of her mouth before swallowing and it is Francisco's gesture, his hand.

Moira says, "I can do this."

So sudden. Pádraig is too surprised to be pleased at first. Then he says, "This means so much to an old man. Thank you."

"I'm a nurse. I assist surgeries. You didn't know that. Even though they're alive and we sew them back together, I think the cutting will be okay. I'm kind of the perfect person to do this." Moira tucks her hair behind her ear. "And I think this will be good for me, too. Catharsis. There's someone I've wanted to do harm to. Violence. Doing this, I think it will let me get this craving, this vengeance, out of my system."

"What?" is all Pádraig can manage.

"My husband. Ex. He beat me. It's still embarrassing to admit for some reason. But I figure the least I can do is be honest. With you. I got him to leave. But I still live in our apartment. Rent sta-bilized, so I can afford it."

"I'm rent controlled here," Pádraig says, going with this swerve. "It's why I'm still down the block from the church I left. Or was excommunicated from, depending on who you ask."

They each drink a large swallow, then another. The air smells good up here, like growing things. The river glints.

Moira nods. "I still see him. He lives in the neighborhood, so I see him out with women and wonder if he hits them. Yells. It's not like I didn't know. He did that all before we were married. And inside the apartment. I see him there too. I know he's not really, I had the locks changed by a smith from another borough, no friend of his. But I don't sleep well. I never talk about this. Not to other people. I talk to myself about it all the time." She stops and Pádraig wonders if she's done. She takes a few visible breaths. "Everyone thinks it's over. Thinks I was brave for getting out but they don't know how bad it was. No one shunned him, he's still living his life"—and this is what Pádraig misses most about being a priest, listening to people, intimacy as healing, but he doesn't say that to Moira, doesn't want to draw attention to what's happening—"so I haven't gotten over it. Not really. Doing this, I wonder if it can help me get over it."

During many intimacies we don't really see the other, pour into a body what we want to see. Sex, confession—Pádraig's been a body, a vessel, his cock or his collar an icon, all the other person sees. And then, a few moments in his life, the gorgeousness of being seen in fullness, wholly held and taken from and given to. "So, you want to chop your ex-husband into bits?" he asks.

"Yes."

"And seeing him there instead of me, you think this will bring you closure?"

"I hope. I think it will help me understand—what? My own capacity for violence. What I'm capable of. I have scars," Moira says, and Pádraig realizes that everything but her hands and face is covered. She lifts her chin and there's a healed, deep notch in it. "I think it might be important," she says. "Let me release him."

Pádraig feels dread. "That isn't what I'd imagined. I thought this would be a holy ritual. To send me on my way. Kind."

"I read about it," Moira says. "The rogyapas aren't solemn. They talk and laugh. It's labor, a practical necessity."

"But your anger, that violence, I fear it might keep me here, when all I want to do is go."

Moira shrugs. "People think souls can get trapped. I don't know if they can."

Pádraig hopes he has enough time to find someone else to break his body gently and with compassion. He says, "I'm sorry. But I don't want it to happen this way. I'm sorry I've wasted your time."

Moira draws together her eyebrows, then relaxes her face. "You didn't," she says. She stands and embraces Pádraig and her body feels so different from Francisco's. Moira leaves with empty hands.

* * *

Violet comes when he calls. "Would a requiem really be so bad?" she asks.

"I'm not allowed to go to services where I used to conduct services. I don't want them to bury me."

"Okay." Violet is drinking a still mostly cold beer. "What about the Episcopalians?"

"I should have become an Episcopal priest. But I didn't. So I'm not their community either."

"You're no Buddhist."

"That's kind of the point. They don't excommunicate. I don't think they would mind me borrowing their ritual."

"You know I can't do this for you."

"I know." Pádraig doesn't want to talk anymore, doesn't want to problem-solve, just wants company. Violet seems to sense this and stays silent. Violet is the best of all of them, Pádraig thinks. The kind of nun who says things like, "Jesus would be hanging with the queers and queens. The lepers of our era. Jesus would befriend them." She works in a Catholic grade school that doesn't have enough students so has been converted to a halfway house for ex-con mothers and their children, a place to become a family again, with help. People tell her it must be hard and she laughs. "The hardest thing about being a nun," she says, gray hair cut sleek, "was figuring out what to wear once they said we didn't have to wear the habit anymore. We're all better off, but we had to get magazines and share them. Who of us knew anything about jewelry?" Today she's trim in a houndstooth suit. In more serious moments she tells Pádraig it is a privilege for her to do her work. "The poor, they've shaped my life. I'm lucky to be a guest in their days." Pádraig knows she's done far more good work in the world than he has. Though she diminishes her service, says her days consist of prayer, reading, studying, singing, gardening, swimming, then cooking dinner at night with her friends. "If there were a similar situation for female atheists," she says, "the waiting list would have hundreds of names on it."

Sister Violet has a wonderful laugh. But she knows the diminishing numbers: "Sixty thousand Catholic nuns in the US now. Three times that in 1965. Ninety-seven percent are forty or older, the median age sixty-five and rising. Who is going to replace me? Us? Nine out of ten nuns say they are strongly satisfied with their lives, even though the majority supports ordaining women, letting priests marry, electing bishops, tolerating doctrinal dissent to a greater extent. How many young women would love to live this life but don't want to be a part of the penis-hat's hierarchy? We've got to shape up, get with the program, desperate times call for desperate measures." Some of the other priests and nuns think she's a pain in the ass, sure, but she is Pádraig's best friend. Her other closest friend was excommunicated after recommending a first-trimester abortion to a woman with a life-threatening condition. Sister Margaret McBride was gone in months, though the priest Sister Violet suspected of abusing children, Father Phillips, was moved to another parish. "High-level fuckery" she calls it, but knows to only say that to Pádraig. "You're one of the good guys," she said to him decades ago when he cried in her room for longer than he thought possible as he tried to explain all he was losing and all he was gaining. She reaches out and squeezes his hand now.

"There's just so much I don't know how to make right," he says.

Violet nods. "I know," she says.

And Yet It Moves

Pádraig is almost too weak to open a beer, but he manages it. He thinks of one of the last times he saw Francisco. "Everyone thinks it's AIDS," Francisco said. "But I tell them neither of us is sick."

"I only ever had sex with you."

"When we got serious I got tested."

"I know. You do look like hell."

"I'm sorry I never quit smoking."

"Cigarettes were a joy. I never tried to get you to quit."

"I miss them, even now. I never think to stop and spend time paying attention to my breath."

"There's always yoga. Or running."

"Too late for that."

"I know." They lounged in bed, reading, Pádraig doing some work, making food when they wanted it. "The new pope named himself after you," he said, pointing to the cover of *Rolling Stone*.

Francisco smiled, effort showing. "The saint. The lover of animals. The man who let birds light on his arms. More you than me." Four years before, the tree Pádraig and Francisco could see from most windows in their home grew too big, too old, its roots buckling the sidewalk, trying to make more space, and it was going to die anyway so the city decided to remove it. Pádraig had known that tree through some of the most important moments in his life. Francisco arranged with the borough somehow and bought all the wood. He made Pádraig an aviary out of the lumber he cut and dried for a year—*That one*, Pádraig thinks, the one over his left shoulder—and he carved a small statue of St. Francis with birds on his arms, and painted it, for their chapel. Francisco said, "This new pope might make things better. People are calling him radical and liberal and lefty because people haven't heard anyone talk like Jesus in the church in a while. I'm excited."

"There's just so much to make better."

"I know."

Pádraig asked if Francisco remembered the mountain they saw in Arizona, the beautiful blue peak rising up out of the forest, a dormant volcano, named after St. Francis. For their honeymoon they'd gone to the opposite corner of the country. Pádraig asked if Francisco wanted to see Mexico and he said no—his parents were from there, not him, and he understood his parents as much as he cared to. They flew to the desert and rented a car and bought an atlas and drove spontaneously. They saw ancient trees and an ocean coast so unlike their own and ate spicy food and swam in salt and chlorine and they were joyful. They toured a reservation in Arizona and saw a ruin with pottery shards on the ground. They had to step on them because there was no place else to walk. The tour guide told them the Franciscans named the mountain after their patron saint, but the Hopi people who lived there, who still live there, have their own name for it. The missionaries and monks, hundreds of years ago, made them stop practicing their religion, their prayer cycle that brings rain in a desert, made them worship the Catholic God. They revolted, killed hundreds of Spanish. The Spanish came back and all the villages said they couldn't stay, except one. The one where they stood. They didn't make the Franciscans leave and the Hopi killed their own people, destroyed their own village, to make sure the Spanish men of faith stayed gone for good. Pádraig said, "No one knows all that was done in St. Francis's name. And that's what the pope, and the church, would actually have to atone for."

"But I'm hopeful," Francisco said. "This guy's a Jesuit. He hung with Jorge Luis Borges. He's better than anything we've had in a long time. He's saying maybe don't judge gay people, we don't see the poor because we're too comfortable."

"Maybe? The hierarchy didn't mean to let this happen. They thought he was a safe choice. The hierarchy will never say they're sorry."

"But small change is still change."

"You're right. We should be glad. It's just hard for me to be glad about anything these days."

Pádraig woke up and Francisco's hand was on the small of his back. He woke up and his hand was flat on his chest. He woke up and his hand curved around his bicep. He woke up and his fingertips touched his clavicle. During their days spent apart Pádraig thought of Francisco's hands and then they came home and they were everywhere and when he slept he was not released.

Violet touches Pádraig on the shoulder, says she'll carry down all the empty bottles and plates, says he should call if he needs anything.

Pádraig wonders—if he can heal something, shouldn't he?

Dusk is nearing. When Pádraig rented the top-floor apartment with exclusive roof access forty years ago he'd started a garden and a compost heap, then bought two birds from the pet store down the block, but the birds kept returning, knew the shop as home. They stood on the sidewalk under the striped awning until the owner let them in. He gave them back to Pádraig at least seven times. Pádraig finally got them to stay long enough to breed, and the eggs that hatched on his roof knew it to be home. He bought birds that aren't homers, bred for their beauty, ones from elsewhere who have no desire to return. He looks at his birds and says the name of each and every one. Aachen Lacquer Shield Owl. Aargau Peak Crested. Abu Abse-Dewlap. Archangel. Nun. Spanish Little Friar Tumbler. King. Fat Shan Blue. Hyacinth. Echterding Colour Pigeon. Thuringian Goldbeetle. Jewel Mondain. Luster Pigeon. Reversewing Colour Pigeon. Moscovite Tumbler. Fish Eye Roller. Giant Mallorquina Runt. Beauty Homer de Lige. Bohemian Fairy Swallow. Clean Legged Fullhead Swallow. Naked Neck Tumbler. Baku Boinije. Elster Purzler. Donek. Dragoon. Taqlaji. Ptarmigan. Smyter. Cambalhota Português. Egyptian Swift. Czech Ice

Pouter. Polish Eagle. English Show Tippler. French Owl. Italian Sottobanca. Spanish Thief Pouter. Swedish Owl. Swiss Self. Syrian Bagdad. Russian Martini. Thai Laugher. Macedonian Turbit. Texan Pioneer. Bukarest Black Hanging Flight Tumbler. Transylvanian Double Crested Tumbler. Romanian Black-Cherry Tumbler. Irish Flying Tumbler. Limerick Tumbler. West of England Tumbler. Krakow Magpie. Lahore. Lebanon. Hamburg Sticken. Dresden Trumpeter. Danzig Highflyer. Warsaw Butterfly Tumbler. Lucerne Copper Collar. Franconian Toy Self. Anatolian Ringbeater. Hindi Fantail. Indian Fantasy. Shiraz Tumbler. Old Fashioned Oriental Frill. Pigmy Pouter. Asiatic Crack Tumbler. American Flying Flight. That humans created such variety from one species proves evolution to Pádraig, which he does not find incompatible with God.

He thinks of the last time his body will lift him up these stairs to this chair. He thinks of vultures, how some say they look like doom. Vultures in flight are a kettle. Vultures resting in trees are a committee, a volt, or a venue. A group of feeding vultures is a wake. Wake. Mourning. Forlorn. Lovelorn. Lonesome. Once. Wants. Parish. Perish. Vultures are endangered in Nepal. He doesn't know what they will do, in that place where the custom he wants was born. He will bring no food with him except for one wafer. He listens to the murmurs and susurrations of his companions. He will take the bottle of holy oil that Sister Violet procured for him and tip it onto his thumb, then smear a cross onto his forehead. He will confess his sins to himself—he has not loved God with his whole heart and he has not loved his neighbors as himself, the only sins he considers worth confessing anymore, the only sins Francisco ever confessed—and eat the Viaticum, bread become body to sustain him on his travels. Pádraig will talk to God for the last time on this earth. He does not know who will be there above,

And Yet It Moves

his lover or his family or no one, but he knows God will be there and he is excited to meet him.

A purple pigeon lands on Pádraig's roof, starts eating with the others. Gleam of amethyst, plump plum body. People think pigeons are banal, mundane. Humdrum. Pádraig knows the extraordinary array, brilliance and magnificence, extravagance of form. But then this creature, making even Pádraig's variety look pale. A purple pigeon, as if a parrot mated with the commonest bird.

Looking at it Pádraig feels the longing that beautiful, impermanent things always make him feel, the desire to save it, keep it, make it all his. Hold it all. He feels no room for anything new because it is something else to lose so why get crowded just to get emptied? Because it stays and leaves, all of it. Why let anything else in. Then others land—saffron, scarlet, emerald, cobalt, turquoise. Here they are. Parakeets amongst his doves. They won't stay and he won't forget them but he will miss the sight of them despite seeing them still in his mind and then he will be gone and he will or won't remember. Pádraig believes he is going somewhere else, but he isn't sure how much of the world is coming with him.

He dials Moira's number. "I know you thought you'd never see me again," he says. "But there's something here I think you should see."

* * *

Moira comes to see if it is finished, if the birds have done their work. She finds a clean, empty bowl. She picks it up to wash in his sink, though it is spotless. Pádraig is gone.

She agreed because—she's still not certain why she agreed, again. Because when he called her back to this roof to show her something she'd never seen before, when he gave her that, she figured she should give him something she was capable of, or at least try. Those jewel-toned birds—she'd looked it up, and it was an art project, regular pigeons captured and airbrushed and released, to make New Yorkers question their sense of normalcy, of beauty. And watching them with Pádraig, they made her feel transported to another place, another time—Moira knew she was on the island where she'd spent all of her life, but she felt both there and somewhere else, in two places at once, between the possible and impossible.

"What if I tried really hard to not think of my ex during the ceremony?" she'd asked Pádraig. "What if I tried to be compassionate the whole time, but didn't promise perfection. Would that work for you?"

"Would that work for *you*?" he'd asked.

"It would let us both get what we wanted, I think."

And then Pádraig said, "I don't think you can try really hard to not think of someone."

And she'd laughed, for what felt like the first time in days. She said, "I do feel like we were fated to find each other," and Pádraig said he still believed that what some call fate is God intervening in our lives.

They decided Pádraig would send her an asterisk as a text every night at eight o'clock and when she didn't receive one she was to come the next day to begin the process. "So long," he said, and "So long," she replied, and they grinned at each other one of the oddest grins either had ever experienced.

The night she did not receive a message she slept fitfully, unsure if she could do what she'd agreed. When she arrived she found Pádraig on the roof, wrapped in a blanket with no clothes on and she was grateful to not have to do that part. Cutting up a body felt much like what she did at her job—inserting a catheter, cleansing a bedsore or bedpan, removing infected stitches—unpleasant, but doable if you just get started. She did not feel angry during

And Yet It Moves

the ceremony. She did not feel violent. The small body in front of her was so unlike the robust body of the man she once loved—not thought she loved, but truly loved—that she couldn't have felt she was damaging the one who damaged her, even if she tried. She kept her emotions contained, after years of practice just functioning. But at the end, when she sliced off each finger, dismembered those hands that had done so many holy and unholy things—who was she to decide? If anything was holy then why shouldn't everything be holy?—fully separating them from what they had been, it was then that she started to sob. Not for Pádraig, but for herself. She wondered if, after all that had been done to her body, after all she'd done to this other body, after all the intimacy and violence, could she ever let anyone touch her again? She wished Pádraig had let her imagine revenge, because anger is so much stronger than fear.

The second time she visited was easier. She was amazed at how bright the bones were, how efficient the birds had been. The pummels, the mixing in of tea and butter and flour, felt like making dough. Pádraig looked like food. Yet she's still not been able to sleep well, worried that someone saw the vultures, someone traced her to her apartment. She keeps the letter exonerating her near at all times. She is glad Pádraig will circle the skies and perch in trees for a time, inside the bodies of other creatures. Devoured. But today she wants this done.

When they sensed the vultures overhead the pigeons hushed to silence but now they're jabbering away. Above their voices she hears a knock at the door to the roof and her heart startles. Moira looks around but there is no blood, no bones, she already threw away the little hair the birds left behind, she washed the blanket, this does not seem a crime scene, the only evidence an empty bowl, but she wonders whether or not to let someone into this space.

"Moira?" a woman's voice asks from behind the door. Moira is glad it's a woman. "I don't want to frighten you. I'm Pádraig's friend." Moira opens the door and a slim woman in a skirt and boots and a blue top and patterned scarf is standing there. "I'm Violet. Am I welcome?"

"Yes. I guess. I wasn't expecting anyone."

"Pádraig told me that after he didn't text me one night I should wait one week, then come feed his birds. I didn't expect you to still be here. I thought it would be done. I'm sorry for interrupting."

"You know? About everything?"

"I do. Thank you for doing what I could not." Violet has a small smile.

"I couldn't come yesterday because of work. But it all went as planned."

Violet looks up to the sky. No birds in sight but she smiles. "Pádraig told me to mail you this envelope he left on his desk. But instead I will hand it to you. I heard you above when I came into the apartment. It's nice to meet you, Moira. I'll feed the pigeons while you read it." Violet hoists a sack and enters a coop and Moira slits the fine paper open with her finger.

Moira,

Thank you. What you have done for me has allowed me to pass in peace.

This apartment is yours if you want it. It can't stay rent controlled without me on the premises, but the landlord will let it to you rent stabilized at a decent rate, more than I paid but reasonable for the area. You can keep what you want of the furniture, give away what you don't, bring down what you want from your old place. I think you might want to leave there. Your birds could join my flock but if you don't want them the local pigeon club will find them all good homes. I'm not sure

And Yet It Moves

if you would want to commute to your hospital but maybe you could transfer to one closer? You shouldn't feel obligated, Moira, but I wanted to offer what I had. I am thankful that God brought you to me and I want to thank you. And God. Five thousand dollars will go to the Episcopal church that buried Francisco and that leaves ten thousand for you, whether you take the apartment or not. A check is clipped to the enclosed will. Not much, but it will help. And thank you, again.

May you have many blessings,
Pádraig

Violet emerges, a feather resting on her hair, nearly the same shade of gray, and asks what she thinks.

Moira asks, "Why didn't he leave it all to you?"

"I'm a nun, dear. Poverty is a vow of mine."

Moira has never met a nun. "How much did Pádraig tell you about me?"

"He told me everything he knew. He said he hoped we might become friends. I live nearby. At the church where Pádraig used to be the priest. If you don't want a friend, I understand. But the offer stands."

The church bell resounds, a gong note reverberating into and through Moira's body and back through the entire neighborhood. She wonders what it was like for Pádraig to hear that gigantic chime every day of his life, to know but no longer see the person who rung it. Moira thinks she could love this small space, the worn leather couches and mismatched china plates and silver forks heavy in the hand and handmade pottery holding plants and art on the walls, not excess, not at all, but a few fine, lovely things to look at. Pádraig feels gone, not a presence, not a ghost. And that other man, she won't tell him where she went.

"I don't think I'll bring much," Moira says, then asks, "Would you be able to help me carry some boxes tomorrow? Nothing too heavy." The bell peals the hour of twelve o'clock and several birds fly away and several land and in the rush of wings Moira feels held and released. She wonders if it rang during those hours she spent with Pádraig but she just didn't hear it.

Ochre Is the Color of
Deserts and Dried Blood

If you want to marry me, the phlebotomist said to the chemist, you must complete these tasks.

She said to him, Get me limonite, hematite, and goethite, for me to dye my dress to a halcyon gilt.

Gather me ebony, mahogany, and teak, for me to fashion a crown.

Dig me up bronze, alabaster, and onyx, for me to craft ornaments to adorn me.

I'll need graphite and ash for my lashes, lapis lazuli and cobalt for my lids, the fruit of prickly pears for my lips.

Brew me chartreuse, absinthe, and claret for our feast.

* * *

They took DNA tests when they decided to get hitched. They wanted to know who they were descended from, who they could combine to create, their lineage, their traditions, what they could pass on. They learned that he was Swedish, Irish, and Polish Jewish; she was German, Armenian, and Red Ocher.

What's Red Ocher? the phlebotomist asked the chemist.

The chemist did not know. They looked it up. The Red Ocher are people named and studied by scientists, and thought to no longer exist.

I draw others' blood and had no idea what was in mine, said the phlebotomist. My family has lived in Nevada for generations. Not Washoe? Not Winnemucca? I'm not Duckwater Shoshone? Lovelock Paiute? Mojave? I'm not descended from the Confederated Tribes of the Goshute Reservation?

Some of your ancestors are from what's now called Illinois, the chemist told her.

I'm descended from a people thought to be extinct, named because they buried their dead under red minerals. I'm glad you study chemicals, the phlebotomist said to the chemist, the things that make us, but you don't study people. You don't put humans in a taxonomy.

We need new traditions, the phlebotomist said. I want to cover my body with things from the land, things the earth made, elements from this place I am from. We need new American traditions, since I don't know my own.

❊ ❊ ❊

The chemist went to deserts, jungles, and caves, and brought her back what she'd asked.

He said, Here is your hydrated iron oxide, my love, your three kinds of ochre—yellow: $FeO(OH)nH_2O$; red: Fe_2O_3; brown: $FeO(OH)$. Here is your wood. Your metal and stone. Your cosmetics. Your intoxicants.

She'd woven a dress from the silk of worms, laced with the pearls of oysters and shells of periwinkles. She mixed the crushed compounds with water and submerged the dress, gilding it. It dried while she painted her face. She donned her crown, gown, and jewelry, and asked her betrothed—who wore a jet velvet suit with a ribbon tied in a bow round his neck—What shall we do? To tie ourselves to each other, and to this land?

And Yet It Moves

The chemist said, To fully commit to what will be, I think we need to tour what once was. He loaded up their red '67 Mustang for a road trip and said, That's my suggestion for a new American tradition.

* * *

They drove to the Nevada Proving Ground, where there once had been mushroom clouds and were now craters. They saw hollows made by bombs named Cyclamen, Lampblack, Sturgeon, Petrel, Kestrel, Baseball, Tuna, Bevel, Cobble, Minnow, Cerise, Sepia, Pike. Deep divots in the pale sand, deviations from an almost-blank expanse, basins, cavities, caverns, where once had been conflagration. The phlebotomist thought they should worry about radiation; the chemist said the longer-lived isotopes like plutonium and uranium would linger for tens of thousands of years, so he wouldn't live on the land, he wouldn't drink the water, but after a quick visit they should be okay. All the atomic glass, fused sand, had been scavenged by previous tourists, but the chemist said that's not something they'd want in their pockets anyway.

This tainted painted desert, he said as they climbed back in their car.

* * *

They drove to the Lost City Museum, full of artifacts that were going to be covered as the Hoover Dam filled Boulder Canyon and Virgin Canyon to make Lake Mead, but were salvaged, put in glass boxes in a building. Woven black-and-white baskets, painted black-and-white pottery, manos and metates, arrowheads. The phlebotomist wanted to hold it all in her palms. But you weren't allowed to touch—the oils in our hands can ruin. Some call those people the Anasazi, some call them Ancestral Puebloans, some call them the Hisatsinom. Some say they disappeared. People of the Taos, Acoma, Isleta, Cochiti, Kewa, Jemez, Ohkay Owingeh, Nambe, Laguna, San Ildefonso, San Felipe, Santa Ana, Santa Clara, Sandia, Picuris, Pojoaque, Tesuque, Zuni, Zia, Ysleta, and Hopi Pueblos say they are their ancestors.

I don't know how to learn this, other than from a museum, the phlebotomist said.

＊　＊　＊

They drove to the Valley of Fire and saw petroglyphs; the phlebotomist wanted to see where people had lived, the buildings they made, but there aren't any left in Nevada. What people call ruins. So they looked at places where people had carved the stone's patina to expose lighter rock underneath. Red-orange under red-brown. Crosses and circles and weapons and animals and people and plants. The phlebotomist looked around her. Some of what the ancients saw is still here, she said.

＊　＊　＊

They drove to the ghost town of Rhyolite, saw its abandoned buildings, the house made out of bottles of Adolphus Busch beer and opium medicine flagons sealed in concrete, crumbled schools, derelict banks, abandoned stores, dilapidated railroad depots. At high noon the shadows stacked under the broken bits of neglected walls that once held roofs, that once housed people and wares. It felt no more or less haunted than all the other places they had been that day.

＊　＊　＊

They drove over the Hoover Dam and saw a white ring showing that the water level of Lake Mead had dropped, lower now because of drought, because of more people using water. They knew the entire canyon below was now white, minerals deposited on top

And Yet It Moves

of minerals. If the lake emptied of water, even the chemist didn't know if the white would dissolve, flake off, reveal the former colors of the canyon. The ruins of St. Thomas are sometimes visible when the water level in Lake Mead drops but they couldn't see the surviving parts of that town today.

* * *

They stopped for gas at the Moapa Paiute Travel Plaza and met the owner. He told them, My mom started this business. She died of cancer. They say it's from watching the tests, being downwind of the fallout. I inherited this place. There are only 329 of us, he said. We've put solar panels all over our land. We sell electricity to Los Angeles, but someday, I want us to be the ones who light up Las Vegas.

They could have gambled in the casino, or bought fireworks, or liquor, or beer, but they just got an Indian taco to share.

We didn't invent this, the owner told them. The Navajo of Arizona did, the Diné, using the flour, sugar, salt, and lard that were given to them by the government in New Mexico, after they were forced to walk three hundred miles away from their homeland. They usually ate vegetables and beans. Most people think it's ancestral food, and I guess it is, in a way. Each tribe serves fry bread a different way. Ours has hot red chiles. Good, yes?

They nodded with their mouths full.

* * *

After their tour, it was time for their ceremony. He drove into the desert, the wilderness. The layers were mauve, magenta, maroon, vermilion, crimson, scarlet, sienna, umber, ecru, puce, fulvous, topped by a cerulean azure viridian sky. The layers were coral, salmon, tangerine, oriole, marigold, canary, saffron, poppy, the striations were eggplant, lilac, lavender, violet, plum, heliotrope, the strata were almond, eucalyptus, fawn, as if they were surrounded by living things, sustenance, rock that could walk away or bloom or feed them. Under the witness of hawks, snakes, and coyotes, under the witness of ocotillos, saguaros, and chollas, under the witness of survival, with knowledge of all the destruction that came before, with no knowledge of what devastation was ahead of them, they married each other.

* * *

To make it official, they drove into the glittering sea of Las Vegas, went to a drive-thru chapel, exchanged palladium rings, signed the papers, kissed, and said cheese into the flash of a Polaroid, without ever leaving their car. They drove to the drive-thru and feasted on grass-fed burgers, organic sweet potato fries sprinkled with Herbes de Provence, and drank the glimmering bottles of hooch the chemist made. They listened to hip-hop, blues, and jazz—the best American inventions, they agreed, far superior to the atom bomb, manifest destiny, and reservations.

Thank you for this ritual, the phlebotomist said to the chemist. I feel bound to you. And this earth, and its people.

I've planned a celebration, the chemist told the phlebotomist. I'm so glad you're mine.

They drove to the neon sign graveyard, where the broken signs go. Neon signs can last for decades, he told her. Eventually they stop. But there's been enough ruin, he said. I want to show you something else. I learned how to fix them.

He tinkered with a cowboy, and then he blazed. He used his tools on a cowgirl, and she shone. He restored a diamond ring, red roses, a horseshoe, a slot machine with three red cherries spilling gold coins, and they all lit up like flames. She applauded. It's so beautiful, she said.

And Yet It Moves

He pointed to red; That's neon. He pointed to yellow; That's helium. Green; Neon and argon combined. Violet; Argon. Turquoise; Argon and mercury. Purple; Argon and xenon. He pointed to white; That's carbon dioxide. What we exhale. What our car emits. What is heating our planet.

Thank you, she said. And here is my gift to you. I learned how to make fireworks. The gas station owner showed me, while you were paying for our gasoline.

She set off a firecracker that sparkled red and she said, Strontium. Yellow, and she said, Sodium. Green exploded next and she said, Barium. Blue, and she said, Copper. She knew he knew but she liked showing him. Every time he gasped. Silver, and she said, A mixture of titanium, zirconium, and magnesium alloys. The last was gold, and she said, Hematite. Like my dress. And he'd never seen her smile so brightly.

The kissed their best-yet kiss. And so they celebrated and solidified their union, surrounded by all the elements, on land that held the bones and bodies of some of their ancestors, others oceans away.

Brightest Corners

I MET YOU AT IKEA—W4M—26

Reply to: anon-2012123@craigslist.org
Date: 2008–08–05, 4:12PM EST

I met you at Ikea. We were both looking for comforters. I'd seen you in Kitchen and then again in Rugs, had tried not to make eye contact too many times because I didn't want you to think I was following you. I wasn't. It's just that there's a path everyone has to follow through the showroom—you know—guiding us all through the natural progression of home furnishings, and I just happened to be a few paces behind you. One time, we locked eyes and I smiled, hoping to give a this-is-an-accident vibe, isn't-it-funny? You seemed to return the feeling.

I don't know if you slowed down on purpose or not, but we both ended up paused near a set of deep cobalt blue bedding, TANJA BODYR—I wrote down the item, the row and shelf number, row 57, shelf 17, so I could pick it up in the warehouse below if I wanted to. It was rough silk, not shiny but with a sheen, and it was displayed with dark brown sheets. I thought it looked grown-up. And okay, I'll be honest, the slight slip of the fabric made me envision throwing you down, fucking you on that bed, sliding along its surface, grinding into it, staining the gleam of that pure cloth, which, if I bought it, would be the finest thing I owned. You were that gorgeous.

this is in or around Ikea
no—it's NOT okay to contact this poster with services or other commercial interests

I SHOULD HAVE DONE SOMETHING
DIFFERENTLY—M4W—34

Reply to: anon-09854302@craigslist.org
Date: 2008–08–05, 4:42PM EST

My friends told me about this site when I told them what a pussy I was yesterday. All I can hope is that you felt the spark too and will look for me here.

We were both shopping at the Whole Foods near Columbus Circle. You had this incredible blonde hair. I've never seen anything like it.

Something about you was amazing.

I don't know why I couldn't talk to you. I should have asked you to go out for a drink.

Write me, and we will.

You know who I am.

this is in or around Columbus Circle
no—it's NOT okay to contact this poster with services or other commercial interests

TO THE EMOSEXUAL ON THE L TRAIN
LAST NIGHT—W4M—23

Reply to: anon-76945390@craigslist.org
Date: 2008–08–05, 5:02PM EST

You were heading into Brooklyn. You were carrying a guitar case, weighed 89 pounds, had no muscle tone or body fat, had an ironic haircut and looked like something 1979 shitted out. I love you and want to have your baby. You are the type of man us hipster girls dream of.

I had on a skirt over my jeans, and my jeans tucked into my boots . . . well, basically I had on the same outfit as every other girl on the train. I had about 30 lbs. on you. We both got off at Bedford Ave. Please write me baby.

this is in or around Billyburg
no—it's NOT okay to contact this poster with services or other commercial interests

I MET YOU AT IKEA—W4M—26

Reply to: anon-2012123@craigslist.org
Date: 2008–08–05, 5:12PM EST

Me, again.

I'm hoping that if I stretch my story out, there's a greater chance that you will see at least one of my postings.

"Do you like it?" I asked, fingering the fabric.

"It might look a little silly next to my Ramones posters and record covers up on the walls."

"You aren't a grown-up yet?"

"I'm wondering if I want to."

"Me too," I said. "So do you want to play house?" I asked you. "Pretend?" I'm never so bold. You smiled right at me, and agreed.

You live in a one-bedroom in Williamsburg, right in the center of too-cool-for-school land, where the hipsters are so fashionable they hurt the eyes, are embarrassing to look at. Skinny jeans and sneakers from the '80s, mismatched colors in a pattern of rightness I just can't discern. But you didn't look like that. You've got a small bathroom, small kitchen. I live in a studio in Bensonhurst, nowhere near you, might as well be another city, my only room with a door that shuts the shitter. Both of us at the new Ikea in Brooklyn, planning to pay for delivery. We began.

We used the bedding we both loved as a basis, shaped our furnishings around that. We agreed that as far as furniture went, HEMNES was the best. Those Scandinavians seemed to like their wood primarily light blonde, but we preferred the dark solidity of HEMNES, its deep black-brown color and clean lines. Like espresso. I wondered if you drank whiskey, what kind of intensity you preferred. A bed frame, end table, wardrobe, bookshelf, and storage bench for each of us—different sizes to fit the different dimensions of our homes. You have a double bed, I just have a single, I envisioned mostly staying at your place. We decided the room needed a little levity then, so added a brightly patterned sofa, KARLSTAD in HEDVIG, a nonsensical pattern that could be viewed as leaves and suns in deep blue, turquoise, red, yellow, then a POÄNG chair in ULLEVI ORANGE, which we both agreed was more like saffron, black-brown frame to match the bedroom.

With the wild chairs we decided to keep the curtains simple, so we got some in the same texture as the bedding, STÅLIS BLUE for near the bed, SKUGGIG BROWN for the living room. All we had left to do was lighting, and I was so delighted when you liked the plastic tulip-looking lamps as much as I did, so a KNAPPA and a KNAPPA KLÖVER for both of us to hang from the ceiling, a tall KNAPPA TULPAN floor lamp as well as a small KNAPPA TULPAN for a table.

Next Kitchens and Bathrooms, both so small we didn't need much, but wanted dishes, dish drains, silverware, glasses, shower curtains, shower caddies, towels, washcloths, dish towels, to complete the designed look we'd just achieved elsewhere in our homes. We backtracked to pick GRÖNÖ chinaware, all different shades of purple—lilac, lavender, fuchsia, royal, plum, eggplant, some solid, some patterned—to give a new tone to the color scheme, dish towels to match, plain utensils and stemware. The bathroom should be green, we decided; we picked the JÄNSJÖ set for its stripes and solids, a calm stillness against the rest of the patterns.

I wrote it all down as if we were both really going to buy it all, pick it all up piece by piece on our way out the door downstairs. I was amazed at how game you were, how willing to play.

After all of the spaces we inhabit were full, we turned to each other, a little amazed at our creation. "Hi," I said. "I'm Elliot." And you didn't tell me it was a man's name, you just shook my hand—I shake hands like a man, I know—and you told me you were Gil. I guess that's how you spell it, but when you said it I looked over your shoulder out the wall of windows to the edge of the sea bumping up against Red Hook, and thought of gills, imagined us jumping in the freezing cold water and just swimming away, across to China or Africa or Connecticut, whatever it is that's out from this bay. I still don't know your last name.

this is in or around Ikea
no—it's NOT okay to contact this poster with services or other commercial interests

And Yet It Moves

Reply to: anon-19482910@craigslist.org
Date: 2008–08–05, 5:41PM EST

Do you think more of these pretty ladies who brighten these men's days (and vice versa) would respond to the posts meant for them if you offered them more than a drink??

Like, "I saw you crossing the street at 5th and 19th. You were wearing a tweed jacket and a blue bag. You are so beautiful, let me buy you . . ."

apple cider? a carriage ride in the park? a frisbee? a bag of chips? Just a thought.

(Though, if someone wrote to me here, I would settle for a drink. Because at least they noticed me among the masses. And that would make me feel special. More so than a beer or a scotch or a mojito or a muffin or a plant or a ride on a roller coaster.)

this is in or around consider it
no—it's NOT okay to contact this poster with services or other commercial interests

I MET YOU AT IKEA—W4M—26

Reply to: anon-2012123@craigslist.org
Date: 2008–08–05, 6:12PM EST

We stood there, the list of our ideal living space between us.

"I really can't buy any of that stuff," you said.

"Me either."

"I do need a new bedspread, but that one doesn't match anything else I own. I mostly just came here because I was curious. I've never been to an Ikea."

"Me too."

"Do you want to get lunch? I hear they've got great meatballs."

We went through the cafeteria line together, picking things to share. Meatballs and lingonberries, smoked salmon with dill sauce, open-faced shrimp sandwich with sliced egg and tomato. We got two beers, even though it was just 1:00 and a Tuesday. Carlsberg. Danish, we decided, but at least Scandinavian. I wondered when I was supposed to ask you for your phone number, just hoped you'd ask me and save me from making the move, then panicked—someone as beautiful as you would never do such a thing with a girl like me.

We sat under dozens of lights just like the one we'd selected for our homes, KNAPPA, and from the windows we could see the Statue of Liberty, the burnt-out factories of Red Hook, the sea. We could see the sky out there, and the sun through clouds did un-urban things to the light; I felt like I could step out into fields.

The best of Brooklyn was all around us: veiled Muslim women; Hasidic Jews in black and white, the women with their hair wrapped and clavicles covered; yuppies from Park Slope with their strollers; hipsters from your hood out to furnish their lofts. There were black people eating Scandinavian food all around us, and I thought those Swedes would be proud of what they'd created here. I felt patriotic, not for my country, but for my borough. I said to you, "I love Brooklyn," gesturing around us, hoping you'd see what I saw, and you said, "Me too," and I took that to mean you did.

We ate from each other's plates, said the food was delicious, and it was so erotic being there with you, sharing sensation, taste, sight. I set my fork down on the table so that its tip touched yours, and you moved yours so that our tines intertwined, and holy shit, that was sexy. The light flaming around, the banter that made us both feel clever, it was like the best first date I could imagine, the

And Yet It Moves

images of beds lingering in both our memories. Hell, I'd have gone to the bathroom with you, done you right there in the stall. I felt brave, like anything we did would be right.

this is in or around Ikea
no—it's NOT okay to contact this poster with services or other commercial interests

YO, SEAN, I REALLY MISS U—W4M—22

Reply to: anon-12398095@craigslist.org
Date: 2008–08–05, 6:48PM EST

U told me not 2 call anymore and I erased ur # from my phone so I wouldn't be tempted 2 so I'm writing u here bcuz I don't know what else 2 do. I know u don't read Missed Connections, but I wish u would c this. I want 2 b w/ u so badly, I think we r dope as hell 2gether—I have never been as comfortable w/ any1, had as much fun w/ any1, been as silly w/ any1, or had as much in common w/ any1 (not to mention the really dope sex). I know u think u were the only 1 freakin out in ur head, but my head was freakin out all the time 2—relationships r scary as hell 4 every1. I thought I did not believe I was capable whatsoever of being in a relationship and you taught me that I can and want 2 b in a relationship even though it is completely scary and hard and my head freaks out 2—the bad parts, like that, always come with the good, but without the bad or sad parts, I wouldn't know the meaning of happy, and being with u, I really felt so happy that it made my head freakin out worth it 2 me. U taught me I can love some1 and am completely capable of loving some1 and I will always thank u for that.

I think we r dope as hell as a "we," but since it can't b, I reiterate what I have said 2 u 2x b4: when it comes down to it, 4getting myself and anything else, I love u and want u 2 b happy w/ or w/out me. So I will leave u alone and try not to be petrified 2 c u around b/c that's when it really hurts. Take care of urself, seriously.

this is in or around the Bronx
no—it's NOT okay to contact this poster with services or other commercial interests

I MET YOU AT IKEA—W4M—26

Reply to: anon-2012123@craigslist.org
Date: 2008–08–05, 7:12PM EST

When the food was finished we both noticed the sign asking us to clean up after ourselves, explaining that this helps keep the food inexpensive, because they don't have to pay people to pick up our trash. I liked these signs that explained things, the one that clarified why Ikea furniture needs to be assembled—if you do it yourself, you don't have to incorporate the cost of having the factory do it for you, and furniture is more easily stored and shipped in flat boxes, so everybody wins. Without saying anything we worked together to clear our trays. I asked if you wanted to buy anything, and you said you really liked the lamps we picked out. You got one for the ceiling, but I was afraid I wouldn't know how to install mine, so I got one for a tabletop. We went through the line together and I didn't think to look on your credit card for your last name.

Once we were in the parking lot, the light still gorgeous, burrowing gently into our skin, we looked to the line of shuttle buses.

"I'm going to Borough Hall," I said.

"I need the Smith Street bus," you said.

And Yet It Moves

We looked at each other. We smiled. I wanted to ask if I could see you again, I figured this was the moment you were supposed to ask for my number, but neither of us said anything, not even, "I had a nice time today," and we turned and walked separate ways, holding our matching lamps. Your bus pulled away first, and though I strained to see you through the window, I couldn't.

I knew I had made a terrible mistake not finding a way to reach you, to let you reach me, again.

So this is how I'm trying.

this is in or around Ikea
no—it's NOT okay to contact this poster with services or other commercial interests

I SAW YOU TODAY . . .

Reply to: anon-90345235@craigslist.org
Date: 2008–08–05, 7:39PM EST

. . . and it answered the question I've always asked myself of what I would do.

I always thought, when I saw you, that I'd be one or more of the following:
graceful
charming
insouciant
violent
mortified
surprised
brazen
nonchalant
vitriolic.

Instead, I grew legs that didn't feel like my own, and off I went. I ran like hell. Quite literally. I didn't punch you in the chest and break your sternum; I didn't spit in your face; I didn't smile, strong and unfazed; I didn't ignore you and keep walking. I ran.

Now I know.

this is in or around Tribeca
no—it's NOT okay to contact this poster with services or other commercial interests

I MET YOU AT IKEA—W4M—26

Reply to: anon-2012123@craigslist.org
Date: 2008–08–05, 8:12PM EST

For anyone else who is reading this, he wasn't the stereotype you're imagining. Gorgeous and living in Williamsburg, he wasn't as typical as you'd think, he wasn't a cartoon. He looked like he didn't know how smokin' hot he was, or if he knew he didn't care, and that was the great thing about him.

I could have made this series of postings quick and simple. You—looking for bedding at Ikea. Gorgeous. Absolutely gorgeous. Curly dark hair, shiny eyes, I have no idea what color, friendly, alive smile, body language that said you were listening, listening, listening.

Me—long reddish-brown hair, tangled. Not good at making eye contact. I have greenish-bluish eyes but I don't know if you noticed that. I talked a lot. More than you. That's weird. I may have seemed nervous. I was.

this is in or around Ikea
no—it's NOT okay to contact this poster with services or other commercial interests

And Yet It Moves

I WAS ARGUING AT UNION SQUARE

Reply to: anon-88556901@craigslist.org
Date: 2008–08–05, 8:36PM EST

I just want to say thanks to all of you who gave me encouraging words after the screaming match I got into at Union Square. After trying to explain why this war is so wrong for over an hour—these wars, both of them, actually—I was too exhausted to really have a conversation with any of you, but I did appreciate knowing that there were some people on my side. I'm usually handing out literature in Union Square, calmly. . . . I'm usually not the one up on the soapbox. So come say hello someday, or write me here. I promise, I won't scream at you that extraordinary rendition is illegal, or that waterboarding is torture, and I promise I won't try to explain the Geneva Conventions to you or that we now have more mercenaries overseas than military and they are paid more and exist above the law. I won't, really—I am capable of stopping myself. And I really would like to get to know some of you compassionate activists.

this is in or around Union Square
no—it's NOT okay to contact this poster with services or other commercial interests

WE WERE BOTH HEADED TO THE BRONX, SON—W4M—28

Reply to: anon-42896540@craigslist.org
Date: 2008–08–05, 8:46PM EST

Man, I've never seen anyone like you. Your dreads were red, and I don't think you dyed them.

Your skin was creamed-coffee colored, but you had these freckles all over, and green fucking eyes. Green fucking eyes. On a black man. I bet your whole life kids told you you were ugly, or a freak. And now you hit your mid-twenties and you are gorgeous. You must be some kinda halfie—Jamaican and Irish? African and Midwestern? I do not know, but I bless the parents that made you.

Maybe you get this all the time now—fly sisters telling you you are fine, just fine. But maybe being the funny-looking kid at school all those years has stuck with you. Maybe you still don't know your goodness.

So here's what I have to say—write me, see me, and you will never again not know how beautiful you are. I see you. I will show you.

And who am I? Guess which girl from the 2 train last night at nine would be writing you this? Am I the blonde girl with the long locks, the same blood running way back? Or am I the halfie who's been funny her whole life? Indian and Korean? Japanese and Polish? Or, was I the Cherokee princess, generations undiluted? The Chinese chick from an ancient Dynasty? Which girl am I? Purebred or a mongrel? Which girl looked at you and saw perfection?

Write me and find out. And in the meantime, baby, whichever lady I am, think of the beautiful babies we can make.

this is in or around the 2 train
no—it's NOT okay to contact this poster with services or other commercial interests

I MET YOU AT IKEA—W4M—26

Reply to: anon-2012123@craigslist.org
Date: 2008–08–05, 9:12PM EST

What the fuck was I thinking? I didn't ask you for your name and phone number. I didn't give you mine. I didn't ask if I could see you again. I got embarrassed and awkward and I let you walk away. For fuck's sake.

I have no idea how that happened. In the light of day, was I not pretty enough for you? Even though I'm grown I still have bad skin, I know. I was just in jeans and a tank top, I wasn't intending to look my best, but I clean up all right, I swear. Do you have a girlfriend? I'm not trained to look for rings, shit, maybe you're married. When we were furnishing all your rooms, you could have easily dropped in a "My girlfriend would love this," or a "My wife would despise this, even though I love it," couldn't you?

I don't have a boyfriend, or a husband. I want one pretty badly. You seemed like you would be a good one. Where the fuck are you now?

Did we just get shy? Was the connection so intense each of us didn't want to admit it, in case the other person didn't feel it? Did we not want to take it further for fear of ruining it? How do I ever make up for this?

Please respond to this so I can stop inventing you.

this is in or around Ikea
no—it's NOT okay to contact this poster with services or other commercial interests

MISSED CONNECTION WITH YOUR SOUL—W4M—24

Reply to: anon-19201834@craigslist.org
Date: 2008–08–05, 9:17PM EST

the most intense moment I ever had as you sat across from me and gazed into my eyes as if you knew me for thousands of years causing me to quiver like a child, never had I felt this way the rush was overwhelming, as you reached your destination I noticed a tear flowing down your face as you left I knew we were never meant to speak in this lifetime, but it was by chance that we saw each other in this one, perhaps a connection with love that happened thousands of years ago

this is in or around my soul
no—it's NOT okay to contact this poster with services or other commercial interests

I MET YOU AT IKEA—W4M—26

Reply to: anon-2012123@craigslist.org
Date: 2008–08–05, 9:22PM EST

Seriously, what is wrong with you people? STOP WRITING ME BACK!!! (Unless you are Gil, of course of course.) All you schmucks, putzes, perverts, freaks, and assholes, knock it off. I'M NOT TRY-ING TO FIND YOU! I'm trying to find him, only him. This is not my attempt to end up on a date with any of you. Please please please knock it off.

And yes, I have figured out by now that to get to Bensonhurst I could have ridden the shuttle bus to Smith Street, taken the F, and walked. Yes, I know. I'm aware it was stupid to go back the way I came, the bus to Borough Hall, the 2/3 to Atlantic, change to the M. I could have spent twenty more minutes with him. Of course I know that by now. You telling me doesn't help.

Who the fuck are you—what kind of people want to read about this shit??? Who *responds*?!?!

Fuck all of you who are out there reading this who aren't Gil, whose business this is none of. I'm not your soap opera. Go away. Go read the message by the girl who told us all that she lied, she

And Yet It Moves

responded to a Missed Connection and said, "That was me!" and met the guy at a bar and fucked him and then posted for all eyes to see, "That wasn't me. I dyed my hair for the occasion, to be your dark-haired fantasy. You didn't even notice that I wasn't the girl you'd glanced on the 4 train." She's number 58906734. She posted two days ago, easy to find, just look for "I lied!" in the headings on the table of contents. Her confession was for all of you. Go read it. Mine is not. Go away.

You don't exist, Gil, really, only my creation of you. But you are out there somewhere, some unimagined version of you, and so I am sending this out. If it reaches you, I am meant to throw away what I have. Move into your apartment, decorate it with you. Start a new life. With you. And you, too. Maybe you have something, something that barely glows, or something that sparks, I don't know. But if you read this, trust me, I am telling you, we are meant to be.

Everyone wants this. Everyone wants to throw away what they have, run into mystery.

Everyone wants to but nobody does. That is why so many people post their wishes on this site. It is easier to send out a message in a bottle than to tell someone "Run away with me" to their face. That's what I should have done. Told you that.

No one runs away together. Ever. Let's be different.

You, you people who are reading this, not looking for your own Missed Connection but instead eavesdropping on my life, admit that you've always wanted to risk it all and never have. Admit it. I know you. Even all you creeps who keep writing me, I know you too. We're all the same.

You know someone, all of you, and you think maybe just maybe if you would have said how you really felt about her, she would have left her life. For you. And you could have made her happier than anyone else in the world could have. And she could have made you happier than anyone else is able. But you didn't say anything, you were too scared you were wrong, and now it's too late. And so you want to take me home, to entertain your broken fucking heart, bang away the pain.

We've all been too scared to follow our desire. The movies are wrong. No one does that. That's why we all are here.

I want us to do that, Gil. Because maybe the strength of doing something fully foolish will carry us through all the years. Maybe if we make our choices based on sensibility, time is bound to erode that bond, like salt water. But maybe time can never kill the bond based on the fact that you both leapt, together. Maybe if you have faith, you can fall always, never land.

this is in or around Ikea
no—it's NOT okay to contact this poster with services or other commercial interests

EVERYONE HERE WANTS SOMETHING

Reply to: anon-99999999@craigslist.org
Date: 2008–08–05, 9:33PM EST

Are you READY to give her what she's ALWAYS WANTED, but was too afraid to ask for?

Are you READY to increase your SIZE by up to 75%?!?!? Even 100%?!?!!!!

Are you READY to finally have the WIDTH AND GIRTH AND LENGTH you've ALWAYS wanted?

Risk-free thirty-day trial size available FREE!!! There's no reason not to start today.

SHE'LL THANK YOU!

this is in or around your desire
yes—it IS okay to contact this poster with services or other commercial interests

I LIED!—W4M—27

Reply to: anon-58906734@craigslist.org
Date: 2008–08–03, 11:13AM EST

Last night was incredible. I wrote you and said, "That was me!" that you saw the other night coming home on the train. We met at your favorite local bar and partied and you took me home and the sex was fantastic. All night you kept saying, "I can't believe it! I can't believe it's you! I can't believe you saw my post!!" You just kept touching my hair.

But I lied. I dyed my hair black just for the occasion. I'm a light brunette, and you didn't even notice that I wasn't your dark-haired fantasy from the 4 train.

It was so easy.

this is in or around East Village
no—it's NOT okay to contact this poster with services or other commercial interests

I MET YOU AT IKEA—W4M—26

Reply to: anon-2012123@craigslist.org
Date: 2008–08–05, 10:12PM EST

A storm has blown in as I've been writing this tonight. Lightning is setting off car alarms, I wonder if the wind will break through my window. It's been years since I've walked in the rain.

I bet most people are inside now, some maybe not even noticing this storm, but I want to be walking with you on a beach, Gil,
wind and rain driving sand into our skin, us the tallest things for
miles around. I want to walk out into the waves, let them rock and
smack us, lift and lower our buoyancy. I want to dance in the ocean
up to our shoulders, I want to swim safely at sea with you, in this
weather, the sky cracking overhead. Take you home, towel you off
with some fine thing, lay you down on new sheets, get sand in the
bed to remind us.

this is in or around Ikea
no—it's NOT okay to contact this poster with services or other
commercial interests

TEMPTATION—M4W—23

Reply to: anon-88203333@craigslist.org
Date: 2008–08–05, 10:28PM EST

(I miss the girl in this story of mine.)
I moved to Greenpoint last night, dropped my shit in my new
room, and went roaming around Bedford, just diggin the scene.
Long story short, I got drunk at a bar, went home with a girl.

So her apartment was like something out of my dreams. She
had a potter's wheel, turntables, a whole wall full of records, a huge
half-painted canvas of some eclecticism-styled flying trees, and
she went into the kitchen to shake me up a Manhattan. I can't explain how small I felt in the presence of her greatness. She handed
me some of her short stories to read, sort of sat sort of leaned next
to me while I read, and then bam, she hit me with, "Do you want
to do a square of Diesel?"

And Yet It Moves

I cursed God at that point. In case you don't know, a square is implied to snort, and Diesel is China White heroin, the best there is. Dealers don't cut it because it has a very distinctive taste. Expensive, hard to get, and pure. A trifecta that renders my willpower impotent.

"Oh, just one more time," I thought. Every good and bad feeling I've ever had rushed through me. I asked where the bathroom was, left the drugs with her, walked into the little room, closed the door and looked into the mirror. Sex on H is amazing. I knew I had to leave immediately.

My sponsor told me this would happen. "Temptation comes from the brightest corners and at the most unexpected times," he said. I washed my hands and face in cold water and flushed the toilet to make it appear like a genuine bathroom visit. I walked out of the bathroom, said I had to go, she scrambled her sorries, and for the first time in my life I meant it when I said, "It's not you, it's me."

On the way home I cried. Temptation is an evil motherfucker that knows exactly what cards to deal: perfect apartment, perfect hot and horny girl, perfect music, perfect art, perfect time, perfect beginning, perfect drug. All designed to get me to slide back down the spiral.

this is in or around impossibility
no—it's NOT okay to contact this poster with services or other commercial interests

YES, I AM A GAY MAN, BUT IT FELT SO GOOD TO GET CRUISED BY A HOT LADY! THANK YOU!!!

Reply to: anon-71439839@craigslist.org
Date: 2008–08–05, 10:36PM EST

I was walking south on 10th and caught your eye and your smile. We even both turned around after we passed for another look! With all the fucked-up experiences I've had with gay men in this town, I thought, HMMMMM!!!??? You made my day!

this is in or around Chelsea
no—it's NOT okay to contact this poster with services or other commercial interests

I MET YOU AT IKEA—W4M—26

Reply to: anon-2012123@craigslist.org
Date: 2008–08–05, 10:48PM EST

You're never going to see this, are you, Gil? I'm being foolish, aren't I, trusting fate too much? All of you out there who are reading this, this public posting I've laid out for all eyes to see, you all are sad for me, aren't you? Sad for my desperation, embarrassed for me and my sureness that someone I was with for an hour and a half…matters.

this is in or around Ikea
no—it's NOT okay to contact this poster with services or other commercial interests

I MET YOU AT IKEA—W4M—26

Reply to: anon-2012123@craigslist.org
Date: 2008–08–05, 10:50PM EST

Or maybe you've read this already, Gil. Maybe you've read each of my nine postings, and maybe you're embarrassed for me. Embarrassed because I'm sure about the first thing in my life for a very

And Yet It Moves

long time, I'm sure that I want to see you again, that I need to, that you could change everything. I'm sure. And you don't feel the same at all. Do you? You've read all of this, you are reading one of my postings right now as I write this new one, and you are choosing not to write back. During that hour and a half, you didn't feel a thing. You must do stuff like that all the time. You don't want to find me, do you? Even though I'm right here, sending out beams of light, trying to guide you to me.

this is in or around Ikea
no—it's NOT okay to contact this poster with services or other commercial interests

I MET YOU AT IKEA—W4M—26

Reply to: anon-2012123@craigslist.org
Date: 2008–08–05, 10:51PM EST

When you're in those hip Williamsburg bars, you won't look into the crowd, searching for my face, will you? Lots of girls look like me. Maybe you don't even remember what I look like.

this is in or around Ikea
no—it's NOT okay to contact this poster with services or other commercial interests

I MET YOU AT IKEA—W4M—26

Reply to: anon-2012123@craigslist.org
Date: 2008–08–05, 10:53PM EST

Why am I telling you people this?

this is in or around Ikea

no—it's NOT okay to contact this poster with services or other commercial interests

JUST ASK—W4W—28

Reply to: anon-10489192@craigslist.org
Date: 2008–08–05, 11:03PM EST

you will probably never read this, but i need to post it. i cannot stop thinking about you. as much as we pretend to be friends, we will never be friends because we both know that underneath it all lie things that we can never forget and feelings that we can never lose. and as long as i see you every day our time together plays over and over in my head making it harder and harder for me to do anything that requires thought or action unless it involves you. maybe you will never know how much you are a part of me. maybe you've known all along. i would leave my life for you if you asked me to. just ask me to.

this is in or around wishing on a star

no—it's NOT okay to contact this poster with services or other commercial interests

TO ALL OF YOU . . .

Reply to: anon-04562937@craigslist.org
Date: 2008–08–05, 11:11PM EST

and your inane, clumsy, middle-class, heterosexual love drivel. . .
    Ugghhh. . . .

this is in or around everywhere
no—it's NOT okay to contact this poster with services or other commercial interests

I THINK I'M GIVING UP—M4W—31

Reply to: anon-02030405@craigslist.org
Date: 2008–08–05, 11:34PM EST

As much as I loooove missed connections, as much as the cheese-ball romantic within me would like to continue believing there's someone out there looking for me as I'm looking for her—I'm just tired of it, tired of it all.... She doesn't exist ... and if she does, she's not here. I'll tell you where she's at, she's with that smooth-talking, sly, charismatic egomaniac who's only bent on earning another hash mark on his bedpost. She's asking herself why she got sooooo drunk last night and hooked up with some random guy—wondering if this one will call, well, cuz he was sooooo much nicer than the rest. . . . She didn't even see me watching from my barstool in the corner, the guy who might not look quite as dreamy as the other guys, but the one who'll treat her right, and it's the same story hun. . . . If you always do what you've always done, you'll always get what you've always got. . . .

this is in or around everywhere
no—it's NOT okay to contact this poster with services or other commercial interests

I WAS LOST—W4M—30

Reply to: anon-88776290@craigslist.org
Date: 2008–08–05, 11:48PM EST

And you gave me directions to the Greenwood Cemetery earlier today.

It was on Dikeman Avenue or Wolcott Road or something, I can't remember the names, but I was on the right road, just heading in the wrong direction.

You were holding a red gas can.

I was in a hearse.

You had the most beautiful eyes I have ever seen.

Please find a way to find me.

this is in or around Red Hook

no—it's NOT okay to contact this poster with services or other commercial interests

And Yet It Moves

Why Things Fall

WHY THINGS FALL

I. Newton

Priscilla led Isaac by the hand, walked him to a tree, placed his back against the trunk. She pulled an apple from between her breasts and placed it on his head. She told him to stand perfectly still. Priscilla strode twenty paces away, turned, notched an arrow into her bow, pulled it back with muscular yet trim arms—at that point Isaac fell in love—and let it fly: the apple impaled, the arrow quivering in the bark. Isaac stepped from underneath, left the apple thrumming above. They both could imagine a crowd roaring.

Priscilla had found Isaac in a bar drawing strange symbols onto cloth napkins:

$$\int_a^b f(x)dx = F(b) - F(a).$$

$$\frac{d}{dx}\int_a^x f(t)\,dt = f(x).$$

He wrote the words *limit, bubonic, infinitesimal, infinite.*

Isaac had left Cambridge because skeletons in rags on slow-moving carts were about to bring the plague. He walked home to Lincolnshire, and before kissing his mother's cheek he went to the pub in the town square. When Priscilla said hello he looked up at her, wrote $f(x) = x^2$, $f'(x) = 2x$. He said, "The slope of f(x) at x = 3 is 6." He wrote $f(x) = x^2$, $F(x) = \frac{1}{3}x^3$. He said, "F(x) at x = 3 is 9. F(x) at x = 2 is $\frac{8}{3}$. So the area under f(x) above the x axis from 2 to 3 is $\frac{19}{3}$.

"Do you see the pattern?" he asked her. "Do you see the beautiful pattern?"

"Yes," she said. "I do." She took his quill and drew the graph, perfectly. He'd never seen anyone but men do that.

Isaac said to Priscilla, "These are the things I know to be true: Geometry is the study of shape, calculus the study of change. White light is the combination of all the colors of the rainbow. Every object persists in its state of rest or uniform motion in a straight line unless it is compelled to change that state by forces impressed upon it. Force is equal to the change in momentum per change in time. For every action, there is an equal and opposite reaction."

She leaned forward and kissed him.

Priscilla said she was an archer, needed a partner for her circus act. She downed the rest of Isaac's beer, plucked a coin from her boot and left it on the table. He picked it up, bit it, said, "I believe counterfeiters should be hanged." She led him outside and showed him what she could do and he was astounded. She said she needed more practice before the audition; they had ten days, so Isaac took Priscilla to his ancestral home. She slept in the library, on a velvet couch, surrounded by gyroscopes and globes and prisms and models of the planets with the sun in the center and a telescope made from mirrors. Isaac visited her there each evening. During the days they practiced against the plum trees, persimmon trees, and cherry trees of the family orchard, but it was always an apple that Priscilla plucked from her breasts.

And Yet It Moves

For nine days Priscilla got it right nine times out of ten. On the tenth day Priscilla got it right ten times in a row, and they knew they were ready. They walked to the field bordered by forest that the circus transformed into a festival for four days every four years. When they arrived, men on stilts were erecting the tent. Isaac peeked under the flap to see a pyramid of clowns lifting the poles that would support all that striped fabric. The fat lady was eating five apple pies. The bearded lady was shaving her legs using a bucket and straight razor. A man with his legs crossed walked by on his hands. A child stood on the tip of an elephant's trunk, spinning a ball on her finger. Acrobats practiced on the fences edging the field, leaping and flipping and landing in the same place. A woman with a python and her hair as her only clothing blew fire. The manager trotted up, his muscular, unclothed torso turning to furred horseflesh, hooves.

"What can you contribute to the Wriggling Smothers Bar None Circus?"

Priscilla answered, "Death-defying acts."

They led the centaur to the boundary of the prairie, to where the forest of apple trees began. Isaac stood dutifully underneath a tree, his spine aligned with the trunk. Priscilla—in her silk striped dress sewn just for the occasion, pinned and tucked to show her lovely legs clad in thigh-high striped stockings, garter straps disappearing under the folds of her skirt—took aim. Her triceps were as taut and curved as bones, her bones underneath were strong enough to support all that tension, and Isaac clutched his side, amazed and pained that his rib could be so improved by being out of his body. The arrow flew, the tip pierced the apple, the sound of contact reverberated through every trunk in the forest, Isaac stepped from underneath, grinning, and thousands of apples, enough for barrels of cider, hundreds of pies, fell from the tree, pounding Isaac's head and shoulders, thudding down his back, burying his feet. He got so many thumps he slumped.

Pricilla explained to the manager that the trees at Isaac's home weren't as laden, where they practiced the trees weren't wild and flush—a cascade wasn't part of the act, but could he see the one apple still held aloft by the arrow, the feathers still shuddering, could he see the one that didn't fall, the one her arrow held? While Priscilla tried to secure them a spot in the traveling circus so that they could see India and Ireland and Jamaica and Africa and the Americas, while Priscilla prattled, Isaac dreamt.

Tuning forks chimed; snakes swallowed apples whole, mounds traveling along the pipes of their bodies; Isaac felt rain, saw a rainbow; a snake in a tree told him, "You, you can understand."

While Isaac watched, God reached into the dirt at his feet, formed animals from soil.

Then God spit, and shaped a man. God pulled a woman from the side of the sculpture. She ate a pomegranate, and she didn't want it undone. She fed seeds to the man, and they didn't plummet. The woman said to Isaac, "The universe can and must be understood by active reason. It is never wrong to know—there will always be mysteries."

The snake dropped to the ground. Night fell. Falling apples glinted silver in the moonlight. Birds were replaced by bats. Their wings resisted the pull downward; an arrow pierced a bat and it fell. *The force extends to them. How high?*

The moon arced across the sky, slashed by each branch it passed.

In his dreaming slumber, Isaac thought, *Apples drawn to the center of the earth. The moon—what makes things fall makes planets orbit. Makes tides. Why women taste like the sea. The same force draws the earth up to the apple, the earth up toward the moon. Attractions across empty space.*

And Yet It Moves

Isaac awoke, his head aching and bandaged. He'd been placed in a bed, a cot for Priscilla near him on the floor.

The centaur said, "Congratulations. You have a job."

Priscilla said, "Together, we will see the world. We will be daring." Moonlight shone through a window, the reflection of sunlight paling Priscilla's skin to a glare.

Isaac spoke. "I've been shown. Gravitas. We fall to the earth in supplication, bound to the clay we were shaped from. The earth is the greatest thing, but every thing moves us—the nearer you come, the more I want to fly in your direction. Each of us is drawn toward each object in the universe. Feeling this lure—instead of just the pull to fall—that is the highest form of praise."

II. Einstein

January 1955
Dear Daughter,

Maybe you are studying to be an astronaut. You may be the
first to orbit this globe, show us what we look like from above.
If so, you will learn what I have discovered. Gravity bends light.
Gravitational attraction between masses results in a warping of
space and time. Free fall is identical to inertial motion—being
pulled by gravity is indistinguishable from being acted upon by
no forces. Will you think we look like blown glass, an uncrack-
able sphere? Maybe you work in a brothel. If so, you know that
matter is energy. The tangible, tactile, is equivalent to that buzz,
that force. The corporeal corresponds to the hum. People stop
me on the street and ask me to explain "The Theory." Instead of
saying, "Energy equals mass times the speed of light squared," I
respond, "I am always mistaken for Professor Einstein!" and flee.
They are asking how to access the energy inside of them. How to
turn bodies into pure light. The same reason they come to you, if
you are there. Maybe you are a trapeze artist. You know without
words what I know through symbols—in motion, time dilates
and length contracts. When you fly through the sky you feel
small and everything slows. Maybe you have become religious.
Maybe you wish what I wish—me, a nonobservant Ashkenazi
Jew—for the universe to be eternal and unchanging. But the
speed of light is the only constant we have. Everything else alters
to accommodate that.

   Did you attend Catholic school, like I did? Do you know you
are a Jew? German and Serbian? You were a mistake we made,
before we knew we'd go on to make more mistakes. Are you

And Yet It Moves

good at figures? Your mother was the only woman who studied physics and mathematics at the Zurich Polytechnic. You have been called Lieserl, Erzsebeth, Erzsike, but I have decided the best name for you would be Tzvipora. Bird. We wanted you. We wanted each other. Children do not want to know of the sex their parents had, but the tryst by the lake, the weekend you were conceived, was the happiest I have ever been. I was poor and jobless. Unmarried. I thought I had time to make a home for you. But the job at the Patent Office, not teaching, all I could find—they would have fired me. Scarlet fever ran through the orphanage. Crimson skin like sandpaper. I asked and asked and finally they told me you did not die. You were not ruined. You still had your wits about you. They would not will not they won't tell me who took you.

Some have said you were handicapped and that I could not abide, that's why I gave you away. But your mother, the truest love I ever had, she was handicapped, walked with a limp, deformed hips I kissed and kissed and kissed. You brother, his mind is not right, but he is dazzling. I do not believe in eugenics. I believe in genetics. I am certain you are brilliant. This is not arrogance—your intelligence is equal parts from your mother as from me. I did not give you away because you were a girl.

Your father,
Albert Einstein

February 1955
Dear Daughter,

I am a pacifist. I am a vegetarian. I am a member of the NAACP. I was offered the presidency of Israel, but I declined. I was short-listed for *Time* magazine's "Man of the Year" but Adolf Hitler beat me. He put a bounty on my head. I helped build the bomb.

I said we should not do it. Had I not done it someone else would have. I carry a replica of the compass Galileo designed. I would will it to you. The electromagnetic field cannot be explained by Newtonian mechanics, so there must be a higher theory of gravitation. I have found part of it, and fear I will not have time to find the Unified Field. I believe it is tasteless to prolong life artificially. My ashes will be spread in an unknown place. They will take my brain from my body and study it but they will learn nothing.

My life's work has been to prove, and I have, that there is no such thing as absolute rest. Time and space change depending on what you fall around. You and I are falling around the sun. We are in the same frame of reference. Taken to its logical conclusion, quantum mechanics says that particles affect each other's behavior, no matter how far apart they are. They've called me senile because I do not believe the world can be as strange as they say. I don't believe in this spooky action at a distance, measurement of one particle fixing the conduct of the other in an instant, even when light years apart. I remedied Newton's calculations at extremes of speed, macro; scientists are trying to remedy Newtonian mechanics on extremes of scale, micro. Very fast, very small—and that is how my life seems to me now. I do not know how far you are from the country where I now live. They call it quantum entanglement. The day I handed you to a stranger, you were less than two years old.

They have said that giving you up let me have my "miracle year." Annus Mirabilis. Me in 1905 a repeat of Newton in 1666. They do not know that all my furious work is an atonement.

This is what I know to be true: I should have shamed myself to keep you.

Your father,
Albert Einstein

And Yet It Moves

March 1955
Dear Tzvipora,

A friend had a handicapped child. He asked if he should cease
his scientific work to care for his son. I said he should not. He
sent his child to an asylum. Years later, my friend went to the
asylum and shot the son he considered to be deformed, in the
face, then shot himself in the head. I am not the reason he
did this. I am part of the reason he did this. I told my friend
Ehrenfest not to care for Wassik because valuable individu-
als must not be sacrificed to hopeless things. Neither wife of
mine—no one—knows what I told him. His son had Down
syndrome. Have you met someone with this disease? They are
much more able to love than I am. They hug me not because I
am the most famous scientist on the face of the earth, but because they like my hair, because they like to hug. The science
my friend did is no better for the world than raising a happy
child. I was wrong. Nothing is ever hopeless. I gave you half of
who I am. If I did not create you, you would have been created.
Your mother and another, so not me at all. Myself and another
woman, so you still half of me. The math of what I made, of
what I've done, is baffling.

> Your father,
> Albert Einstein

April 1955
Tzvipora,

Walking through the market today, I was certain I saw you. My
hooded eyes. Your mother's timid smile. You are fifty-three years
old. Beautiful. And I knew—you are a baker. Recipes your math.
You ceased your singing—something your mother never did,

something I never do, which gave me hope—and you said hello. Can I help you? You said, "Do you have any questions? I make every loaf myself."

I said, "You feed people."

You blinked those eyes, mine, improved, above such lips I have not seen in years, and said, "I like to nourish strangers."

There was no ring on your finger. I love the laws of the universe, the God who made them, more than the God who intervenes in our lives, who makes bodies. I want you to be me and better than me. There is no ring on my hand, long into my viduity. Giving you up poisoned me and Mileva. We got what we wanted—two legitimate children—and then we didn't want each other anymore. Elsa is dead, my second wife. Gravity is not what makes us fall in love. If it were we would stay in love, as long as we stayed in the same frame of reference. You said, "I would be honored to feed you, Professor Einstein," you whom I never fed, whom my wife fed with her own body, then you turned away, to let me look without being watched.

Today, I stole your bread. I have not eaten much for days. I picked up a loaf, dark, heavy with nuts and seeds, then turned and walked away. You kneaded this dough, put it in a small, hot oven, and it leavened. I wanted someone to say, "Stop! Thief!" I wanted to be chased, cuffed. I wanted to be found out. Everyone let the doddering old man wander off with his bread, the forgetful scientist who certainly could pay but did not. I sat in my bright kitchen, cut jagged slices with a serrated knife. I smeared a thick layer of creamy butter right to the edge. When I lifted the slice it oiled my fingertips. I ate four pieces of bread, then one with blueberry jam. I drank a glass of milk and felt full and then washed the stickiness from my mustache.

Someone will carry these epistles to you. I do not think I will be going out again. I did not cover the loaf and after I sign this letter I will check to see if it has already started to harden.

Your father,
Albert Einstein

III. *Tesla*

"It would seem as though the Creator, himself, had electrically designed this planet just for the purpose of enabling us to achieve wonders which, before my discovery, could not have been conceived by the wildest imagination."
—NIKOLA TESLA

My father was a priest. My mother's father was a priest and had the poems of my nation memorized. My mother invented household appliances. She was never photographed. I was born during a lightning storm and the midwife thought it a bad omen but my mother knew I would be a child of light. Every photograph of me gets my good side. I cannot speak to a woman wearing pearls.

I almost died of cholera but I read Mark Twain and that helped me not die. We later became friends and my high-frequency oscillator, what made small earthquakes, frightened him. I had to smash that device with a sledgehammer to keep it from ruining Fifth Avenue. I constructed an electric bath that would destroy germs so no one else would get cholera. Some think it strange that I wash my hands three times, and shake hands, when I shake hands, up and down, three times.

I gambled away my tuition but later won it back. I was unprepared for exams and they did not give me an extension so I never graduated from university.

My friends thought I drowned once. In the Mur. I'm not sure what kept me away so long.

I do not visit doctors. I work from 9:00 to 6:00 and dine at Delmonico's at 8:10. I work again until 3:00. I walk eight to ten miles a day when I am not working and before sleep I squeeze each toe one hundred times, each toe of each foot, to stimulate my brain.

I am slim, stable, regimented, and some call me elegant. A man asked how I could have such light eyes and be a Slav. I said my eyes were once much darker, but that using my mind a great deal has made them many shades lighter. I live in the top of my head. I do not yet consider myself successful. I speak Serbo-Croatian, Czech, English, French, German, Hungarian, Italian, and Latin. Anyone can speak Latin, still, of course, anyone who wants to.

Chastity helps my scientific abilities. Women will be the dominant sex in the future.

My boss, Thomas Edison, said he would pay me fifty thousand dollars if I could complete a task for him; I worked for months and did it, but he said it was humor he was using. He said I would understand when I was an American. He tried to make it up to me but I quit. They say he invented the light bulb but he didn't; he sold light bulbs. I had four cents in my pocket when I arrived and a letter from Edison's former employer, Charles Batchelor, which read, "My Dear Edison: I know two great men and you are one of them. The other is this young man!"

I feed the pigeons. Thousands of them. For years. I healed the bones of one. One could read my mind, a pure white one with light gray wingtips. I would know that pigeon anywhere. When I asked her to come to me, just wished it, she would fly to my room, 3327, three times eleven, three times nine. She loved me and gave my life purpose and I loved her as a man loves a woman. I find the ways beasts speak soothing over those of humans.

Once I was supposed to be in a banquet hall receiving the Edison Medal but there were pigeons in the park below so I went to see them instead and they stood on my body, on my head and on my arms, their blue bodies on my black suit. My pigeon, the one that I loved, she came to me. They made me come back inside but that was a good day.

Neither Edison nor I won the Nobel, because of our quibbles.

Gravity makes some things fall and some things orbit. It depends on what's in the way. I have never been pulled to an elliptical revolution around someone else as my center, forward motion drawn from a line into a curve, a change in trajectory. My bird flew to me and I was most drawn to her but neither of us ever fell into a cycle around the other. She died in my arms. She never fell from the sky. When she came to say goodbye there came a light from her eyes, two powerful beams of light shining brighter than any light I ever made.

I will die alone in a different hotel room.

I walked away from millions, billions, because Westinghouse never tried to swindle me and he couldn't afford the royalties he said he'd pay, so I said he didn't have to. I will die less than penniless, in debt, but Westinghouse will pay my room and board until that day.

Unlike Einstein, I am more interested in physics than in metaphysics.

It was my childhood dream to harness the power of Niagara Falls, and I did, I made hydroelectric power. In the dirt with a stick I drew the first rotating magnetic field motor. I improved dynamos. I experimented with harmonic vibrations. Electricity can pass through the skin without harming the heart or the brain. I am the father of robotics. I discovered x-rays at the same time as someone else. I discovered radar before someone else. My technology made radio—Marconi used seventeen of my patents. My technology could be used for interplanetary communication. I made neon light. I made fluorescence. I hold the record for length of manmade lightning. I made ball lightning in the laboratory. Alexander Pope wrote, "Nature and Nature's laws lay hid in night:

And Yet It Moves

God said, 'Let Newton be!' and all was light." But Newton didn't light up the planet. I made a speedometer for Cadillacs. I made remote control. Many of my schematics are only in my head, so people cannot duplicate what I've done. This is not strategic—I do not need to write things down.

I made a tower that would give free wireless energy to everyone on this earth. There is no way to make money off such a thing, so it was never given. Some say it was responsible for the Tunguska Event, a ten-megaton detonation that deforested hundreds of miles in central Russia. Yes, I created a weapon one thousand times more powerful than the nuclear bombs that will destroy Hiroshima and Nagasaki, but I did not use it.

I cannot know that they will name a unit of power after me. I cannot know that I will be printed on Yugoslavian money. I cannot know that they will name a corner mine in New York City, Fortieth and Sixth. Only one of those numbers divisible by three. I cannot know that Edison was wrong about fossil fuels, that the bodies of dinosaurs cannot give us energy for fifty thousand years; I cannot know that I was right that the world needs hydroelectric, wind, solar power. That the earth can sustain us—I cannot know if I am right about that. I cannot know that a band will be named after the War of the Currents. A war I won, no longer a war. A ridiculous band that will make far more money than I ever made in my life. I cannot know that the one invention they named after me, the Tesla coil, out of my 278 patents, will be used for entertainment at musical festivals. I said I could make a device to split the world in two but no one dared me to prove it so I didn't. I cannot know if I could have done it, except I did everything else I said I could.

Electricity runs through the bodies of birds on a wire but it does not hurt them because the wire has so little resistance, very little detours through the bird. Pigeons can perch on electrical wires as long as they don't touch another wire with their wing, above or below, a wire with a different voltage, as long as they don't reach across and complete the circuit. I cannot know how birds can know this.

Something I made is in nearly everything. Everything I have ever said is true.

IV. Galileo, Hawking, Rabinowitz

Galileo Galilei had a lovely courtyard in the house he was not allowed to leave. Someone found an abandoned bird, one they weren't sure could survive on its own, and brought it to him, a man with nothing better to do. Galileo put mesh over his atrium so the bird could fly and not shit on important documents inside the house. We do not know what kind of bird this was. After, those returning from the new world would sometimes bring him birds unseen on his continent. Parrots. Small jays. He became a repository for what other people couldn't hold on to. And it brought him visitors, people came to see the specimens brought across an ocean. Returning explorers sometimes brought him trinkets, jewels, maps, drawings of the people indigenous to that other land, rewards for his loyalty to the mission of conversion.

His church believed birds don't have souls and souls are all that matter. Birds seem to not be falling but they are in fact flying while falling. Galileo mopped the tiles of his courtyard daily until he could no longer see well enough and then his daughters did it for him.

* * *

I am learning these things from Galileo's journals. I am supposed to be writing a research paper but instead I keep typing these notes, anecdotes. Deleting them, retyping them. The assignment is to research how one physicist built on the work of others. Learn from the past to be inventive in the present. The professor thinks that physics has become too in-the-lab, too in-the-skull, we don't get enough of a chance to survey the field. I work in unified field theory. I do not think my professor understands my research. He says, "You are getting ahead of yourself, Elizabeth."

Galileo dropped a book and a florin from the Leaning Tower of Pisa and they struck the ground under his wrists at the same exact time, proving Aristotle wrong. Paper falls more slowly—he understood that our perceptions often don't match the things he knew to be true. But if he could suck the air from the earth, his body and a feather would land at the same instant. Laws work best in the purity of a vacuum.

Galileo improved the compass. Galileo used pendulums as timepieces. Galileo invented a 30x magnification telescope, the most powerful yet.

Galileo did not discover anything. He saw Jupiter's four moons first. To not know something and then know it—but they were always there. No law or constant or field or theory is named after him. What counts as discovery? Gravity was there before Newton had a name for it. The new world was only new to the people who hadn't been there yet, not the thousands or millions of people who'd lived there for thousands or millions of years, or forever. Did Einstein discover relativity, that $E = mc^2$? Or give symbols to truth? I don't want to *discover* the Theory of Everything. I want to describe what I am certain is already there.

Galileo did not discover that the earth travels round the sun— Copernicus proved that, more or less. Others suspected. Galileo made it popular, a controversy. People borrowed his telescope or bought their own and looked up and Jupiter had moons circling it; the universe wasn't concentric, not anymore, anyone could see.

That's what I want to do. Show that the world isn't so simple as it seems.

They've got a GUT, a Grand Unified Theory, which reconciles electromagnetism with the strong and weak forces. But no TOE yet, no Theory of Everything. Gravity still can't slot in. General relativity and quantum mechanics make sense—Newton has been overthrown, but Einstein, Heisenberg, Schrödinger, Planck,

　　　　　　　　　　　　　　And Yet It Moves

Oppenheimer, Fermi, what they did still works. It just doesn't work together. Relativity only needs gravity, but quantum can't deal with gravity. Gravity is still a problem. We've got a gut but no toe. I do not know what that means, can't turn acronyms into metaphor. I don't know what's next, but I want to be the one to do it.

I've been working on string theory but it hasn't fixed the problem of forces and fields. I've worked on perturbative heterotic string models, eleven-dimensional M-theory, orbifold and orientifold singular geometries, D-branes, flux compactification, warped geometry, and nonperturbative type IIB superstring solutions. But some part of me knows that the answer isn't there.

※ ※ ※

Galileo was told to stop advocating heliocentrism and he did. In 1616 he asked if he could write a book, *Dialogue Concerning the Two Chief World Systems*, describing the Aristotelian/Ptolemaic/geocentric system and the Copernican/heliocentric system. Both possibilities. The Inquisition said sure, but when the book was published, Simplicio advocates geocentrism, and while yes, his world system can be seen as the simpler of the two, he also comes across as a simpleton. Advocacy by showing the idiocy of the other side.

The idiots in my reality say things like, "Oh! A woman physicist! How does it feel to be so rare?" Some even say, "And you're so pretty," as if I am meant to have any response to that sentiment at all.

They charged Galileo with heresy. He recanted in front of many men in gemstone-toned robes, then spent the rest of his life under house arrest.

They used the Bible against him, of course. In his journals he wrote that Ecclesiastes 1:5 tells us that "the sun rises and sets," and it looks that way, yes, of course. A poetic way of describing how reality seems to be. Poetic language feminizes the earth in Psalm 104:5:

"He set the earth upon her foundations, so that it shall never move." The Bible is not always literal, Galileo said to the men trying him. It is, they responded. That shift from *her* to *it*, alongside that tense—*shall*—got Galileo interested in translation. He wondered what the original said, so he found all the varieties of the Bible he could. Chronicles 16:30 is translated variously as (in my translation from his Italian—my Italian is passable, learned when I was an art student, like Galileo once was, when I wanted to study perspective and chiaroscuro, represent figures, before I fell in love with mathematical figures—but I use a dictionary to help me):

Tremble before him, all the earth! The world is firmly established; it cannot be moved.

Fear before him, all the earth! The world also shall be stable; that it be not moved.

Fear before him, all the earth! The world won't be shaken; it is immovable.

The tenses: è = is, deve essere = shall be. Is it stable now, or will it be at some future time? Is it immovable, or cannot be moved? Galileo wanted to learn Aramaic, but his eyes failed him. "Say among the Nations, The Lord reigneth. Surely the world shall be stable, and not move, and he shall judge the people in his righteousness." Psalm 96:10. Someday. Not now.

Galileo Galilei never went to Galilee. He wanted to eat seafood and bread where Jesus increased the loaves and fishes, read the Sermon on the Mount in the place where it was spoken, swim in maybe the same water Jesus touched, evaporated and rained down into the same sea many times since then but essentially the same. Galileo thought he would be a priest, after he thought he would be an artist. But he read the Sermon on the Mount time and time again, and didn't feel he could actually hold people to those standards. Couldn't hold himself to them. And when he stood in front of the Inquisition, he said yes, yes, he believed everything in the

Bible to be the literal truth, and he was deeply sorry that he implied science said otherwise, and he humbly repented.

As he walked off the little stage they made him stand on, his journal confirms the rumors every student of physics and mathematics and astronomy and cosmology has heard ever since: as he walked away from them, he did say, loudly enough for all to hear, "And yet it moves!"

Galileo felt what others did not feel, his body told him, then his observations of the heavens confirmed it—we orbit, gravity makes it so. The earth feels still under our feet, yet we are moving at incredible speeds. Falling through the cosmos. This he knew to be true: we are all falling together around a ball of light, another ball of light falls around us, we are caught between two spheres, tumbling through space around fire while a reflective stone plummets around us, again and again and again.

* * *

I have one week to turn these notes into a research paper. I have no thesis, just these saved pages. I'm not the type to keep a diary, but this feels more like that than like any essay. I'm not doing science here, I know.

I went to the laundromat today and a fairly attractive man, roughly my age, watched me fold my panties. I own only black underwear and they are attractive enough, some have lace, boyshorts and thongs and bikinis, not too many choices so I don't have to think about that too hard when I get dressed in the morning, just put on whatever won't show under clothes. Cute enough that no one would be embarrassed to find them on me, nothing so fancy I'd seem to be someone in bed that I'm not. On occasion I go home with men when I go to bars. I've had boyfriends that lasted months, never years yet. This man did not try to hide the fact that he was watching me. I am a meticulous folder. He saw the MIT T-shirt my dad bought me when I got into the physics PhD program, a big step up from the local state school in the New Mexico desert where I did my undergrad, and he asked me if I went there. I said yes. He said he went to Harvard Business and what did I study? When I said theoretical physics, he scoffed. That's the only word for the sound that came from his throat. I looked at him, threw my unfolded clothes in my bag, and we both went home alone. I finished folding my clothes, tried to work on this paper, typed these notes instead. Now I will read one of my three-hundred-dollar textbooks. Men like him do not make me think I can't do this. I do not know what they make me think.

*　*　*

Six days left.

These days his daughter says his penance for him. That's how Galileo phrased it, so he must have done it himself awhile. He was commanded to recite the seven penitential psalms weekly. His daughter Virginia had become Sister Maria Celeste. His daughter Livia had become Sister Arcangela. They had no dowries. They were sent away before they were old enough to choose the convent for themselves. Maria Celeste wrote letters to her Illustrious Lord Father telling him that her love for him was "infinite." For Galileo, infinity was a mathematical concept. Galileo never married Marina Gamba, his housekeeper, though she bore him three children. He did not send his son away.

It's unclear whether or not Galileo loved Marina Gamba. He mentions her rarely in his journals. Mentions his children rarely. They were not what was on his mind. The Inquisition seemed unbothered by the fact that he had children and no wife. I am unbothered. In his journals, Galileo draws sketches, writes numbers I don't see the pattern of.

And Yet It Moves

* * *

Five days.

He writes this: a visiting Franciscan monk handed him a doll, but it couldn't be for children. Too spooky. The monk said it was carved from the root of a cottonwood tree. The doll had the broad shoulders of a man, but wore a skirt of animal hide. Its skin was black and its tongue stuck out far from its grimacing mouth and its eyes bugged out of its head. "I wanted to pay respect to your piety," the monk said. "And to a former countryman of yours, whose good work laid the foundations for the work of God I now have the privilege to do." The monk was Spanish, Galileo Galilei was Italian, but each man spoke enough of the other's language that they could communicate. The monk, whose name is unrecorded, told Galileo a story.

Álvar Núñez Cabeza de Vaca and six hundred other men left Spain for Florida in 1527. They got lost in the swamp and their numbers were reduced to 242. They slaughtered and ate their horses. They made bellows from deerhide to fan a fire hot enough to forge metal tools and nails, and made five boats. They sailed to the mouth of the Mississippi and a hurricane reduced them to two boats and forty men. They sailed on to what is now Galveston, Texas, which they called Malhado, misfortune. They were enslaved by native peoples. Only four men survived and escaped: Cabeza de Vaca, Andrés Dorantes de Carranza, Alonso del Castillo Maldonado, and a Moorish slave called Esteban. They wandered the desert for eight years. They were occasionally enslaved. Cabeza de Vaca healed some with the faith he never lost—"Never," the monk said, "like you, Galilei, you have always believed that the church knows best." Finally the four men reached Mexico City and other Spaniards, and sailed back to Europe in 1537.

I've since read *La Relación*, and it's all true.

"Here is where this story connects with your gift," the monk said. "Fray Marcos de Niza was born in Nice, which was under the control of the Italian House of Savoy. That makes him a country-man of yours. He'd heard stories of the Seven Cities of Cibola, made of gold. He and Esteban de Dorantes of Azamor guided Francisco Vásquez de Coronado there."

Esteban traveled days ahead of de Niza with a group of Christianized Pimas and Tlaxcalans. The first nonindigenous man the Zuni people met was an African slave. Other native people had previously treated Esteban like a god, gave him turquoise and women. He expected the same from the Zuni people. Or he interrupted a ceremony. Or the gourd rattle he carried there offended them. But he did something wrong and they killed him.

"This is Esteban?" Galileo asked, looking into his hands, horrified.

"Yes. A kachina based on him. A doll to teach children of the different spirits. He is an ogre spirit now. He frightens children into good behavior. His tongue hangs out and his eyes bug because they garroted him. The story does not end there. I have returned from the same village. We have since sent many more explorers and missionaries. We have brought faith to the pagan indigenous tribes of the new world."

Galileo hadn't realized he was considered to be a part of the Christianizing mission. He writes, "Since I recanted my beliefs all know me to be faithful. Those returning from the conversion of souls bring me maps they trace my hands along since I can no longer see. They bring me bundles of birds broken by the long journey over the sea and hope I can heal them. They bring me more and more dolls of spirits the Natives once believed in, but no longer do. They have recanted, too, of course."

* * *

Four more days to turn this into something I can turn in.

The middle finger of Galileo's right hand is housed in the Museo Galileo. Part of me wants to go there and stroke it.

Manhattan Project. Los Alamos. Oak Ridge. I was born near proving grounds. Born near where bombs were used. Not against people. Just sand blown upward, desert plants and animals destroyed. I was born near the place where the doll was made, before it was carried to Galileo's hands. Trinity. The name of the test site was taken from Donne. "As West and East / In all flat Maps—and I am one—are one, / so death doth touch the Resurrection." Who thought this was about resurrection? Oppenheimer, that charmer. "Batter my heart, three person'd God." Trinity.

I do theoretical physics because it can't be used against anyone.

If I quit, they will say I was too emotional all along.

* * *

Three more days until the deadline. In a three-hundred-page textbook, not one woman's name is mentioned. Can I be the first whose name is known to households with a woman's name before the last? Elizabeth Rabinowitz added to the list.

* * *

Two more days. Last night I couldn't work anymore so I went to a bar for a beer. I met Stephen Hawking. The only heroic scientist still living.

He was with an aide who helped him drink beer through a straw. I asked if I could join them and she could tell by his eyes that his answer was yes. I told him I was a great admirer.

He spoke prefabricated sentences that are easy for him to find and click on, sentences he must tell to a lot of people he meets. His mechanical voice is not hard to understand. He was born exactly three hundred years after Galilei died. He calls him Galilei, by his last name. Hawking's boyhood nickname was Einstein. He held the position at Cambridge that Newton held. Nothing is bigger or older than the universe. Space and time began with the Big Bang and end in black holes. Because there is a law such as gravity, the universe can and will create itself from nothing. Life appeared on this planet within half a billion years of when it was possible, pretty quickly in the ten-billion-year lifespan of a planet, so the probability is high that life could also spontaneously arise on other planets. "But," his machine said, "I do not think there is life within one hundred light years from us. If there were, we would have heard from them by now. And if there is no other life in the Milky Way, then we really should survive. The exponentially increasing use of the finite resources of the planet makes me believe the only way for us to survive is to move into space. That's why I believe in manned, or should I say personed, space travel, the sooner the better. I've done my zero-gravity trial. I'm scheduled to go on Richard Branson's trip to space next year. For a long time, the biggest danger to our survival as a species was comets. Now, our problems are man-made. Or should I say human-made. We will destroy ourselves if we stay here."

I asked him if he'd ever known a stupendous female physicist.

"No," he said. "But I do not think that is the fault of females. They have not been given the same opportunities as men."

It took him about seven minutes to type this three-sentence answer. Apparently no one had asked him this before. I asked if I could buy him a beer and he didn't ask his nurse for permission. When I returned, he wanted to talk about black holes. Everything he said, all the preprogrammed sentences in the memory bank of his speaking device, felt like they were about me.

Matter falling into a black hole forms an accretion disk heated by friction, the brightest object in the universe. For an outside observer, time slows for object falling into a black hole, taking an infinite time to reach it. An indestructible faller can't tell when the event horizon is crossed. When an observer falls in, information—its shape, its charge—is evenly distributed along the horizon and lost to observers. A gravitational singularity is a point of zero volume and infinite density where spacetime curvature is infinite. In a nonrotating, noncharged black hole, the observer falling in gets added to the singularity. This can be prolonged by accelerating away, but it can't be avoided, so it's best to just free-fall in. The observer is torn apart by tidal forces.

"It's called spaghettification," Hawking told me.

"I know," I said. I'm not the type to pretend to know less than I do. "In a charged or rotating black hole," I said, "the singularity can be avoided, and the observer can exit into another spacetime, so that the black hole functions as a wormhole. One could exit into one's own past."

"That's why your work on unification is so important," Stephen Hawking told me. "None of these peculiar effects would survive a proper quantum treatment of rotating and charged black holes. You might be the one to unify quantum and gravitational effects into a single theory."

Symmetry. Infinity. Saturating this inequality. Naked Singularities. Unphysical. Cosmic censorship hypothesis. Little Boy. Fat Man. Dark stars. Frozen stars. Photon sphere. Gnomon shadows. Circumpolar stars. Neutron star. Ergosphere—the space where it is impossible to be still, where you would have to accelerate at greater than the speed of light in the direction opposite the black hole in order to stand still. I feel myself being pulled into myself. A collapse. Gravity's relentless pull.

"It's not that I can't do it," I said. "It's that I might not want to. Or, rather, I want to—my work is the most fun thing I know how to do. But it feels awfully pointless sometimes. The weather as strange as it's been. War. Famine. My thought experiments and tinkering in a lab, what good is that to Ukraine? To a kid whose family was killed by drone strikes? Drone strikes, for Christ's sake."

Dr. Hawking laboriously typed by twitching his cheek muscle. His machine said, "More fun than sex?"

I laughed. Then thought about it. I really did. Nothing worthwhile came to mind. "Yeah," I said. "Much more fun." He didn't type. Just looked at me. "Should I say it for you?" I asked. "That's a big part of my problem? Great sex would make me feel better about the world? Probably. There are just so few men I want to sleep with. They're so stupid. Or boring. Or unkind."

His response? "I want to sleep with everyone."

I looked at this man, all the muscles I could see still, save one. His internal muscles still worked, digestion and breathing, which is why he was still alive over fifty years after his diagnosis, after they gave him two and a half years. "I'm sorry," I said. "You have it harder than me."

"It is not a competition."

"I know. But now I feel bad for feeling bad." The aide lifted the beer to his mouth and he sipped. "Would you like me to do that?" I asked her. She said no. No reason. But a kind of responsibility, I assumed, devotion. She's the one to do it. "I wish you could speak as quickly as me, as I, so I could know what you're really thinking," I said.

He found the prepared quote he must have said to other people. "My disability has not been a significant handicap. It has probably given me more time than most people to pursue knowledge."

And Yet It Moves

I wondered if he would consider depression a disability. I wondered if the time spent in my own mind, more than most, has been beneficial.

"Can I see your work?" he asked.

"I just have scrawls with me. Most of my calculations are in my office. One wall a window, the other three chalkboards. I've been thinking about the limits of string theory. I don't think what I'm looking for is there. Thank you for asking."

His aide held the notebook. She must know the speed he prefers to read, turned the pages with no obvious signal from him. When Stephen Hawking was diagnosed with amyotrophic lateral sclerosis he and his lady friend married, thinking it would be intense and tragic. He's since had three kids, divorced the wife who was supposed to be short term, and the nurse he left his wife for. This nurse is just a nurse, as far as I know.

He typed for ten minutes, then said, "You are missing something. I do not know what. But I believe you will find it."

I shook my head as if to sling my thoughts out my ears and said, "Thank you. I just want what's in here to matter. You matter. I want little girls to know they can do this. I'm sorry. I must be a little drunk. Morose."

"Are you a betting person?"

"Not usually."

"I would like to make a wager. You will find the Theory of Everything."

"If you're right?"

"You take me out for a night on the town."

"So I'm betting against myself? And if I don't do it? If I win?"

"I take you out." This man who must be fed. And then, the last thing he said to me that night, typed while I finished my fourth beer and he finished his second: "It matters more, for some, for others to believe in them, than for them to believe in themselves. I am betting on you. I am drunk. Good thing I am not driving this machine home. Thank you for a lovely evening. I hope you become less lonely soon."

This morning Dr. Hawking's chalkboard arrived. The one he used in Cambridge. A note, printed in the same early-nineties computer font his machine uses, green ink, a weird joke I loved, says, "You are part of the lineage. Good luck and go for it." I will not turn in this research paper. The chalkboard covers my window so that I can write on four surfaces without distraction.

All Those Stairs

I've worked hundreds of eight-hour shifts in this box pushing buttons, making this elevator—its dented metal walls, its gum-blemished floor, each blotch blackened by hundreds of shoe soles, its folding card table unfolded and folding metal chair unfolded in the back corner where I sit, with my puzzles and my papers and my lightened, sweetened coffee and my fan or my heater plugged into the outlet below me—go up and go down, making the doors open, making the doors shut, and I've gotten used to how long it feels, eight hours, here, underground, but this shift, I fear, will feel much longer than the others. Because I'm waiting for something. After this shift I will see my son for the second time in twelve years, the son I'm shocked to have raised, the son who has now asked for the help I have not given, for twelve years—and I usually don't feel anticipation. Hundreds? Thousands? I wonder if, if I counted the number of times we go up and go down today, the number of times I make the doors open and shut, could I count today as an average, and then count all the years I've worked here, twenty-six years now, and figure out how many shifts a year that is—two weeks vacation, five shifts a week—and then do the math to know, approximately, how many times I've gone up, how many times I've gone down, how many times I've opened the doors, and how many times I've made them shut? More or less? If I ever saw someone spit gum on the floor of my elevator, I'd make them pick it up. How do so many spots get on the floor without me noticing? Does it happen on someone else's shift? Someone who seems more lenient about such things? I've never seen someone do it. No one has ever done it in front of me. Who would ever think it's okay to put gum on the ground, where other people walk? In front of someone else or not? About once a year the first few years I would scrape it off with a trowel meant for paint, but it would come back with a quickness that upset me so I gave that up, who knows how many years ago.

That one is as big as me. A woman, too. Harder to tell, at that size. She stands in the corner opposite me, as if to balance the weight, as if to keep the elevator from tipping. People filter in as they always do, fill the empty space evenly, leave the same amount of distance on each side of each person, condense closer only when the elevator is full and people still want to get on. But they leave slightly more space around her. As if everyone agrees that since a bigger person takes up more space, she deserves more of a buffer around her. Proportional. Or, people don't want to touch her, want to ensure they don't rub up against her surface. But don't mind touching other people quite so much. People file in as always, though because she came in and stationed herself first they look to her, look to me, their faces don't betray anything but they eyeball both of us then they turn. Two big women in the same elevator. Maybe we'll crash. People look at me and think I have a man's job, I know they do. But this job, it doesn't take strength. I push the buttons, we go up, we go down, I'm friendly to those who are friendly to me, I'm polite to everyone who walks through those doors. This job requires no strength, just patience, and since when do men have more of that than us? I don't fix the elevator if something goes wrong. They hire people to do that—yes, usually men. Always men, in my experience. Men carrying heavy bags filled with large tools. Not my job. I'm a big woman, I may be big

And Yet It Moves

as a man, sure, but that has nothing to do with my suitability for this job. I'm strong enough, but not very strong, and I don't need to be. It'd be harder for a small woman to do this job, I guess. But she could. We're here for safety, our presence prevents anyone getting mugged or raped or shot on the elevator, on that long ride up from underground, up something like seventeen stories to 168th Street, up to the small flight of stairs that you walk up to get outside. We don't actively try to stop those things from happening, it's not like I search anyone, no metal detectors ring the doors, and it's true, someone could shoot someone else right under my nose. How could I stop that? But it's less likely they'll do it with me or someone else sitting here. I'm here as a witness: people generally don't want to do their crimes with someone watching. A small woman, she could watch just as well as me. But maybe she'd be less intimidating. I'm not intimidating, I wouldn't say that. But my size implies something, something like I can handle whatever happens. Even if I'm reading my papers and not really looking around, doing my puzzles, even all of us who don't really pay attention except to push the buttons and say, "Have a nice day"—we prevent crime. Simply by being here, by our bearing. I pay more attention than most. People ask me if I carry a gun. I do. If it's ever just me and one other person on the elevator, I don't want to be raped, mugged, or shot. So I carry a gun to defend myself. We all do. Comes after the training. And yes, I do know how to shoot it. People wouldn't ask a man that. I have handcuffs. I'm allowed to use them, but only on the elevator. I'm not a cop, I can't do anything up on the street if something's happening—though myself, I would. If I see an old abuela getting robbed of her bag of groceries? Sure I'll shoot. At the knee, I'm not like those cops who shoot to kill. But I've never seen a crime being committed up there, at least nothing worse than kids selling bags of weed. They look at me like, "What're you gonna do about it?" and I shrug as if to say, "Nothin', really," and they keep selling. Myself, I don't care if people smoke weed or not. Doesn't bother me at all. I've never seen it turn anyone mean. Lazy, maybe, and we do have enough lazy as is, but it's not my job to tell people they can't be lazy. People say the Heights is dangerous, but those are people who've never really been here, or have just been here and seen all the brown people and thought, *Danger*. They don't know anything. It's not the most dangerous neighborhood in New York, and New York's not even in the top ten most dangerous cities in the country. The Heights is safer than Bed-Stuy and safer than Baltimore. Detroit has had us beat for some time now. People selling drugs don't scare me. That kind of crime doesn't make me feel unsafe. People are poor up here, but they aren't likely to shoot you because of it. Well, not real likely, at least, but likely enough to need me on the elevator I guess. Cops most likely to shoot. Robbery. We do have robberies up here. I can't pretend like that isn't true. And I know that some of the kids selling dope carry guns. That graffiti on the walls of the station, though? That's nothing. Sure, there must be gangs up here. 188 block talking shit to 169. But that's all I've ever seen of them, their marks on the wall. Nothing else. And I don't read about them, either. I read about kids getting shot by the people meant to protect them, and some say they deserve it, and some say they don't. I'm not one to say who deserves what. I keep people safe on my watch, that's all I can do and know. I read all three papers daily: the *Times*, the *Post*, the *Daily News*. Then I give them to Dan who comes on at four, when I leave. Three eight-hour shifts scheduled, we ride these things round the clock. No lunch break, we eat in the elevator, and they frown on us using the pisser. I don't see what the big deal is if I'm gone for a few minutes. There's always two attended elevators, and two unattended. So what if for five minutes there's only one person to ride with? There's always someone. I'm not abandoning the patrons to their own devices, I'm not forcing them to ride the

And Yet It Moves

elevators alone, they can always have company and the safety of company if they want it. I take one bathroom break every shift. That seems more than civil.

I haven't been counting the rides. I didn't think to do it until a few rides in, haven't been doing it since. For accuracy, I wonder if I'd have to do a whole day, or if I could count only an hour and extrapolate? That wouldn't work. Because the traffic each hour is so different. I bet I've only been here about an hour so far today, it's probably only about nine o'clock, still rush hour for all the folks going to work, though I don't look at my watch yet, don't want to know yet if I'm right or way off. I can usually guess the time to within fifteen minutes, almost always, but my sense of time might be skewed today. Because of what happens when I get off work, seeing him. Sebastian. Sebastian coming home. My son. I'm waiting for that and don't know if that will slow things down today, or speed things up. A group of teenagers gets on the elevator and they clearly aren't going to school today, but it's not my job to say anything to them about it. I'm not here to enforce all rules, just the immediate safety of my patrons. They don't look dangerous. Standing like they're about to ditch school, shuffling their feet and looking at the ground; not standing like they're about to shoot someone, feet planted, jaws set, chins up. They were joking with each other before they stepped in, now they're quiet. Maybe they think I'm judging them. Maybe they think I'm like their moms. When Sebastian went away he was their age, about. All teenagers in baggy jeans and baggy jackets remind me of him. Some see that as the costume of a criminal. A costume over the skin of a criminal. I see swarms of young boys and think of him. He didn't run with criminals. Not for most of his life. He got good enough grades that I thought he had a future, college or maybe not but a job. Clothes that aren't the costume of a criminal. All our skin is the costume of a criminal. But slacks and a button-up help. Clothes to put over the costume of a criminal. Whether he was or wasn't he was always presumed a criminal. We all knew that about our sons. He is a criminal. Where he is now, until tomorrow, the cops protect him. Well, not cops, guards. Like me. I looked at him and saw a fortress, others looked and saw a felon before he ever was one. My son didn't get shot in the street like so many other boys, he was not murdered by a man meant to uphold the law, and I don't know what else to say about my son's lawlessness. Even criminals shouldn't be shot in the street. Someone is watching over my son, keeping him safe from other men, other sons. Starting today, he will be mine to watch over again. I hope he does no more harm but I do not know how to enact that hope. I did not fail to protect him but I did fail to protect others from him. Now Sebastian is much older than these boys, much bigger, thicker. I saw him last week for the first time in twelve years. The only time. Now I know he doesn't look like he did when he left. After today, I'll be seeing him daily. I see these boys, I see someone who doesn't exist anymore. The doors take a long time to close and the boys seem a bit nervous. They don't know what to say to me. I want to tell them not to worry. I'll get them wherever they're going. The elevator never breaks down during my shift. Not once in twenty-six years. I've never gotten stuck on the elevator, like the horror stories from other operators, what you read about in the papers. The elevator always runs well when I'm running it. I can tell when it's near to breaking down, I feel it. It settles into its floors differently. Not as smoothly, whether we're settling down at the subway level, or up at the station level. It's not like the patrons can feel it, they don't jolt or lose their balance or anything. But riding all day, I can sense how the cables run through their pulleys just a little more roughly, and one's about to slip. I'm right over half the time. I'll tell the next operator, Dan or Joe or Hank or Sheridan, what we call the other Joe, whoever's been on after me throughout the years.

And Yet It Moves

I'll tell him, "It's gonna break down this shift. You wait. Tell me about it tomorrow." And the majority of the time, they tell me I was right. "How did you know?" they say. "How could you tell?" I tell them I can just feel it. There are other times when the elevator feels like it's swaying back and forth. It doesn't balk when settling up or settling down, it shimmies, just a little, side to side. I know there isn't a lot of room to do that, I've looked inside the shaft when an elevator's been broken down and the doors are open, into the column it travels through. There are only a few inches on each side between the room of the elevator and the walls of the tube it runs through. Not much space to move, I know. Most people wouldn't notice the swinging back and forth, it's true. But if they rode the elevator all day like I do, over hours, over dozens of trips up and down, maybe hundreds, they could tell. It rocks. So instead of going straight down or up we draw waves, sine and cosine, the shapes of sound waves and light waves. It's soothing. It's the only time I think I could sleep in my chair in the corner. I don't of course. But I feel soothed. But when the elevator moves like that, it means something really bad is going to go wrong with its gears soon. Sometimes the elevator is out of operation for days while men tinker with its innards, adjust its cords and cables and turning mechanisms. When I look in when they're working, it amazes me that in order to lift and lower, things aren't lifted and lowered—cogs turn. The mechanism of up and down involves circular spinning. Incredible, whoever thought of that.

People who fly, I don't know what airline it is that has it, I don't fly myself too often—never have flown at all, if I tell the truth—they get me the magazine that has the Mensa quizzes in them, and they bring them to me. All sorts of people, I don't even know their names, people who see me doing the quizzes one day and ask if I like them. Then they always ask if I've ever gotten enough right to be in Mensa. That question's always bothered me. I don't know; for starters, they base Mensa membership on some other test, not the quizzes in the magazines, and I've never looked into taking it. But it just seems kind of rude. It's like they're saying they don't think I'm smart enough to get in, but they're asking in a way that's pretending like they think anyone, even me, even an elevator operator, could be much smarter than she seems. They're asking like they want to show they think I might say yes, though they're expecting me to say no. I tell them I've never taken the real Mensa test, and as for these, I've never gotten them all right. Consistently I get four out of five, or four right and part of the fifth one (some of the questions have three- or four-part answers). My best score yet is 4 and 6/7. But the one part of the seven-part question I got wrong, I don't agree with their answer. You had to unscramble "transportation" into seven words that are six letters or longer. Shorter than six letters is easy: snap, spit, star, spar, rasp, rips, sort, torn, noon, toot, root, port, snort, start, rapt, sport. For longer words I found transit, ration, nation, rotation, notation, and tattoo. I didn't think "transport" counted, because you didn't have to unscramble anything to get it. It's just part of the original word. I tried and tried to get the seventh answer, and then finally looked in the back, and they had all of my words, plus "transport." I don't think that should count. I know lots of words, even though my dictionary isn't the best and I always forget to look things up when I'm using the computers at the library. I find I don't use all the words I know. There are words I recognize, and I can say what they mean, but I never use them in my sentences. Only when I talk in my head. I don't know why that is. Maybe I'm shy about using the word wrong. Or saying it wrong. Maybe I'm more shy about people thinking I'm a jerk for using big, fancy words. Like, who does this elevator operator think she is, saying the Mets' five-game losing streak is egregious? Those folks in their business suits, they can use any word they want and no one will blink. Hubris or pulchritudinous or onomatopoetic. They could even use them the wrong way, and no one'll notice, because no one will think to check them. If it bugs me so much that people don't think I'm smart, why don't I get a job that shows I'm smart? I guess I don't know what else I can do. Or, at least, what else it looks like I'm qualified to do. I didn't finish school, dropped out in the eleventh grade to have my baby. When I was sixteen, I got my first job at Dunkin' Donuts, the one right outside the stairway to the subway station, the one I still stop at on my way down sometimes, most days, to get a cup of coffee and sometimes a maple-glazed in the fall, like now, or a cherry-filled in the summer. Starbucks wouldn't hire me, even though they pay better, and give benefits. They require a diploma. There wasn't a Starbucks in the Heights back then, I would have had to travel down to Thirty-Fourth, or even Fourteenth. But I worked at Dunkin' Donuts for two years, and then when I turned eighteen, I got this job. Thirty years to retirement sounded impossible; I thought I'd just do it until something else came along. Then, no surprise, I never looked for anything else. I started on night shift, so Mama watched Sebastian while I worked. The baby mostly slept through the night early on, so it wasn't too bad for her. He was a good baby. I had days with him. I tried to stay awake while he did, napped when he napped, cleaned up the apartment while following him around, handing him toys, taking away things he couldn't have, finding the toy he wanted. I didn't get a lot of sleep those days, but I guess I was happy. I don't remember them very well, those days. And now I'm four years from retirement. I won't be too old to work then. I could just take my pension, and start working somewhere else. But what else is there to do? Who would hire me? Randall, one of my favorite operators, the one who listens to classical music during his whole shift, a tape player from the '80s plugged in under his fan, and he never plays it too loud, even though he's got those big hearing aids on each ear, he's studying for the GED. He's about my age, early forties or so, I haven't asked him exactly how old, but we both have some salt in our hair. I haven't asked him what he wants it for. But I looked over his shoulder one of the rare days I rode the elevator down to take the subway to run errands after my shift instead of just walking home, and I could do the math he was practicing. It was algebra, FOIL, how to multiply two parenthetical phrases. I'm not sure if that's what they're called, but like this: $(x + 8)(x − 4) = x^2 − 4x + 8x − 32 = x^2 + 4x − 32$. I didn't even have to look at the answer or the explanation, I just remembered how to do it all. But then I went home and wondered why that's helpful. After writing some of my own, I remembered there's a reason to do the reverse, to solve a quadratic equation. But you have to set it equal to zero for it to work. So, if I'm given $3x^2 − 6x = 24$, I can un-factor it to solve. $3x^2 − 6x − 24 = 0$, and I had to play around with making the parenthetical phrases work, there might be a way to do it more efficiently, but I figured out that $(3x − 12)(x + 2) = 0$ works: $3x^2 + 6x − 12x − 24 = 0$, $3x^2 − 6x = 24$, which was the original problem. So, looking at the parentheses I made, x = -2, or 4, since one of those terms has to equal zero. I liked all the scratches and x's and numbers on my notepad. I wouldn't have to study too hard to get the GED, I don't think—though I'm not sure what else is on it besides math. I could ask Randall.

But what would I get it for?

This job is kind of meaningless—but I look around this neighborhood, and I know I don't have an education, so I never expected better. Now it's nearly over. I can do something else. Though, I keep people safe, that's the meaning. I could be a cook, maybe. I might like to feed people good food. There was a time when I didn't know what good food was, thought all food was good, didn't know food could be bad for you. Some nights we had pork chops and potatoes, some nights my mom made us fish sticks in the microwave, some

And Yet It Moves

nights we baked a frozen pizza from the grocery store, some nights when she worked late Mom brought home McDonald's. Every night we had dessert. I thought food was food. My mother was an excellent cook though she didn't always have time to do it, so we often had store-bought. At school I ate what the other kids ate, Mama didn't have time to make me a lunch. They served us chicken patties, chicken nuggets, mashed potatoes, French fries, pizza worse than the kind in the grocery store, then they started serving us Pizza Hut pizza, and Taco Bell, which was pretty good. We never got McDonald's in school when I was there, which is what all the kids wanted, and what the kids who had pocket money left school to buy for lunch. Today, they just go ahead and serve them McDonald's in the cafeteria. I bought candy with the twenty-five cents Mom gave me every day. I drank soda. I didn't know there was better food I could be eating, I ate what was put in front of me. I didn't think to ask for fresh fruit, vegetables. I didn't know how good those things could taste. Now, I'm a real good cook. My mother didn't know better. I didn't have much time either. Like her, I worked. Full-time. But I cooked. How did I get to know better? I really don't know. I packed a lunch for Sebastian. Every day. One for him, and one for me. I often gave us leftovers, but I tried to not make it what we'd had for dinner the night before, exactly, so we wouldn't get bored. So if on Thursday we'd had roasted chicken breast with garlic-sautéed kale and quinoa, the next day I'd pack leftovers from Wednesday's dinner, veggie lasagna. Or, I'd at least make sandwiches out of the chicken, so it would be a little different. I checked out cookbooks from the library on my days off. I learned how to make stews in the Crock-Pot, simple homemade breads, lots of vegetable sides that actually tasted good: Brussels sprouts, pureed turnips, roasted butternut squash, sautéed broccoli rabe, garlic mashed potatoes, carrot and cumin salad. Some people will tell you mashed potatoes aren't healthy, with all the butter and fat. I do use butter and cream in mine. But I read that you should leave the skin on, because the nutrients are there, and garlic is good for you. I figure if something has vitamins in it, and tastes good, then it's good for you. I don't mind eating butter and fat along the way. I never bothered taking home the low-fat cookbooks. I'm willing to put time into my food, but I'm not willing to eat food that doesn't taste good. I'd bring home a book, *Simple Italian*, or *Weekday Meals Made Easy*, or *Main Dishes and Vegetable Sides*. I'd take two or three at a time, make a few recipes to see if I liked how the book was laid out, how it explained things. If I liked it, I'd copy down on index cards all the recipes I thought I might use. I don't have a recipe box. I just keep the cards held together in categories with metal clips: Mains, Sides, Desserts, Appetizers—which I don't make unless I'm entertaining—and Foreign, which includes all my Italian recipes, and the ones for tacos, fajitas, I even have a recipe for hummus and one for sesame noodles in there. I can make pesto from scratch, bought a food processor on layaway like one cookbook taught me. I sometimes have to ask at the grocery store if they have basil, because they keep it in the back, with the roots and dirt still on it. Pesto pasta with chicken pieces and salad was one of Sebastian's favorite meals. I still make it for myself, it keeps well, and I like having pasta with a glass or two of wine after work. When I packed up pasta with grated cheese on top, when I made sure most of the chicken pieces went in Sebastian's lunch, when I packed up a salad with dressing on the side so the lettuce or spinach wouldn't get soggy, was he embarrassed to eat with his friends? Did his lunch seem too homemade? I'll admit, I never knew his friends well. Met few of their mothers. I don't know if they had the kind of mothers who packed food for their sons. Maybe he ate lunch mostly with girls. Would they approve of a lunch sent in Tupperware containers that had to be brought back home and washed? I'll never know unless

I ask, which I won't. I wonder if he just wished I'd send him to school with five dollars to buy a processed, packaged lunch someone else made with more machines than I use. He never said so. He complimented my cooking at night, every night. The boy had manners. I taught him, sure, but even as a child please and thank you came natural to him. He had a talent for compliments. "This rub on the pork roast is really bright, Mom. I like it." "That necklace looks nice on you, Mom. You should get yourself the bracelet to match." Telling the neighbor lady past her prime, "I like that color on you, Ms. Whitfield. It looks good with your eyes." A charmer, sure. But not the kind that had you rolling your eyes, saying, *Oh please*, thinking he was shady or playing games to get what he wanted. Sebastian always sounded sincere. I wonder if he threw my lunches in the trash, bought other food with his own money. He always brought the Tupperware home. I bring my lunch to work every day. We don't get a lunch break, so that the three eight-hour shifts work out the same every day. I eat on the elevator, so I bring something that can warm to room temperature and still be good, like quiche from the night before that's been in the fridge, or a hummus and avocado sandwich, or sometimes I put a bag of ice in my insulated lunch bag to keep it cool if I bring salad, or yogurt and fruit. For dinner, I always eat something hot, at home. I have the most seniority, so I have the best shift, 8 to 4, so I eat my meals at normal times. Early on I worked the midnight to 8 AM shift, had "dinner" when I got home at 8:30 in the morning, lunch at 4 AM on the elevator. There would hardly be anyone riding the subway those hours of the night, but that's when we're the most important: if a crime is going to happen, it'll happen late at night, most usually. From six till eight was busy with people going to work and school. Young white folks in business suits that live up here because the rent is cheap, riding the 1 to Ninety-Sixth, changing to the 2 or 3 to go express to Wall Street to work their fancy jobs. A starter apartment up here. Kids in braids and pigtails or with their hair cut close riding to school, sometimes with their moms, sometimes by themselves, sometimes with an older brother or sister. Teenagers obviously not going to school, riding the train anywhere else. Students riding to City College at 137th, or the Columbia Med students from the campus up here riding down to the main one at 116th. So many people starting their day. I'd feel like I was finishing mine, but then I'd go home to Sebastian, my mama still drinking her coffee, him ready to play. We'd take our first nap at about ten o'clock, another around one. I'd put him to bed around six, get a few hours of sleep, the baby in the crib next to me, then go start my shift at midnight, Mama snoozing on the couch. I always told her to go sleep in my bed when I left, but she never wanted to move after she got settled in. I only get the end of the morning rush now, and lunchtime can be busy, though a lot of people walk from work, don't bother with the subway, and people are just starting to get off work by the time I do. So my elevators usually aren't too crowded. But sometimes. When you work the other shifts, four to twelve, or twelve to eight, rush hour can make it so bad you actually have to tell people to get in or out of the elevator, you have to tell people to cram together, to pull their bags inside so the doors can close. Then they go down to the trains and do the same thing in them. Miserable. They're more polite to me than to each other, apologize if they bump me, try not to invade the space my card table blocks out for me. Sometimes I bring leftovers to the boys who work the other shifts, especially the single ones, since I know I won't eat it all when I make big meals for just me, and they likely don't eat as well as they should. Sal and Vinnie, Italian cousins, they don't cook for themselves, expect their girlfriends to do it when they have one, or they ride the 1 up to the Bronx on Sundays and get leftovers after lunch from their mamas and grandmamas. I don't do too much Italian, but they appreciate the beef stew, the baked ham slices, even the sides of collards I sometimes bring them. I don't do low-fat, but I cook fresh food, no preservatives, and I think that makes it good for you. I'll make lasagna tonight. With meat. The men in my life that have come and gone have certainly appreciated my cooking. Not that they stuck around for it—though I didn't expect that to be enough reason. I do think I am enough reason to stick around for, but I can see why some don't agree. I live in my head a lot. There might not be enough of me in a room to feel like you're really living with a person. I mean, bulk, I take up some space—I cook wholesome food, but I make a lot of it, and I enjoy eating. I know I'm big. And if someone asks me what I'm thinking, I'll say. But I usually don't meet the kind of men who ask questions like that. I can see how I might seem a little hard to reach.

I've been lucky. Men who like a woman like me, wide at the shoulders and wider at the hips, quiet, hair not too flashy, not a lot of jewelry or makeup, more comfortable in my uniform than a dress, likely to break things with an elbow or a bump of my hip, the kind of men that like a woman like me tend to be pretty rough, gruff voices, gruff hands. I'm lucky that none has ever laid a hand on me. They aren't exactly delicate, several have threatened, but none ever did, so I have that to be thankful for. No means no for me, always has. I know it makes me rare. I always said a man could hit me once, learn his lesson from it, then never do it again. But I never had to follow through on that bargain with myself, or make that bargain with him. A history of heartbreaks, sure. A couple that made me hopeful, but didn't work out. But nothing too bad. Nothing that left a mark. The daddy of my child made it clear real quick he didn't want to be a daddy. We were teenagers. I'm sure I was heartbroken for a time, must have been. My sixteen-year-old self, with thick hips and a thick rear, I see pictures of myself then, now, and wonder when I ever looked like that. I was shocked and amazed my body could make a baby, and it seemed worth losing a man over. I wanted it. It didn't occur to me then that men wouldn't keep coming along the way they always did in high school. Well. I have two cats. They like to be in my lap, rubbing a small space all over in that wiggly feline way. They are very kind and perceptive, can read my moods. They stay near when I seem low. They're also whiny and needy, and make it clear my primary role is to feed them. I really wanted a dog when I went to the pound, but figured keeping a dog in an apartment for over eight hours a day would be cruel. The cats live inside, only. I worry about what would happen to them on 172nd if I let them out the door. They don't seem to mind. That one-bedroom apartment is their world. I rubbed one's back, Jeremiah, after dinner one night, while James—the most recent man of mine, gone just a few months now—and I watched television with a glass of brandy. Jeremiah kept squirming into my palm, purring, purring, purring. I said that it was a good thing all domesticated animals like to be touched, us included. Helps us all get along. He asked if I really thought we were domesticated, and animals. I said of course. Our instincts are still there, we still respond with fight or flight, we still crave to sleep around and murder, even though society tells us not to do those things anymore. We care about food, shelter, and sex a whole lot more than anything else. We're animals. But we've lost the ability to do those things, the food and shelter part, on our own. Who could survive a night out in the woods? Who knows how to hunt and gather anymore? "People in Idaho," he said. "And Montana, Arizona, places like that. People hunt and gather there." I asked if he'd ever been out west, and he said no, and I hadn't either. But I told him sure, people hunt out there, and gather, whatever that means, but they don't do it to survive. If they don't shoot a moose, it's not like they starve. We can't live the way our ancestors used to anymore, because we don't know how. We're domesticated. That

And Yet It Moves

night he stayed, which he sometimes did and sometimes didn't, and Stephen, the other cat, curled up on James in the night, and purred, and kneaded his pudgy stomach. I was still awake, and it made me smile to hear. James woke up, scooped up Stephen in one hand, and slung him down on the ground.

A lady gets on the elevator on probably my thirtieth trip of the shift and it's just us and we trade hi-how-are-yous and she's familiar to me and then she asks, "How did your visit go last week?" She remembered. I don't talk about Sebastian often, really, hardly ever, but with her, I don't know her name, but last week when she asked me, "How are you?" I'd answered, "I'm okay. Nervous. I'm going to see my son after work, and I haven't seen him in a while." I don't know why I said that to her. Maybe because the elevator was almost empty, only a few other people in with us, ignoring us. Maybe because she asked. I don't think she meant to really ask, I think she was just being polite like almost everyone who steps onto an elevator and feels obligated to greet the person who's pushing the buttons so that they don't have to. I guess I wanted someone to know that I wasn't feeling my best, someone out of the hundreds that had walked near me that day. Thousands? And she was so nice. She just said, "Well, I'd be nervous, too. But I hope it goes really well." I didn't tell her anything else about him, that day. I never talk about Sebastian. But I remembered to say, "Thank you. And how are you?" She told me she was looking forward to a weekend with her grandchildren, and she thanked me for asking. So now, by remembering, by asking after it, she's made the feeling in my stomach stronger, that feeling that never goes away, the feeling of being truly frightened of something, that feeling I've been trying to ignore for years. And so I say to her, "I'll be seeing a lot more of him in the future, so I guess it went better than expected. Thank you for remembering. For asking." She must take that as the best possible answer, because she just beams. "Oh, I'm so glad," she says. I don't bother telling her that it's more complicated than it sounds. I remember to ask her about her grandkids, and she says they're getting so big so fast it almost makes her sad, the usual. And I hope she won't ask after Sebastian every time she sees me. I didn't give her a name, that's good. And it's my fault. I mentioned him. When I named him, I liked that his name sounded like bastion. I thought he could be a fortress. It never occurred to me that the kids at school would instead hear bastard. Which he was. But so were some of them.

She leaves, and I'm alone on the elevator for a while. I don't check my watch. Time passes funny down here, fast and slow, usually slow, so it's best to not check too often. It's discouraging to think your shift is half over and then realize you've only been underground two hours. I sit up top with the door open for quite a few minutes, and nobody comes in. I don't ever really feel alone though, at work, not really. There are people around me all the time, nearly every minute of the working day. Many of them talk to me. Some remember things, like that woman, and they ask after what they know—how're my Mets this year, if my cold's gone (one whole week I had to tell people to stay on the other side of the elevator I felt so achy, and when I sneezed really loudly one guy said, all nasty, "Why don't you stay home, so we don't all get sick? We can run our own elevator," and I realized he was right), they ask what I think about the cover of the *Post* or *Daily News*, A-Rod's latest scandal or our governor's latest wrongdoing. They laugh with me about the punny headlines. Except "Tali-BAM!" That was a bad one. I always have people to talk to. And when I don't, I have plenty to think about. One young man gets on the elevator, a student at Yeshiva I guess by his yarmulke and book and strings hanging out from under his shirt. I take him down to the subway and he reads while we descend, swaying, his finger tracing from right to left. He's davening, that's what they call it. Praying. They do it three

And Yet It Moves

times a day. Even if they're in public. I'm not one to pray. I bet it's a nice thing to do, to believe that that matters. I thought the Yeshiva up here was just a religious school, but the students go to college. It's a university. All boys. They keep the girls 150 blocks away, near Thirty-Fourth Street.

I hadn't seen Sebastian in twelve years, not since he got locked up, until I went to go see him last week. I don't know when I would have decided to go see him, I hadn't gone to see him at all in all those years, but then I got this letter from him, saying he was getting out on parole, good behavior, after twelve years instead of twenty, and he needed a place to stay. Said he didn't know who else to ask. Since he'd been in he hadn't kept in touch with any of his old friends. Hadn't wanted to, he told me. He didn't say he thought that the life he'd lived had been wrong. He said he knew I hadn't been around for the past twelve years, he said he couldn't say whether he understood that or not. But he didn't have enough money for a hotel once he got out, and he wouldn't stay long with me, just long enough to find a place and a job—but could he stay? The job first, of course, and then save up enough money for the place. They told him there he'd need people on the outside, to help him, to help keep him outside. He said he didn't know who else to ask. He'd written to the address of our old apartment, he'd remembered it, and he hoped I still lived there, but he wasn't sure. Could I write him back and let him know? I wrote and said he could stay. I kept it brief, didn't say of course he could, didn't say how happy I was to hear from him. I wasn't sure how he would take that. But then he wrote again and said maybe I should come visit, see him one time before he came back to the city, maybe that would make it less strange when he came back to the apartment. Strange, he'd said. So I went. He told me I looked good, and I said I must be bigger than when he'd seen me last, and he said I was, but I carried it well, I always had. He was big. A grown man. Without the same expressions on his face, the teasing grin, the direct gaze, I wouldn't have known him. He's big but he's not fat. Maybe he works out, or maybe he just doesn't eat enough to gain like I do. I expect the food isn't any good there. He's not so big he's fearsome, but he is a bit startling, not doughy enough to imply cuddling. He seems like someone to leave alone. But then, if he wants, he can open his mouth and pour out charm. I wonder what people think of him there. He asked me, "Do you still have that same job?" and when I said yes he asked, "What do you do in there all day?" I looked at him like, *You're asking me this?* I just shook my head, I didn't even try to tell him. In less than eight hours, he'll be in my apartment. I'm not sure when he's showing up, but he'll get there before me, that's all we decided. I left him a key when I went to go visit; well, gave it to the guard to put in his things for when he leaves. I wrote down directions for him, the reverse of what I'd done to get to him, left him some money for cab and train fares. I asked if he had a change of clothes to wear out and he said yes. I didn't make him tell me what he had ready to wear. I don't know how that was arranged but I wouldn't have known what to buy him. What does one wear out of prison? Who got it for him? Who knows his size? I couldn't guess it. He's adult-sized now, not a child. Twenty-eight years old. He'll get to my home before me and let himself in with his key. How strange, to have some of the first smells you smell after release be your mother, your childhood. I hope he feels comforted by my meager home. My mother, she lived with me until recently, couldn't stay in her own place alone those last few years, but she doesn't anymore, so there's room for Sebastian again. There wouldn't have been, with me in my room and her on the couch. I won't offer him my room. I think it would be best if he stayed on the couch. Make it clear to both of us this is temporary. I showed him nothing but the straight life. I didn't like my job, but I did it for him. I didn't finish my education, but I

And Yet It Moves

found an honest job. Union. We didn't have much, but we always had food, electricity, a clean apartment, we even had cable TV and he always had basketball shoes. We only had one bedroom, so once he got too big for his crib his bedroom was the living room, and he slept on the couch. I felt bad about that. When he was twelve, I offered to trade with him, but he declined. I don't know what else he wanted. Maybe he wanted other basketball shoes more than the ones he pointed out to me, but didn't say so because he knew we couldn't get them. Maybe he wanted to take girls out on fancy dates. I don't know where kids go together, then or now.

I never asked why he did it, and he never said. Maybe part of why we never talked about it, why I never visited, was embarrassment. I hadn't seen the signs. He didn't start staying out later, or wearing different clothes. He didn't act different toward me. He didn't flunk out—I wasn't sure, but when I went to withdraw him from school they told me he was passing everything. Doing well. He had absences, but not more than he was allowed. I didn't see the change in him, I didn't know he'd become a criminal, that kind of criminal, I hadn't known anything was wrong until I got the call from juvenile hall, saying they were sending him to the youth felon prison the next day, awaiting trial. Felony charges. Carjacking. And rape. That. Took a girl's car, not a girl he knew, at gunpoint, made her drive to Jersey, raped her in her car, then told her to get out, sold the car for parts. The money was to buy drugs to sell. Not weed, cocaine. To sell, not to use. That's what they told me. He'd been selling, he and his friends wanted to upgrade. That's what they said he did. And he never told me he didn't do it. I never asked, he never said. I wasn't at the trial, but the state, I guess because he was a minor—sixteen, the age I was when I had him—the state had to keep me informed. Found guilty of armed theft and armed rape, sentenced to twenty years. There was just one of me, he never had a father or anything that even looked like a father, but I gave him a good home and he spit on it like that. I kept making plans to go see him while they kept him at the temporary prison, awaiting trial, but I kept finding reasons not to. Tired, worked a double, had a cold. He never wrote me or called me, so I didn't know if he even wanted me to come. Then there was the trial, then they gave me the address for where he was being sent. I wrote him then. I didn't know what to say. I said, "If you need me to come see you, I will." Something like that. Not that I wanted to, not even that if he wanted me to I would, but if it was necessary, I'd do the necessary thing. Like I'd been doing with him, and with myself, all along. He never wrote. So I never went. I blamed him. Never admitted to myself or anyone else that I didn't give him much opportunity to feel like he could ask me to come, or should. Or that I wanted him to. Because I didn't. And then. Twelve years of a twenty-year sentence served. Good behavior. A twenty-eight-year-old man writes me, same apartment, it's rent controlled, he knows I'm not going anywhere, and tells me he has no one else to write. Can I give him a place to stay, just for a little while, until he can figure out what's next?

My job is to keep people safe. But I couldn't even keep my own son safe. Safe, not exactly right. He harmed, he hurt, he tortured another human, he's the one that did wrong. But could I have kept him safer, so he didn't need to do it? How is it that a good kid can do an evil thing? A kid that seemed good to me. The plan was they would each jack a car, each take it to a different chop shop in Jersey, each get the money they could, then meet back, buy a package, be in business. Three of them. Bigger business; they'd been selling weed for over a year, but wanted to move on to real money, and needed some money to start out, to finance the upgrade. Carjacking seemed the easiest way to get money fast, the way least likely to get caught. He's the only one who hurt the driver. He's the only one who took the driver with him. All the others, the other two,

And Yet It Moves

with their faces covered, wearing all black, they kicked the drivers out of the car, they used a gun to scare them, but didn't shoot, they left the drivers on the curb and by the time the cops were looking for them, the car was in pieces and they had their street clothes back on, Yankees jerseys, old-school Dodgers jerseys, matching hats, matching sneakers, one in shades of purple, one in shades of green. Only Sebastian took the driver with him to Jersey, parked in an abandoned lot before turning in the car for cash. I don't know how they caught him. All I know is what he did. Did someone else see the gun, hear the screaming girl, did someone else call in the plates and they were waiting for him? Did he take off his mask, and she could recognize him later? I don't know. His friends were only charged with armed robbery, I think they found them through him, they did less time, I think eight or so years, maybe just six, have been out for a few years now. I don't see them around. I don't know what they do. I'm not sure I would recognize them now that they're grown. I don't know if they own businesses, apartments, have families, left and went out to the suburbs of Long Island, I don't know if the best job to get after prison is full-time criminal. I only know Sebastian did not ask them for help, now. My son is alive. My son wasn't shot in the street. I do not know how to have him in my life.

I take a sip of my coffee. I always let it go cold before I finish it. Every day. Not on purpose. I've been going to the same Dunkin' Donuts for years, the one I worked at for those two, though the staff changes so often I have to be relearned every few weeks by the new girl at the register. Once she knows me, though, when I walk in the door my coffee is made for me without me saying anything. I bring my own travel mug to save paper, I hand it to someone behind the counter and they fill it with lots of cream, lots of sugar, then coffee, and the girl rings me up for a refill, only seventy-five cents. I drink coffee before work at home; this is just one final jolt before sitting still for eight hours. They don't automatically give me a donut, though, they make me ask for that. They know I'm trying to cut back on sweets. Been trying to cut back. It's hard to ask, hard to say out loud what I want and know people will look at me and think I shouldn't be eating donuts, at my size. Whoever is behind the counter hands it to me with a blank smile that glosses any judgment. It's hard to say what I want, but sometimes I want it enough it's worth it. All the girls who work there are skinny. They change, but they all look the same. Tight pants. Tucked-in uniform shirt. Hair slicked back into a ponytail, then poofing out past the rubber band into twists so tight they can't really be called curls. Lots of jewelry. Nails always done. Clear skin, eye makeup, accented English. Names I never bother to remember—Yessenia, Rosario, Maria, Jasmine, Yahaira. The only person who's stayed the same all these years is Guillermo. I worked with him back then. He doesn't speak much English, and I don't speak much Spanish, but every morning I say, "¡Hola! ¿Cómo estás?" and he replies, "¡Buenos días, bonita!" He doesn't work the cash register often, because even though most of the customers up here speak Spanish, they want to make sure an English speaker can be served, too. He mops the floor, and stocks the shelves, and always seems to be busy. He has a wife and two children. He's a hard worker. I think he must be here legally, because I don't think this company will hire you without a Social Security card. I had to show mine. Though I don't really care if he's legal or not. That's never bothered me too much. I bet he still makes minimum wage, has all these years, feeds his family on that. I don't know how that's possible—they must not eat much fresh food, no vegetables, mostly beans from a bag, rice, cheap stuff. He works with teenagers, works harder than all of them combined. I wonder if his wife and children will ever betray him, after all he's done to provide, I wonder if his kids will flunk out of school, if his wife sleeps around on him while he's out

And Yet It Moves

of the house. I wonder if he knows how trapped he is, or if coming here every day feels like a choice. I sip my cold coffee, think how different chilled sweetness tastes than hot.

I didn't tell Sebastian it was hard for me to go up there. Two subways to Grand Central Station, a Metro-North train to Beacon, then a taxi to Fishkill. It makes me nervous to go places I've never been before. The circle I usually walk is small: my apartment on 172nd, to work four blocks down, two blocks over, then back. Associated grocery store, bodega with some Latin groceries, laundromat, liquor store, Dunkin' Donuts, Duane Reade all less than five blocks away. I can get the clothes I need at the stores here, usually discount things, very simple, but a couple stores carry my size, and I don't dress fancy. I only go each place when I need to, and a good day is when I just go from home to work and back, have enough food in the fridge to make a meal so I don't have to stop. Since I have to carry my groceries home I can't get much at one time, so I have to stop a few times a week. But it's a good day when I don't have to stop at all. They deliver groceries, but I never do it, just to save the couple-dollar tip. Same reason I don't order pizza, I'll pick it up myself, but really I can make it better on my own. They say New York pizza is this special thing, but if I make my own sauce and use good mozzarella, mine's better than theirs, easy. But maybe I'll start getting my groceries delivered. Maybe it's worth it. It feels like giving in to something—laziness, or my weight, but it's really not that, just the anxiousness I feel having to go out in public, stand in line, talk to someone, not drop something, pay. People do these things every day, so it seems I should be able to, too. I am able to. So since I am able, since I can do it, it seems I should. Asking someone to bring me boxes of food, it seems like saying I'm an invalid. The people at the grocery store, they'd think it was because I'm big. They've seen me drop my wallet, the slow way I have to get down and back up to get it. I move slow, I know it's obvious. But my body isn't the problem. I can move this bag of bones around just fine, I've got my soreness and my pains but it's not as hard to be inside of it as it looks. People expect fat people to not live a long time. But I'm healthy. I wonder how many decades I have left. I guess I shouldn't care if that's what they think, the workers at Associated, they can think I'm weak in a way I'm not. Weak in the body. I know I can still get around, take care of myself. And it may be better than them knowing the truth, that I'm weak in a way most people aren't. I guess it would embarrass me for anyone to know how nervous the fluorescent lights of Duane Reade make me. That buzzing, it's like it's just waiting for me to make a mistake. Knock over a display or try to use a coupon that won't work. I don't want to be the annoying, old, fat lady who can't do what everyone else can do: ask where the Q-tips and Depends are (instead I just wander and wander and wander until I find them), reach the bottom shelf for the natural toothpaste I like, communicate that I think the clerk rang me up twice for the same box of deodorant, without it seeming like I'm complaining, or daft. Other people go places with ease. Hell, other people go to China, Australia, Brazil. I'm finding it harder and harder to not be in a place shaped like a cave, a cage. Cave. Cage. What makes them different? A cave is earthen, where the world invites us into its body. A dark, damp, frightening place. People paint pictures there, in the body of the world, touch the walls and give that texture color. A place with no light. A hollow. But not square. This place is square, and brightly lit. The light shines off the metal walls. A cage is square, but it has holes, gaps to see out, to let in light, to see what's outside. A cage, one cannot exit by choice. A cave, one can come and go. Unless one gets lost, loses light. Here I am, underground, in a box. I can leave anytime I want. I do not draw on the walls, but other people do. Symbols to tell others who recognize such symbols that they were here. Warning others to go away. Some silly lines

And Yet It Moves

and designs: who loves whom, the simple statement that "Alex was here," not meant to scare away rivals, instead just label a fact. Assert an existence. I scrub away what can be removed. I no longer scrape the floors, but I still wash the walls. They stay cleaner longer. The other elevators, the ones people ride without a watcher, they must have many more marks on them. I don't know how the drawings get made here, with someone always watching. But in an empty elevator, or one with only one other passenger in it, a person who's certain not to make eye contact, why not? No sky all day in this place, just ceiling. Not a cave, not a cage. And then I walk up to the sky, walk up a small flight of stairs into a place that has no roof, but has a sky. It is bright and pounding.

I mostly feel the physical discomfort in my knees. The left one particularly. All my joints are a bit creaky, as if they get stuck at a certain point in their journey and don't want to move past it. But they do move past it. My shoulder doesn't like the gesture of shrugging a shopping bag up on it—I bring my own to the store, to conserve paper and plastic—but it'll do it. All my joints do what they need to do, they don't stop and lock. But there's a point where each protests a bit. The knee, well that one feels like it's going to give out on me when it's asked to do some serious walking. Up hills, and there are a lot of hills in this area, hence the name. Down the stairs to work. It makes me hobble a bit, though I try not to show it. Take it slow. Let kids and impatient people off to work pass by me, let them let go of the rail and go around me in the middle of the stairs, sometimes rubbing up against people coming up the other way. I worry sometimes they'll trip when they're in the middle of the stairs like that, with nothing to hang on to. I'd feel responsible. But I didn't make them hurry. Still, I wouldn't want to see them stumble and splay, the gash on the forehead or ankle already swelling, I wouldn't want to walk around the tangle, trust someone else will come and fix it. If I were walking down the stairs to my shift, I think it would still be the responsibility of the workers in the booth, the ones who survey the lobby area, not me, not us in the elevators. I'm only responsible for accidents in my space, and only when I'm on duty. I'd help if I could, of course. Took first-aid training as part of the job, of course. But I don't like stepping on other people's toes, doing their job like I think I can do it better. Maybe doing it wrong. I try sometimes to tell if my one knee swells, the left one. But to me it looks the same size as the other. I suppose I should admit that it would be hard to tell on me. Comparing a cantaloupe to a honey-dew, my knees. It's got two kinds of pain in it. An ache I feel always, from when I wake until I sleep. It ebbs and flows; up hills and down, the soreness makes me think it can't do it, might crumble, and me down after it. But when I sit at work, it's a gentle tenderness, just reminding me it's there. I've taken to rubbing it sometimes. I don't know I'm doing it, until suddenly I realize, and then I wonder how long I've been sitting there, my fingers circling and circling, kneading down into the inflamed-feeling bones, though I can't get to the tendons and ligaments that are the real hurt. It makes me feel like an old woman, to be rubbing at my pains and not even know it. I suppose I've asked a lot of that joint, carrying the bulk of me around for so many years. I don't have a car; wherever I want to go, my feet or the subway have to take me. I don't go as many places as I used to, can get all my groceries and clothes and light bulbs and shoes and wine and movies and papers right here in the neighborhood. I walk down into the subway station five times a week for work, but I don't remember the last time I took the subway to somewhere. Before last week, when I took it to the Metro-North at Grand Central, up to see Sebastian, I mean. I hadn't been to Grand Central since I was a girl, and it seemed impossible for me to walk without running into people. I brushed shoulders with several people, and though it felt like they hit me, I feared it was my fault. I couldn't negotiate the swarms and currents, couldn't

And Yet It Moves

predict which way people would swerve when we were walking toward the same spot. One collision was so jarring a man cursed me, and it was then that I felt that other pain in my knee. The searing. What the doctor called a hot stabbing pain, not an ache, the one time I went to see him, oh about five years ago. It's coming more often, that jab. It happens when I try to move quickly, or sometimes for seemingly no reason at all. The man cursed me, and went on his way, and my knee seemed to shoot bolts of heat into the air around it. When I saw on the big lit board that you can catch the Hudson Line in Harlem, I was both sick and relieved. I wished I hadn't come there, felt like I was doing it all wrong. But I knew I could manage for the rest of my life to never come to Grand Central Station again. Not that I may ever need to—once Sebastian is out, after tonight, I'll have no need to go upstate anymore. I have to believe he won't be going back. I asked the clerk just to make sure, after getting my round-trip ticket to Beacon—she asked, "Peak or off-peak?" and I said, "Right now, coming back in a few hours," and that must have been a good enough answer—I asked her, "Could I have gotten this train in Harlem?" and she said yes, my train would stop there on the way. She answered quickly, which made me wonder if it was okay that I asked, but the line wasn't that long, and I only talked to her while she was making my change, right when I had my tickets and my money back I walked away. I didn't hold up the line. Maybe she just didn't want to encourage chitchat. She was standing, selling her tickets there. It doesn't make sense, to keep them on their feet all day. They don't make us stand at our job for eight hours. The floors are too hard, bad for our legs. And backs. They talked for a while about getting us rubber mats to stand on, the kind bartenders have back behind the bar, but we all asked why we couldn't just be as comfortable as possible. I mean, I don't have a La-Z-Boy down here, just a folding metal chair, but sitting is better than standing, we all agree. But I don't feel too much pain. I fear that if I ever feel too much pain, if it's ever so hard to walk down stairs, walk up the hills of this neighborhood, walk along flat ground, if it's ever too hard to do all that then I just won't. I'll just stay home. Have a reason to order in my groceries. I wonder if Duane Reade delivers medicine. I bet they'd mail it to me, if I ordered in advance. I don't take any pills yet, but that would be good to know. And if it's ever hard to stay in bed, if the pain is ever so bad I don't want to be awake, then I just won't be anymore. Being alive is only worth enduring so much. I hope I never get to that point. I don't have diabetes, which my doctor is pleased with. My blood pressure isn't great, but it isn't terrible. My cholesterol and triglycerides are only a point or two high, nothing to be too concerned about. Turns out I'm a lot healthier than I look. I bet I'm a lot healthier than some of those skinny women in skirted suits that ride the train every day. So brittle they look like they might break their cardboard cups, not crush them, but just shatter them, right there in their hands. Some of them, I swear they may shake to bits in the elevator. This one woman, she rides my elevator most mornings, she hasn't lived up here long, still has that wary look, like she can't believe she's the only white woman in the elevator sometimes. I didn't see her this morning, but I see her most mornings, she must start work at nine. She's so trim. I've never seen her in workout clothes, so she must walk to her gym, not take the subway. I'm not sure where there's a gym up here; maybe she carries a change of clothes in her briefcase, goes after work. But her tennis shoes wouldn't fit. I don't know how or when she exercises, but she must, to be so small. Long, shiny hair. I've never seen her wear the same suit twice. Colorful shirts underneath, with interesting textures and extra designs. One has a fabric flower at the neck, so you can see it poking up from the collar of her jacket. It's a coral color, not an orange, but a really warm, girlish shade. She must live up here to save rent to afford her wardrobe. And heels. She isn't one of those women who wears sneakers on the subway, then changes into pumps at the door of the office. She wears her high heels from the minute she leaves her apartment. Clicks down the stairs, clicks into my elevator. The floor is hard, so her clacks clang once she gets in this room. Maybe she stands so uncomfortably because her shoes make noise, or because she's the only nicely dressed businesslady on the elevator, or because she doesn't want to lean up against the walls like everyone else does on the edge, petals bending away from the center of a flower, because she doesn't want to mess up her clothes. The walls aren't dirty, they just look dirty. I scrub them, but some of the writing and smears won't come off. No matter who's on the elevator, she always acts the same way—tense, rigid, and jittery, as if she's going to fall over or expects to be punched. She doesn't seem scared. She just seems like she's having a very, very hard time staying still. I wonder if she's so busy, if she has so many things running around in her head, a to-do list of really important items, that she just wants to go do them, she can't wait to get started. She seems so purposeful. But I get exhausted just looking at her. It seems like so much effort for her to just stand there, which is one thing that should be easy to do. When she enters the elevator, people fill in around her, and it's interesting how aware of her they are. I only see people's faces when they walk in, not after they stand behind me or beside me for the ride, but I see so many of them glance at her, then try to pretend like they aren't looking. Exotic businesslady. She must get tired of being stared at, no matter how hard people pretend like they aren't. It probably takes her as long to get ready every morning as it takes the kid standing on my elevator right now, baggy pants tucked into the tongues of his Timberlands, with his blue Yankees hat, blue T-shirt, matching blue hoodie, matching belt. He probably ironed his jeans like she ironed her suit. No one looks twice at the kid, he's got dopey eyes, a slouchy posture, not that jagged edge and twitchy stance of someone who, if he hears the train rumbling into the station right before the doors open, might grab a purse and run out the doors and down the stairs onto his escape vehicle. This kid, wearing the same outfit as hundreds of other kids throughout the city, in all the colors of a rainbow, he doesn't merit much notice. When she gets on the elevator she stands in the back like she's supposed to, though she doesn't lean against the wall like most would, and everyone who walks through those doors sees her face, then turns their back to her and faces front. In those few seconds, every time she rides the elevator, I see them study her. Maybe their eyes narrow a little, maybe they lift their chins, maybe they cast their eyes quickly to the ground after making contact with her eyes, but some move they make tells me what they're thinking—*Why are you here, what do you want from us, you don't belong, this is our place, what will you do to our neighborhood now that you're here, and, what do you think of me when you see me?* They probably don't even know that they think those things. Would likely deny it if I asked them. But we all think that when we see a white person or a few amidst our brown and darker brown. I was born and raised in Harlem, but when I looked to find my own place rents were cheaper up here. Mama would make the short commute on the A train to watch Sebastian while I worked. I know the people who were born and raised here don't like the white folk that move in, raising everyone's rents because they can pay more, like what's happened to Harlem. I couldn't go back even if I wanted to. I don't mind them too much—white folk want cheap rent too, just like the rest of us. But it makes me wonder how people in the neighborhood view me; this neighborhood is still mostly Hispanic, and I'm clearly not. Dark dark. They can look at me and tell I don't have much more money than them, though. And enough black people live in the neighborhood that it's not just me: below the South Bronx and above Harlem, what do they expect? Of course we're going to creep in. And

And Yet It Moves

Dominicans are part black, have that African slave blood in their veins too, though I don't know how many of them claim that. This neighborhood used to be Jewish, still is on the eastern edge, in the apartments alongside the Yeshiva. Most of the people who live here have been here a while, years, but not generations; mostly immigrants, parents came here from DR, children born here. I understand being more suspicious of white people than of me; it's stranger for them to appear up here. They do take over anything they think can be theirs—I'd be nervous too to see too many white faces on my block. None yet in my building. When people look at me funny in the grocery store or the street, I don't think it's because I'm not Hispanic. There are other stranger things about me, I guess.

I wonder about my mind, if I will lose parts of it. And if I have, how would I know? I try to keep it active and strong. But there are entire parts of my life I can't access, entire things that I know happened that I just can't reach. The birth of my son. I hardly remember it. Just flashes. I don't know how long we stayed in the hospital, I don't know when we came home. We lived with my mother the first two years, I got our apartment when I got this job, I remember that. My father, he was a strong presence in my life, he was there, he died when I was ten, he never met Sebastian, he was not shot in the street, his heart gave out, I cannot see his face. I cannot picture Sebastian's father's face. I would need a photograph to remind me, but I don't have one. I have cousins all over this country, they used to come visit the city when we were all little, dozens of cousins spread all over our apartment, sleeping on pallets on the floors. I can't remember any of their names. It's been decades since then, over two decades, nearly three, but I would think I would be able to remember their names. Or faces. I can only see hordes of them, hair and skirts and denim shorts and running children without space to run. They didn't like our playground, at Mama's place.

I remember that. Too small, no grass, broken swing. But I don't remember who said anything about it. Can I see my mother's face? Not really. I remember what she feels like, but I can't quite bring up her appearance. There are some customers who ride this elevator, who've ridden it all or most of these twenty-six years, and I don't know their names but I know their faces. I can see them. The old man who still wears three-piece suits, ones that I bet have been his since the '40s, his wrinkles in his face are so deep, so a part of his expressions now. I haven't seen him get older over the years, he's the same as he was, wears the same brown houndstooth suit, the same fedora with the green ribboned band. But there are entire parts of my history I can't recollect. I wonder what I might call forth, if I hadn't been down here for so long.

It's rare, rare to see an Oriental person in this neighborhood, but there she is. Carrying her orange grocery sack with her, way up here where there are no Oriental markets. The bodegas here carry Goya spices and plantains, you can get Jesus candles and Olde English forties, but none of that stuff you'll find in Chinatown— no shrimp with their heads still on, crabs still moving their claws, whole dried fish, fruit with spikes on it, the whole place smelling up the street for a whole block up and a whole block down. My first subway station I worked at, when I first got this job, was in Flushing, Queens. Nothing but Asians. Really, I hardly ever saw black or Spanish people. They all stay so close to each other. Subway seats are one size, with ridges between, so the same amount of people can sit down in a subway car, whether big or little, whatever shade, but they crowd in on the people sitting, and hover so close. Try to fit twice as many people on an elevator as will fit. Don't mind pressing up against every side of me. Normally, people try not to touch me. Any proximity of bodies makes me uneasy, that space that isn't meant to be crossed. The smaller the space, the more charge there is in it. But it's even worse when that gap isn't

And Yet It Moves

regarded, people's clothes against my clothes. I had to take the 1 down from the Heights to Times Square, then change to the 7 and go up again, to the end of the line. No other way to get there—have to go into the web and back out again, no way to go across. Midtown Manhattan is the center of the universe. Ridiculous subway ride. I did it for two years, turned my eight-hour shift into being away from home for ten and a half, Mama watching Sebastian. I couldn't do it now. Why she's carrying vegetables with her, or whatever's in there, I don't know, and why she's here, I can't guess. She's one of those old lady Chinese people, ragged and bent, thin thin thin, with hair still mostly black, but the wiry texture of gray hair, not soft and smooth. I don't understand how Chinese women get used up so fast. We all work hard. When they're young, every single one of them has lush hair, shiny and vibrant, smooth skin, and none of them are fat. They get old and they stay skinny but I've never seen a group of people fade so fully. All the shine gone from their faces and hair, hollow eyes. Russian woman don't hold up too well either, they go from skinny with big boobs to just big all over. Their faces sag but they don't give up, keep loading on the makeup. There'll be a Russian lady in her sixties with full makeup on—thick eyeliner, lipliner, eyebrows drawn in, lipstick, too much mascara, and blush. Who wears blush these days? Their hair dyed a deep pink or black, or blonde, and teased. Many of them still have bangs. And their puffy bodies packed into jeans and sparkly shirts and heeled boots, all covered by a full-length fur coat. The young ones are so pretty, with big eyes in their small faces, they all have long hair, and they dress American, in tight shirts and tight jeans, but a little off. You can tell they get their clothes in their neighborhood, not a department store. Teenaged Russians are so well behaved, so quiet and calm. They get old, they get twice as big, and they get loud and brassy. We used to go to Coney Island as kids, and you take the Q through Brighton Beach, Russians everywhere. They were as exotic to me then as Eskimos would have been. I still find them a little strange. I don't know if anyone who lives in Brighton isn't Russian.

What's the good, telling myself these stories? To pass the time, sure, get rid of these eight hours that need to be gone before my son comes to stay. But what came before won't do either of us any good now.

Except. His crime. And my silence. Those things aren't over and done, the way our old life seems past.

He feels I betrayed him. Well, I did. But he let me.

In the face of his protest, had he asked me to be present, I couldn't have stayed gone. But his indifference, he allowed it.

This man, wait, I know this man—the man who just walked into my elevator. He's—I know him: but how? He's, no—it couldn't be; is he the one I used to see all the time? That nice man? Could it be him, so changed? He always said hello to me, and goodbye, every single time he rode the elevator. Every time. For years it must have been. He brought me presents. And then gone, and I forgot to wonder about him after a while. Now he's here. "Hello," I say to him, and I know I smile in a way I haven't yet today, don't most days. My smile could be called beguiling, by someone who isn't me. He smiles back, but his eyes are clouded over so I'm not sure if he knows he's looking at me. He always used to say hello, and smile in a way that implied he'd say more, but he had nothing to say. I assumed he didn't have much English, sensed by the way he nodded his head after each greeting. I guess you can look at me and assume I don't speak Spanish, and you would be right; he must have figured that out because he never spoke to me in Spanish. And when he said goodbye, he always added, "Thank you," and smiled and nodded again, and I always said, "You're welcome." I've always thought it a little funny when people thank me for doing what they could do themselves, push buttons, but I guess the

And Yet It Moves

whole point is that they can't do what I do, they can't provide a safe space like my presence does. Some people thank me. Many people tell me to have a nice day, every day. This man seemed to really mean it, like he appreciated what I did. I liked him for that. He still wears a mustache, but it's white. I don't know many men who wear mustaches, didn't know any then, know fewer now. It suited him though, made his eyes above more sparkly. He squinted when he smiled, but doesn't today. The rest of his face isn't clean shaven, has prickles all over. He looks like an old dog. If I were to stand I think he would be shorter than me, stooped. I remember him being tall. Tall and thin. I may have grown in bulk since the last time we saw each other, but he has grown more slim. He's wearing an old hat, and it makes me remember that he always wore a hat, not a fedora, different kinds, I never saw his hair, just his mustache to let me know he was dark-haired, and his eyebrows, but now hair sticks out from the back of his brimmed hat, hair not white but going white. Sunk-in cheeks, wizened face, grizzled, he looks like a bear after hibernation, wasted and starved. Too thin to be dangerous. He smiled at me, but he didn't say hello. Just now. He seemed to still have all his teeth, and they weren't more yellow, they always had been, a bit, but yellow teeth are common up here. I'm not sure if he knows who he is smiling at. Does he remember me? Can bones shrink? Of course they can. Isn't that what osteoporosis is? What could have possibly happened to this man, my friend? We ding to a stop and he shuffles off my elevator. I imagine him walking slowly up the stairs to street level, he slowly leaves my box and he doesn't turn to smile or say thank you. "It's nice to see you again," I manage to say, to his back. I want him to know. I know nothing more about him, just that he was a presence for a time, and then he wasn't. I mean daily, I saw him daily for a time, and then not at all. One time I saw him on the streets of the Heights, and it was like seeing your teacher at the grocery store as a child, or your doctor at the movies. We weren't sure how to interact. He said hello, of course, and this time he waved, when he recognized me from a distance, but of course he didn't say thank you, because I hadn't done anything. I said, "Have a nice day," and he nodded. He smiled so much, it made having no words not too awkward. He filled the space with his smiles and nods. The next day, he brought me an apple. It was the strangest thing. I felt like a teacher. It didn't look like the apples in the neighborhood—the produce in the grocery stores and bodegas around here is never great, we get the worst fruit and vegetables, lettuce nearly wilting, bruised bananas and plantains, flavorless citrus, and apples only bright green and sour, or bright red and mealy. This apple was yellow, and spotted. I wondered where it was from, but didn't ask. I told him thank you, but didn't bite into it right then. I felt funny assessing it in front of him. He just held the apple out to me, and nodded, and smiled, and I took it and wrapped both hands around it. On my walk home I ate it, when people wouldn't be paying attention to me—for some reason, a worker on an elevator eating anything draws a lot of attention, as if we can't keep people as safe if we're eating a ham sandwich, as if peeling a banana lessens our vigilance. I guess it's something to look at, something to pay attention to, out of the ordinary as they sink or rise. No one asks me about the food I eat every day, but they all notice it. The apple was delicious. Tart but not sour, sweet but not cloying, very crisp with no hint of mush, a bright, sharp flavor. I ate to the edge of the core and carried the core home, threw it away in my own trash can, didn't dispose of it on the street. When I saw him next, I thanked him. I said the apple was incredible, and I asked where he got it. He nodded and said, "You're welcome." A week or a few later he brought me a coffee. A fancy coffee, with whipped cream and a dusting of chocolate over the white foam, the lid on the side so I could cap it once I drank it down. It was mint flavored, so it must have been near Christmas, when they make stuff like that. What a bold move, to assume I like mint. I do, but some people hate its pointed, acrid flavor. It must have been from Starbucks, no other shop around here would make something like that. Starbucks must have just opened. And they must have been having some kind of a special. I can't imagine this man spending four dollars and change on a fancy coffee for me. Maybe the mint kind was on sale. But I really enjoyed it, that extraordinary coffee drink. I never drink coffee like that. I savored it, something I wouldn't have bought for myself. And when I saw him again, I thanked him, and he smiled. I don't think he was flirting with me, I think he was being kind. He saw me every day, or at least a few times a week for, well, what was it? Years, for certain. He wanted me to be happy. I don't know why. But I wanted him to be happy too. Though, I never gave him gifts. I thought about it, but the idea of carrying a gift in my bag and then not seeing him and having to carry it home embarrassed me. He always knew when he'd see me, Elevator Three, eight to four, Monday through Friday. Over the years he gave me a bagel, the good kind, he must have gone to the Jewish deli where they make them right, and a donut, and an orange. A good one. One that tasted like real fruit grown on a real tree. Not a lot of presents for the decade or more we saw each other. What's that, five? But enough that I remembered him more than the rest. When he didn't have something for me, he didn't shrug in apology, or comment in any way. The days he had something were treat days. And then he was gone. I'm not sure how long it took me to notice. A shift doesn't usually feel like a day, there are no light markers to note the passing of time, there's a rhythm of busy, slow, starting to get busy, and the difference is that in the morning more people get on up top and come down, and in the afternoon more people get on in the bottom and go up. Sometimes I forget which direction we're going, and push the wrong button, and we don't move. So I don't know how many days or weeks it took for me to notice that I hadn't been seeing him. And how many more days or weeks it took for me to realize it had been a long time, and to wonder if he was okay. There was nothing I could do to find out. I didn't have a name. For years after, I'm certain I didn't see him for years, I'd think about him off and on. The Starbucks has been here five years now, so it could have been up to that long. Occasionally I'd wonder if he'd moved, if he was happier, if he got a new job and so took the A or the C instead of the 1. And he was just back. On my elevator again. But not himself. And—what now? Will I see him tomorrow?

I shiver. He was warmly dressed. It's getting cold aboveground, I may soon need to change my fan down here for a heater. Not yet—in a few weeks, maybe. It's always stuffy, so I keep the fan as long as I can. I reach down and pull the plug from the socket in the metal wall. I don't need the heater yet. But maybe tomorrow I should bring a blanket. Something for the time between machines. The elevator always runs a bit more jerkily when it's cold. Just slightly. It never does break, but winter is the only time I feel like it might jolt to a stop, yank the cables from the fasteners, shriek to a halt. But we always make it through the winter with nothing snapping, no slipped gears, we never crash to the bottom of the shaft, never get stuck in the box for hours, wondering how much air is needed for fourteen people, I've never had to mentally do that math to know how many hours the rescue crew has to come get us. Spring always comes again, and the kinks in the journey up and down always get smoothed out, and I always feel a bit foolish for having been certain something terrible was going to happen this season. I don't feel the waver in the course yet, just felt the coolness in the air this morning that reminded me to look for it. I wore my medium jacket today for the first time this season, had been only needing my light jacket until I heard the weather this morning on the TV. My light jacket is really just a lined man's work shirt,

And Yet It Moves

flannel on the inside, dungaree material on the outside. It's plenty big, easy to get in and out of, but my next-warmest jacket has a bit of a poof to it, it's thicker, filled with cotton or down, I'm not sure which, and so it fits me a bit closer. I remembered when I sat in my chair and took it off to hang behind me, I remembered the way it gets stuck around the shoulders a bit. I had to wiggle out of it, claw a bit at the fabric to peel it off, and I felt clumsy, bulky. There was a time when shrugging out of a jacket might have looked sexy on me, the way you have to shake your shoulders, and everything jiggles a little. I might have done that in high school without a thought, without realizing how I looked, or maybe I knew, felt like I'd accidentally drawn a bit of attention on myself. There was no one on the elevator this morning when I tugged my coat off, no train had arrived below when someone from above called the elevator back up, so no one saw my struggle. Nobody really looks at me all day most days, even when my elevator is full. They just enter, glance, turn, exit. But all those glances are starting to feel burrowing. All those stares. When people look at me, I know it never occurs to them that I was once smaller. I haven't always been this size. I suppose I shouldn't worry about getting raped or robbed when I'm alone on the elevator with someone; it's clear I wouldn't have much money on me, and I can't imagine I'm an attractive target. Though I do understand it's not about that. I used to have an attractive shape. No one sees that lingering inside this vastness, this mass. Well, in the next few days it'll get easier to negotiate my coat, I just have to get used to it each season. The elevator won't break down during my shift, it never does. The quicker the cold comes, the quicker winter will be over, trees budding down the block, the only sign that it's time for things to grow from the ground. The leaves haven't fallen yet, but they don't put on much of a show. Not enough of them. Too far apart to make a collective spectacle. There is a tree on 171st that is brighter than the rest. I wonder if the original tree died, and they replaced it with a kind that doesn't match. Its leaves are bright red on the outside, yellowish green closer to the trunk. That tree hints at what's happening in other places that aren't this city.

I finally check my watch, without really meaning to. Just flick my wrist and look, then realize now I know. It's 2:13. I never took my one bathroom break. Now I'll just wait. I skipped lunch. I'm not hungry. Less than two hours to go. And then I'll go home and make dinner for my son. Eat with him. Feed him. Tonight I'll be able to eat, because then it will be happening, then I won't be waiting for it anymore. I used to get so excited about good-tasting food I'd eat it quickly. Bite after bite because it was so pleasurable, because each bite was gone before I stopped wanting it, so I had to put more in my mouth, quickly, to not lose that taste. Sometimes I'd get full and be disappointed because I wasn't yet done with that flavor. Roasted garlic smudged on crusty bread, red sauce heavy with basil, richly browned meat, the resistance of al dente pasta— tonight's meal, there will be so many flavors it will be hard to stop. Salad with so many veggies each bite is different, the sweetness of olive oil against the tang of balsamic in the dressing I made. But I've gotten better at savoring each bite I chew, tasting each part of it. I've been working on that. Once we're eating, it will be okay. And then, after—well, and then? *How could he* is not the exact response I had when I learned. More like, How could something that came out of my body do that to another body? But not that either. This isn't about bodies. I know that, read one self-help and healing book at the library: it's about power. Why he did what he did. Why he hurt another body. The pain of the body we forget. I would have had another child if I'd have ever found someone to have one with. That birth was painful, I know it must have been. I don't remember it, only have flashes. Barnyard flashes of not feeling human. Dumb animal pain that my mind could not understand. I

And Yet It Moves

remember wishing it would stop. I remember wanting it to be over. But I don't remember how it felt. I can't bring up that feeling, feel it again, now. So, I would do it again. Marvelous, that humans forget pain so easily. Or else women would never birth more than one child. Boxers would never get back in the ring. People who've been in accidents would never ride in cars again. When you're in it, pain, it's the only thing that exists, and you need it to stop. Even when I bang my knee on the table in this elevator, I think, Stop. Please please stop. And then it does. Then I can't, like now, recall the feeling. I can't call it up from the depths. When I birthed my son, I remember crying, I remember defecating in front of strangers and being thankful they would just deal with it, I remember wanting it to be over. Maybe I asked for drugs. Maybe I asked them to kill my child so it would be over. I would have threatened the man who did this to me but he wasn't there. I know I said awful things. And then that son, that son who'd turned me into an animal, then he goes and does this thing. Uncivilized. This non-necessary, brutal thing. He didn't just hurt her body. She must remember that night. Not even night. Afternoon. Daylight. The physical pain wasn't so great to erase it from her consciousness, so she's left with a worse pain, that doesn't fade. Maybe it pales. But it doesn't go away. This woman—this teenager, then, funny that I don't know how old she is, was—this woman, now, she must have sex. She must want to have sex. We all do. And how does she do that? How does she will-ingly participate in something she once didn't? Or, maybe the pain was great enough to wipe it from her mind. I don't know details. I'm not sure I want to live with a man who can do something like that. Who did that. I said yes and I can't go back and say no now. But he's not been in my house since I knew he could do something like that. He's not been inside my house and I'm not sure I want him under my roof, there with me. I'm safe. I'm not in danger. But, just to know he could. What else is he capable of? What else did he become capable of in the years he's spent with people like him? People worse than him. Are they worse? Existing there, will he be able to exist here? It's hard enough for me to exist out here. How many men I see on the street, how many men in this elevator, have done something like that? Could? They aren't marked. Looking at them, you wouldn't know. Looking at my son, he doesn't look like the type of person who would do something like that. I know I'm not in danger, no one would do that to me. I know. But living in a world where people can do that to each other, why does it make me feel in danger? All of this is in my head. What will I say out loud to him? We never talked about serious things. Now, there's just more to avoid. I'll ask him about his plans. How does someone hold a woman down and make her do this thing? He was big then. He's much bigger now. Does she stop resisting at some point, lie calm? Where's the pleasure in that? It's not good for me to think about these things. It frightens me. I think of the moment, I think of after . . . shoving a flower into someone, into where it can't bloom, can only rot in the damp. This isn't good. I've managed to think about this so little for the past twelve years, I've thought about it hardly at all, and now it all comes burrowing in, the awfulness. Maybe he shouldn't be here. Maybe I can never help him anymore. Did he turn her over?

If you think about breathing, you can do it in any pattern you wish. If you don't think about it, you do it anyway. Survival. I just have to stay calm. Less than two hours, and then it will be happening.

* * *

I brought a blanket with me to work this morning—it was just cold enough yesterday that I think it's time. When it gets really cold we each take a small heater from the storage closet, plug it in the socket that powered a fan in the summer. I don't think I need

And Yet It Moves

the heater yet, but a blanket will make the day easier, make this day easier. People look at me and wonder how I get cold, with so much layering. But my surface, my skin, it can get cold just like anyone's.

The blanket I'd washed and folded for Sebastian is the one I've used every winter. It's seen about a sixth as many elevator rides as me. Two months. Or so. I'm sure he didn't realize, yesterday, all the miles his childhood blanket has traveled. Didn't realize as he threw it on the ground. Or, as it fell. I couldn't tell if the blanket on the ground was purposeful or not. I meant to buy him a new bedspread before he came back, but just never got around to it. This morning, I thought maybe I should leave the blanket there, on the couch—I'd picked it up off the ground, refolded and placed it back where I'd put it—for him, in case. But it seemed better to just admit I knew he wouldn't be coming back. This has been my blanket for so long down here, ever since he left, ever since it wasn't his blanket anymore; I didn't want to take the one off my bed, or go buy another one.

That cake, with the gouges across it. Two purposeful slashes. Gashes, lacerations. It would have been better if he'd never walked through my door.

I don't unfold it and tuck myself into it yet. There's something delicious about the moment when you finally admit you're colder than you want to be and wrap warmth around yourself. I'll wait.

It is morning. The elevator fills and empties. People go to the same jobs they had yesterday. Go to school, or skip, again.

Then the man, the old man, my former friend, the man I saw yesterday for the first time in years and found him wizened, on maybe my thirtieth trip of the day he steps onto the elevator and I smile at him. Yesterday frightened me, seeing him so transformed, but I am glad to see him again. He smiles back, looks a bit more alert, more cognizant today.

He hands me a white paper bag, unpatterned, unmarked. The top is folded over twice, backward, like a collar. I look inside and there are small red mounds, little irregular orbs so dark some are nearly black. With stems. Out of season and ripe.

"Cherries for a cherry," he says. "Cerise."

My name. He must know it from before. From then, from when he knew me back then. I didn't know he knew it.

"Thank you," I say. "But I'm sorry, I don't know your name."

"Xavier," he says. "You are welcome. I hope that you enjoy."

I want to eat one, show him I'm pleased, but cherries are hard to eat in public. They stain, and you have to reach into your mouth to get out the pit, or spit. "I'll eat them later," I say. "With lunch. Thank you." There are more cherries than one person should eat, and I start to tell him I'll share them, but then don't say anything.

He hands me two crumpled napkins. "For the pits."

"Thank you," I say again. "How thoughtful."

I remembered to push the button before we began this exchange and we are moving and I look around and no one looks like they're listening to us, but I'm sure they are. Not much exciting happens on an elevator ride, so people eavesdrop. I imagine everyone as bats, all the passengers clinging to the ceiling, Xavier as a javelina, rooting for grubs and seeds to give to me.

He takes a red knit hat from his pocket and puts it on his head. He's right, it is chilly. I pull my blanket over my lap, tuck the corners under. My heat hasn't begun to warm it yet, but I squirm a little, thinking of how cozy it's about to be. Xavier pulls his cap lower. The elevator grinds to a halt and everyone on it gasps, including me. We all stay still for a few beats, just waiting to see what will happen. Then it falls, maybe just a few inches, but the floor gives out from under us and we drop and at least one person screams. Not me. We hold our breath. We feel like we're teetering on the edge of something. We feel like we may tip over the cusp

And Yet It Moves

and plummet. Everyone looks to me and then we drop one more time. Again, just a tiny distance, not enough to lose your stomach or knock anyone off their feet, but even a small drop feels momentous in a metal box. Then we are still, the gears stop turning, their teeth still inside each other. Nodes and nodules still clasp, hold us aloft.

I look to the old man, the only person who knows me here, and his hat is pulled down low. He has notched it down so that it is nearly covering his eyes. His face is perfectly calm. He reaches up to pull it down farther and I know he should not, I know something bad will happen if he does. I stand and pull the blanket from my body, I never stand in an elevator full of people, show my full bulk, but I stand and pull off the blanket covering me and drop it to the ground, the dirty, gum-covered ground that has seen thousands of shoes since its last cleaning.

We're tipping, the floor isn't perfectly level. I reach out and it feels like I'm falling forward a little and I snatch the hat from his head before I know what it is that I'm doing. The gears make a screeching sound, as if half are saying sink and half are saying rise, they work against each other, but then there is a little jolt, the floor cranks up and clicks into the right place, and the elevator begins to lift.

He doesn't seem upset at all that I've taken his hat, exposed his gray hair poking up from his head, full of static. "Don't panic," I say to everyone, and no one is panicking. We're moving in the right direction.

The doors open at the top and people shake their heads, wiggle their bodies as if ruffling feathers, as if shimmying water from fur, and they step off, not sure what just happened, glad it wasn't worse. The old man doesn't try to take his hat from me. I don't want him to have it. I put it on my table. He looks at me, holds my gaze, then turns and walks away.

New people walk onto the elevator, into the box, and I try not to show in my face that anything is wrong. Nothing is wrong. Nothing happened. And as we descend, I feel the elevator's motion. I feel how it moves. And I can tell, I can tell now that it's working better than it ever has. It's running perfectly straight, impeccably along its column. No wavering. Any potential kink that used to flare up in the cold, it's gone. The joggle fixed it. Everyone gets off at the bottom and they couldn't feel it, they didn't notice the perfect glide that just brought them underground. No one gets on at the bottom. I wait a few minutes. No one gets on, but I decide to take a trip up anyway. I know exactly how long I have to ascend; I can't say the amount of time, but I feel its length in my body. As soon as we begin to move I stand, and there's no creaking in my hips, my knee doesn't feel like it's going to give out. I move my chair to the middle of the square room and stand on it, reach up, push up a tile in the ceiling, and look to the gears. At first it's like looking up into a sky full of stars and I almost stumble, almost fall wondering if it's gotten dark outside. But then I see the sparkles are just light from my room reflecting off twisted wire cables, thick bent metal, the edges of turning gears. The shaft of light spilling upward shimmers off all that metal as it gently raises me through a tunnel. Gears turn, wind metal, and I lift. And all I can think is, *Glorious.*

I lower the tile, step down from my chair, and my body feels loose, strangely graceful. I move and sit and pick up my blanket and tuck it around my body again, and then the doors open, and I greet the people stepping on with a smile.

Under my table I slowly lift my left heel from the ground, and lower it again. I feel all my joints smoothly shifting, easily working together to change the lines of my body. I feel like a machine that's gotten a tune-up, I feel well oiled.

I decide to eat my present.

And Yet It Moves

I bite a cherry and juice oozes in my mouth but it doesn't drip down my chin. Astounding. I eat with one napkin in my hand, spit the pit in my palm. I push the elevator button with my knuckles to not stain it crimson. People enter and exit the elevator and they don't look at me strangely, doing this messy thing when I'm supposed to be tending to them. They look at me with envy. I offer cherries to everyone who looks at my chewing and smiles. Some decline, but some take a handful, end up with scarlet palms, realize they hadn't thought of that. I look at them and shrug; I don't have extra napkins. And they aren't angry, they look at me and decide it's worth the blotch, that taste. Out-of-season and unbidden, a treat.

I keep eating them. They are the most delicious cherries I have ever eaten. Each one is different—some sweet, some tart, some have a layer of Chardonnay and butter, some taste like garlic inside a date dipped in orange juice, the sugar hint is molasses not honey, and as I swallow one it leaves behind a bit of pepper and sage in my mouth. They are a cornucopia, a banquet.

Last night, I came home and saw what my son had done. He got to the house before I did, used his key to get in, and he realized I planned to make lasagna that night. I had already made the sauce, the dressing for the salad, I had planned to shred the mozzarella and parmesan then assemble the layers of sauce, noodles, and cheese, I planned to cut the veggies and mix them into the spinach, to give my hands something to do in those first hours together. I'd planned ahead so that I could make a meal that would take half an hour to assemble, an hour to bake, I could make the salad then, while it was in the oven, I made the chocolate cake in advance, I planned ahead so most of it was done so it wouldn't take too long, but not all of it, so I would have something to do, and so I could feed my son a wholesome meal. After dessert I had a room I could go into with a door that shut. Leave him with more space than he'd had in a while. He went to my home before I did, he used his key, the key I left him, and he figured this out, and he made the lasagna himself, and he ate three slices of it. He must have remembered how, from watching me. I am glad he enjoyed it. Three big slices. He ate most of the salad, and he included every vegetable I would have except the cucumber. He ate the broccoli and the tomato and the avocado and the carrots but not the cucumber. I don't know what he likes. I bought him beer. I didn't know if he'd had a beer in twelve years; if he had, it would've been illegal, not the same as cracking open a can at the kitchen table. My small, two-person kitchen table. He drank all six and I'm glad. I hope he enjoyed himself. But the cake I made. I'd put it in a box saved from the bakery, to look fancier than it was, the box only had a few marks, one oil stain, the cake I made was dark chocolate with rich icing, and he opened the box but he didn't eat a slice. He dug two fingers through its surface, gouged out two gorges. I guess he licked his fingers. And then he left. He left the key inside and locked the door so when he closed it he couldn't come back in. He can't come back. My son left. He has the one hundred dollars I left for him at the prison, he has the clothes he said he had. I don't know if he has a cell phone. I don't know if my son knows what money is worth now. I don't know if he remembers the subway lines. Some have changed. I don't know where he went. I don't know if he knows how to use the internet. He washed every dish and dried them and put them away, he brushed the crumbs off the table, the small table with just two chairs in my small kitchen, he left the lasagna covered with foil in the refrigerator, the salad in a covered bowl, for me, and the cake box closed with the slashed cake inside.

After I saw I left my house, bought Twinkies, grape soda, and Cheetos at the bodega, and I knew I'd still be hungry if I just ate that so I got a Quarter Pounder and large milkshake and fries at

McDonald's, then I went home and ate. I know the French fries are frozen, I know the meat might be contaminated, I know the milkshake is just syrup and milk and ice, I know grape soda has nothing to do with grapes, the Cheetos left my skin an orange that has nothing to do with cheese, the Twinkies would not spoil if I left them on my shelf for forty years, but I ate it all. I ate all the food I could find that isn't food, I ate until I was full but I knew I hadn't consumed enough nutrients to survive. I was overfed and undernourished but my body has plenty of fuel stored to make up the difference. It was both delicious and awful. I didn't bring lunch with me for this shift because I couldn't decide what to bring. Lasagna is fine when it warms to room temperature, but I didn't want to eat that.

This, these cherries could be a meal.

When my doors part I hear bells. A bell choir is practicing in the lobby of the 168th Street subway station. Synchronized and serious. Half the group gets onto my elevator, half get onto the elevator next to me, so as we descend I can only hear half the song. When we get to the bottom and they step out they are all still playing in time, the two halves come together seamlessly, and even though their backs are turned to me I can tell they are all smiling. This seems to have been the experiment, to see if they could separately keep time well enough in their heads, in a collective half. Turns out, they all agree on the time signature for Canon in D, sensed the time signature within each other, kept it without a conductor, without the entire symphony being together. They knew it in the rhythms of their arms, and each half stayed true. They didn't diverge. They walk away and keep playing, down the stairs and onto the platform I hear the swelling and jangles of their bells, then the train comes, and when the doors close, silence—the silence of footsteps and chatter, people getting off the train and climbing the stairs, no music.

A group of children get on the elevator, only children, all dressed alike, each in the same uniform, they must be on a school trip, and each one of them is holding a small, clear bowl with one goldfish in it. Their teacher must be on the elevator next to us, because in this one there are only children. They are all very grave, or maybe just well behaved, very quiet. No raucousness—they want to get this right, this time away from their teacher. When we arrive at the top each one quietly thanks me.

On the ride down I finish my cherries, and the elevator is empty enough that I feel comfortable licking my fingers clean. No one notices. I haven't touched the elevator with my fingers, just my knuckles, so I don't feel like I'm licking dirt or metal tang. The doors open, the people get off without looking at me, and then the businesslady gets on the elevator and she makes me check my watch. 12:37—more time has passed today than I thought, I'm over halfway done, but I usually only see her go to work, and I didn't see her this morning. It's too early for her to be off work. She must be going to lunch. She looks relaxed. She smiles at me as she walks on, and I don't think she usually does that. As we lift she looks around the uncrowded elevator, then her eyes still. She gazes into the corner. "You're handsome," she says to a man standing by himself. He's not dressed like her, but also not quite as informally as everyone else on the elevator. Slacks and a button-up.

I've never seen her look so confident, so strongly in her skin. She's not meek. But she's not trying, exactly, I don't think, to hit on him; it's like she simply wants to tell him.

"Th-th-th-thank you," he says, then looks to the ground, not in her eyes. Ashamed.

But she just stands there and smiles at him. He's not looking at her, but she keeps looking at him. Really, quite adoringly. Like she's curious.

And Yet It Moves

Finally he looks up. "You're v-v-very pre-pre-pre-pre-pre-pret..."
He takes a deep breath, then says, "beautiful. Y-you're beautiful."

"Thank you," she says, with a look on her face as if to say she
couldn't possibly care less how she looks, it's so irrelevant. Then,
gesturing to her clothes and shrugging, she adds, "I'm off work.
Early. Would you like to go get a cup of coffee? Or a cocktail? A
beer? If it's not too early? And talk? I guess it's nearly lunchtime."
She's not mocking him with that word, talk. She isn't. Somehow I
can just tell. And he can too. I think she's trying to find a way to tell
him that it's okay. That his stammer is okay. That it doesn't bother
her. He can still talk, and she'll listen.

I've never seen a black man blush, but if he could, he would. The
elevator doors open. He looks up from the ground again, and he
smiles at her. "Y-y-y-y-yes, okay. I'd l-l-l-l-like that."

Her smile is so sincere. "I'm glad," she says. "Do you know a
place? I never go out in this neighborhood. I wouldn't know where
to take you. Do you have a place to take me? I'm buying." I don't
think she's looking for a one-night stand. I think something happened to her, and she just wants some company. She's a cause for
suspicion, this woman, but she deserves to be happy, too. She turns
and smiles at me, and I hope I give her the most encouraging, con-
gratulatory smile she's ever seen.

I hope they go to the Dominican seafood joint, the one on the
corner with the amazing fish stew and the strong, fresh margaritas.
Really excellent mofongo. I only went there one time, with James,
when he took me out on a date, must have been at least a year ago
now, but I thought that place was good. Homemade hot sauce.
Seasoned beans and yellow rice. Sweet plantains. I bet that guy,
I bet he knows the place. I bet he takes her. I bet it makes her like
this neighborhood a whole lot more.

A child walks on, holding her mother's hand, maybe getting
picked up from kindergarten. She smiles that childlike grin, like

I'm interesting to her. When she smiles, I see she has tiger teeth, two sharp canines hanging down below the rest, snaggletoothed in a way that would be goofy and charming if it weren't so sinister. They do not make sense in her round, shining face. I wonder if she'll grow into them, if they'll even out when she loses the rest of her baby teeth, gets her adult set. I wonder what she craves, if her appetite is appropriate.

Behind her a teenager with crutches gets onto the elevator; she's not old enough for it to be polio, but something deformed her legs and made her unable to walk without sticks to help her. Bullets? Car crash? We ride down and the elevator is still running the best it ever has. Pushing buttons seems easy today. A kid looks at the girl with crutches and asks, "Doesn't being crippled suck?" A kid from the neighborhood, baggy jeans and tight T-shirt showing muscles he worked hard for. "All those stairs," he adds. He doesn't say it with malice, he seems genuinely inquisitive. She has light hair and light eyes, but she's dressed like all the other girls in the neighborhood, tight jeans, big bling, tight shirt. Her hair is pulled back into the same slick ponytail, light shining off the curve up to the rubber band, light getting lost in the curls that spring out after it. She might be pretty, she might have a nice body, if she weren't crooked.

"Yeah, it does suck," she answers. She pauses for a beat, thinks. "But doesn't something in your life suck?" she asks with a shrug.

He actually thinks about this for a moment. He stands there, and we can all see him turning things over in his mind. He must land on something. "Yeah," he says, nodding slowly. "Hell yeah." And then they smile at each other. The doors part and he gets off first, doesn't wait for her.

I see the glowing Exit sign, lit red above their heads. If I think to notice, I can see the sign every time the doors open at the top, the sign that says "Exit" with an arrow telling them which way to turn,

And Yet It Moves

which direction to walk out of the elevator to get to the stairs that will take them to street level. I exist to help people exit. To protect, exit safely. I've wondered why there are stairs from the lobby to the street, why we don't take them all the way aboveground, save them that last walk. But we need a lobby for people to buy tickets and ask questions. We need a place for the turnstiles so people can swipe their cards, pay to take a ride. Many stations do have lobbies at ground level, but the street here is congested. There is a business above us, at street level. A bank, next to the Dunkin' Donuts. I sip my coffee, cold of course. I do feel badly bringing people up from underground and the doors open and they're still underground. They still have to climb. I never see outside during my shift. A glimpse of the subway platform at the bottom, signs above everyone's heads that say Downtown with an arrow, Uptown to the Bronx with another arrow, a glimpse of the lobby at the top. I don't see the street or light, though it is always daylight during my shift, all year long. Soon it will be dark right before, dark soon after, but it is always light out while I work.

Teenagers get on, and as we sink one asks the other, "What happens if the elevator breaks?"

"We get out and walk back up, I guess."

"Up stairs?"

"How else? I don't know. Hey, lady," he asks me, "if this thing breaks, do we have to take the stairs?"

"No stairs."

"What do you mean?"

"There aren't any. At this stop, no stairs connect underground and above."

The boys don't like the feeling of lowering. "What do we do if the elevator breaks?"

"Take another elevator."

"What do we do if all the elevators break?"

"Walk along the tunnel to One Hundred Eighty-First. There are stairs there."

"Are you serious? We walk, what, thirteen blocks underground in the *subway* tunnel, getting run over by trains and shit, and then walk up? How deep are we?"

"If the emergency was that bad, they wouldn't be running trains. You wouldn't get hit. At One Hundred Eighty-First, we'd be about seventeen stories underground. Here, about the same, though I'm not sure since there aren't stairs. One Hundred Ninety-First is the deepest, twenty stories below ground."

"Holy shit. I hope the elevators never break while I'm on them."

"No shit," the other kid says.

"I've worked here twenty-six years, and they've never broken. Not all of them. At most, two at a time. That's only half. The MTA must think they won't ever all break, to not give us stairs here."

"This is freaking me out. I want to be aboveground."

"Goin' the wrong way," I say. The kids are not impressed. "This station opened in 1906," I say. Still not impressed.

"Now this lady's got me all creeped out," one of the kids says with a shoulder roll as he exits the elevator. Some people—most I'd say—don't want to know of the doom that might await them, the doom they may face, the inevitable doom that will destroy them, the doom they will avoid, the doom that won't raze them but that will seem impossible to endure.

Exit. Exist. I exist to help people exit. But in the event of an emergency, I cannot help them. Would I be the one to lead them through the tunnels? Confident enough to know how to get them out, aboveground? We never ran a drill about it during training. They just told us what to do. We don't ever get reminded. I wonder if my other elevator operators remember there aren't stairs here, only above us, and below us, down at 145th.

And Yet It Moves

The boys exit and don't say thank you. I bring new people aboveground and they don't sigh the sigh of relief I do. I don't like being reminded that every time we arrive up top safely, a bit of luck is involved. At the top of my route there are no people who want to clamber on, but there is a bird, a pigeon, waiting patiently. He, or she, walks in between the parted doors, taking tiny steps. The doors do not catch its tail feathers between them. I push the button, we descend, and the bird circles around himself, I decide he, in these little jabbing steps so that he faces the doors again. He waits, doesn't look at me. When the doors open, he walks between them, then soars away, over the heads of the people standing on the platform, out of my sight.

A flight of stairs. A flight of birds. A flight of butterflies. A flight of wine. A flight of fancy.

Some groups are herds, some swarms, some are called a pride or a pod or a caravan or a gaggle or a flight—when on the wing. But each group of birds has its own name, too. A murder of crows. An unkindness, or a storytelling, of ravens. A muster, an ostentation of peacocks. A charm of finches. A bellowing of bullfinches. A wake of buzzards. A gulp of cormorants. A piteousness of turtledoves. An aerie of eagles. A flamboyance of flamingos. An implausibility of gnus. A kettle of flying hawks, a boil of spiraling hawks. A scold of jays. A pandemonium of parrots. A murmuration of starlings. A watch of nightingales. A parliament of owls. An exaltation of larks.

And there are others. A romp of otters. A scurry of squirrels. A gaze of raccoons. A prickle of porcupines. A crash of rhinoceroses. A shrewdness of apes. A business of ferrets. A wisdom of wombats. An obstinacy of buffalo. A zeal of zebras. A glorying of cats, or a nuisance of cats; an intrigue of kittens. A tower of giraffes. A congregation of alligators, a bask of crocodiles. A rhumba of rattlesnakes, a quiver of cobras. A hover of trout. A fever of stingrays.

A shiver of sharks. A smack of jellyfish. A troubling of goldfish. A fry of eels. A cloud of bats. A plague of locusts, always called a plague, whatever size the group.

A book from Sebastian's childhood, with pictures. He loved the names, the group names of animals. I remember so many of them.

I haven't forgotten everything. There are things I still recall. Can call back.

This, this life alone, in my head, it's not so bad.

I haven't had to rely on the regular markers of time today, the regular passers of time, the things I rely on to get me through— first this, then wait, let the anticipation build, then this—I haven't had to pull out my papers, read about cops accused of rape and excessive force, haven't had to look at the pictures from the latest red carpet event, haven't had to see how badly the Mets are blowing it right now, haven't had to hear the latest politician's latest insult. But I have a Mensa quiz I didn't take yesterday because I was too nervous, someone brought it to me last week, and that seems like a satisfying way to pass the rest of this time. Today has offered me so much more than my regular entertainment, and yet there is still this to look forward to, this bonus. I open my magazine.

1. What three-letter word can be placed in front of the following words to make new words?
   SIGN, DONE, DUCT, FOUND, FIRM, TRACT, DENSE
2. What is the following word, when it's unscrambled?
   H C P R A A T E U
3. What number is missing from the following sequence?
   1 8 27 ? 125 216
4. Only one other word can be made from all the letters of INSATIABLE. Can you find it?
5. Four years ago, Jane was twice as old as Sam. Four years from now, Sam will be ¾ of Jane's age. How old is Jane now?

And Yet It Moves

I spend half an hour or so on it. Most come to me almost right away. Some take skipping, then scratching possible answers all over the glossy page, then coming back to it. But this test, this one is easy today.

CON. CONSIGN, CONDONE, CONDUCT, CONFOUND, CONFIRM, CONTRACT, CONDENSE.

PARACHUTE

$4^3 = 64$.

BANALITIES.

$J - 4 = 2(S - 4)$. $4 + S = \frac{3}{4}(J + 4)$. $J - 4 = 2S - 8$. $4 + S = \frac{3}{4}J + 3$. $J = 2S - 4$. $4 + S = \frac{3}{4}(2S - 4) + 3$. $4 + S = \frac{6}{4}S - 3 + 3$. $4 + S = \frac{6}{4}S$. $4 + \frac{2}{2}S = \frac{3}{2}S$. $4 = \frac{1}{2}S$. $S = 8$. $J - 4 = 2(8 - 4)$. $J - 4 = 8$. $J = 12$. Right now, Jane is twelve, and Sam is eight.

I answer them all. I check the back of the magazine, and I get them all right.

That felt too easy. Maybe it's because there were no multiple-part questions? Those are the ones I usually think are hard. I just got my first perfect score on a Mensa quiz. Internally, I exclaim. I don't tell anyone.

Splendor. Marvel. Grandeur. Glory. Magnificence. Today, my space is charmed.

Is this the kind of stuff that would help me be a student again? Find a job to do next, after this one? Find out what to do with myself? I don't think these are the kinds of things I need to know. But still. The pleasure in figuring things out.

Only twenty-three more minutes until the shift is over. I wasn't restless today. The time went well today.

But I don't yet want to go home, with so many hours before sleep. Strangers get on and off this elevator, enter and leave this box, hundreds of times a day, and yet it feels safer than my own home. My home is my nest. One violation. I can decide who to invite in, who not to. I will go back. It is safe. But not yet.

Dan arrives to work the shift after me. He always brings me the end-of-shift paperwork, because he's thoughtful like that. I tell him about the jolt. I tell him it feels fine now, to me, I'm sure, I'm not worried about the elevator, but I thought he should know. I fixed it. Or, at least, it is finally fixed. I don't say this. He looks worried. I step out of the elevator and fill out the incident report, writing sentences on forms clipped to a board. Paperwork is not the kind of puzzle I enjoy—it seems there is only one way to answer every question, but that is not true—but I understand its necessity. I walk my forms to the booth, you only have to bring them over if there's something to report, so now everyone knows something happened on my watch. But not my fault. They'll probably have someone check the cables just in case. I walk back to the elevator and when the doors open Dan is surprised to see me. I say I'll ride down with him. I took the subway last week, again this week—but he doesn't comment.

"It's running real smooth," he says as we descend. "It seems fine," he tells me. I agree with him. I say I think it's better than ever.

This ride, when I am not responsible for it, when I'm not the one making it happen, feels so swift. But I still feel the even way the elevator is sliding down its column, I still feel in my spine the way it isn't faltering, the gears perfectly synchronized, turning to lower us, releasing the wire like a rope, stringing our box down a tube burrowed into the ground.

Dan has his own blanket today so I don't offer him mine. I step off carrying it, not folded, just bunched in my arms, the old man's red hat clutched in my fist.

As I step into the cavern I remember how beautiful and bizarre it is. Lit with old streetlights like the ones that must have been aboveground decades ago, white globes on wrought-iron posts. They aren't gaslights, they couldn't be down here, but they emit that eerie glow, bluish green, so the air is faintly tinted the shade of

And Yet It Moves

young grapes. The air makes it seem as if gas escaped from them, thickening the air so it's tinted, tinged. If that were the case then the air could light, burn. That must be why I always feel nostalgic in this station for a time I've never seen—and on edge, wanting the train to come before the whole dome combusts.

Mercury vapor lamps. I have no idea what that means, but that's what they're called. I don't know if mercury is volatile. Mercurial. Maybe the place won't flare into flame, but will transform. No. It always stays the same. Since 1906. Just filthier.

This is the biggest subway station I've ever seen, a gigantic room underground, a huge tube with an arched, vaulted ceiling, as if the trains that pass through here are five times their normal size. They say train stations are like this in Paris. And all of it tiled. Tiled walls, white that used to be shiny with the number of the stop every few feet, and on top a border, a mosaic of tiny tiles drawing a tangled design, where lines twist and intersect. Men on ladders had to smear on mortar, lay in each square. I wonder how many dropped and shattered before they adhered. This place looks like it could have once been a grand train station, where people in fancy clothes waited for a train to take them to exotic places. Now, the tiles are more gray than white, chipped, pieces of the mosaic missing. Thick brown sludge runs down the walls in some places, stalactites hang off some of the overhangs. I don't know what it is. The grime of the place turns that pure green light spooky, so dim the shadows seem slick. Dilapidated. That's what this place is. And if it were the stop for the Met, or even just along the park, it wouldn't be so run-down. It would be scrubbed, and it would still look grand.

Pigeons live down here, dozens of them. Only a few must have come down from the outside, like the one I gave a ride to today, and the rest must have been born down here. There's no way so many rode down on elevators. Maybe some of them have never seen sunlight, only know colors tinged by this aerated green. They swoop and roost and have their nests under the bridge that crosses the tracks, the bridge we walk across from the elevator if we want to go downtown. They must live off the food scraps people leave down here. Maybe they hunt rats. Would a pigeon eat a roach?

There is a man sleeping on the bench, and he may live down here too. He is filthier than the walls or the ground. Paper bags lie slightly crumpled below him, filled with remains of food or bottles or syringes or books. I cover him with the blanket in my hands, the blanket I no longer want to carry, and put the hat near him on his bench. It feels good to release those things.

I hope that someone is helping to care for Sebastian. I feel I will never see him again. Wonders may happen to him. Or calamities. I hope something presents itself to him out here, something that makes it possible for him to not go back there.

I stand and wait for the train. There is no schedule. One will come soon.

The rush of the arriving train blows wind through the tunnel, rustles newspapers and feathers, makes us feel like we're suddenly outside. A door opens right in front of me, what I've always considered good luck, and I step onto the subway car. I'd like the pigeons to fly alongside the train, companion us along the tunnels.

All the people who ride my elevator are here, in the subway car. That kid in the do-rag; that man in the suit, tie loosened now that it's time for happy hour; that mom with her stroller she's going to have to carry up stairs—she'll wait near the bottom for someone to grab the front end and help her, and someone will, a teenager or a businessman or a mom whose kids are grown. All the people that step into my box, all these people that I watch, all the people I see in slices, they're all here in front of me in this space. Here I can see all of their faces I want, and here, I don't know when they will exit.

And Yet It Moves

A kid with blue streaks in his hair steps through the doors, a few pieces of metal in his face, I don't see them all before he turns and starts studying the map framed on the wall. He looks at it for a while, then looks around. He sees me and walks over and I'm so startled—why would he want to talk to me?—until I realize I have on my uniform.

"Can you tell me the best way to the Bowery?"

He has such an interesting face to look at. He's wearing eyeliner, and it does the same thing it does to women who wear it, it makes his eyes huge and spooky and magnificent. And metal slid through his eyebrow, his lip, his nose, many loops in his ears.

"I'm sorry," I say. "I actually work in an elevator. On One Hundred Sixty-Eighth Street. Near my house. I don't know the system very well. I'm sorry."

"That's okay," he says, and smiles. He seems like a sweet kid. He seems like he may sit near me for a minute, then the businessman says, "You going to a show at the Ballroom?"

"Yeah. Thought I'd go early, wander around."

"The J, M, or Z lines get you right there, but you can't really get to those trains from this one. Take this to Fourteenth Street, walk underground to the L, take it over to Union Square, get the Six Downtown. Take it to Spring Street. If you walk east you'll run into Bowery, and the Ballroom is a few blocks down. Four stops or so on the Six."

"Thanks," the kid says, making a face like he's trying to memorize that, then nodding. He tucks his headphones into his ears and walks to the other end of the car.

I'm not certain what I'm doing here.

My station used to be for the 1 and the 9 trains, now the 9 doesn't exist anymore. Black stickers were placed over the signs where it said "9" in a red circle, so they wouldn't have to replace the entire sign. I don't have this web memorized. I didn't pay for this subway ride. When I walk into my station the attendant in the booth buzzes me through. At the end I usually walk home. People who ride to their station from other places, do they have to pay at their booth, swipe their card, or can anyone in a uniform get buzzed through the gates, never have to pay at a turnstile? I don't remember if I used to pay to go to Queens.

This station we just pulled into is a bright beyond fluorescent, or it just seems so after the dark of the tunnels. I get out, stay at the same track, wait for the next train going the same direction, which is probably a different kind of train, a different color, this seems like the kind of stop where lots of different kinds of trains pass through, and I step onto it. This one will at some point diverge from the path the other train was on, they make a few stops the same, but then they each have their own tunnel, they each have a different end of the line, this one will take me somewhere else.

It's nice that it's now almost night. The train isn't crowded. I can take up two seats without embarrassment. Lots of people are taking up two seats, their things next to them, their bag resting to their right or left.

Several stops later the station looks particularly dim and dismal, so I get out, walk to another track, just as gloomy, catch whatever train going whatever direction, step onto the train that comes first. I don't count the stops. I ride for a while. None of the stations are lovely here. I must be on the edges of the city, they wouldn't let their stations look this eerie in Midtown. Some people get mosaics, others get unpainted columns, chipped walls. After letting these trains lead me along the tracks of a map I don't own, moving me horizontally after a vertical day, this box with many entrances, many exits, after riding for I don't know how long, I don't know where I am. I look up, I look into the dark tunnels, I know people live in some of them.

And Yet It Moves

I need a map, and this station doesn't have one posted. Dim, dingy, the walls are tiled but the columns running along the platform aren't, are painted red. I climb steps to get to their lobby, it makes me pant and heave a bit, so I catch my breath at the top before I go to ask someone in the booth for a map. I won't ask for directions. I can figure it out. There must be a sign somewhere telling me which stop this is. I would feel funny asking. Letting show that I don't even know what borough I'm in.

There's a person behind glass in the station, a person in a booth, and I don't really want to go ask for help wearing my uniform, I feel foolish. I consider walking into the street, hailing a taxi. I have enough money in my bank account to take a taxi. Even if it cost over a hundred dollars, I could pay for it, if they'll take my debit card. I could get a hotel room, eat in a restaurant, deal with it all tomorrow. But I can't imagine telling a taxi driver that I don't know where I am, I can't imagine walking into a hotel lobby, eating in a restaurant alone, in my uniform.

I walk up to the cubicle and with the light behind me I can see my reflection on the glass. I also see the man behind because of the light inside. As I walk closer I get bigger, and when I stop in front of the booth my silhouette engulfs him, my edges extending beyond his. I am over twice his size, and we are dressed the same.

He smiles at me, so wide.

"Can I help you?"

It's so nice when someone offers help, and you don't even have to ask for it.

I did not withhold my help. I offered it.

"Yes, I need a map, please."

"Can I help you get somewhere?"

"Yes. Well, yes, you can. I'm not sure where I am. Actually, I have no idea. After work, I just started riding trains. Changing trains. I didn't want to get lost, exactly. I just, I wanted to do something I never normally do. Today is different from yesterday, so I wanted to signal that. Be brave." I feel ridiculous. Such bravery for me is such normalcy for other people, riding trains. How to explain? The freedom of releasing an obligation. He released me. I didn't have to be the one to do it. "I'm not sure how I got here. I'm not sure which line this is, even."

"Are you wanting to go home now?"

"Yes. I'm hungry."

"Come in and have a snack, and I will show you how."

"I shouldn't come in there. I'm not official."

"You are an employee! Please, come inside."

He isn't fat or thin, tall or short. Not too dark or too light. He looks so normal. What would it be like to move through the world like that, like no one in particular?

He opens the side door to the booth, and I step inside. There's not really enough room for both of us, I bump him a little as he reaches around me to close the door, but I don't feel claustrophobic. We aren't shoved inside or squished. It's just a little close.

"Here," he says, and hands me an orange. "This is not from this place, but maybe you will like it. I think they are good. They are from where I am from. My daughter, she came to me this afternoon. She lives at home, my country. I send her money. She came to visit America for the first time, and she brought me oranges."

When I peel it, the mist seems to fill the entire booth, the scent of groves and white flowers and sunlight. I almost feel I have eaten, being so ensnared in a scent. As I peel, he opens a map. There is no counter space, so he unfolds it and presses it against the glass. He spreads the map to show me, and covers the window. Someone outside could need his assistance, and he wouldn't know. If someone comes to the window now, we will not see. He's helping me. I bite a wedge and the skin is thin, unlike the oranges we get at the

And Yet It Moves

stores in my neighborhood, where the covering of each sliver is so thick and dry it's nearly inedible. The skin disappears when I bite a chunk into my mouth, and all I taste is chewable juice, flavor so rich it has thickness, a texture I can grind between my teeth. It's both sour and sweet, both sugary and sharp. I have been given such treasures today.

He says I'm in Brooklyn. In another borough. On a different island.

"How did I get here?" I ask. "We didn't cross a bridge."

"Most trains go underwater." He points to the map, all the colors crossing blue. "These are all tunnels," he says. They're drawn like they go over the river, but they go under. He then shows me his stop. "You're almost at the end of the line," he says. "Newkirk Avenue. The next one down, the last, is Flatbush Avenue/Brooklyn College." I touch the map. The lines in the place where I am are red and green. Close to us are yellow and orange lines. Then over some more, orange and a different green. Then more orange. Then more yellow. Lines spread out, touching all the parts of Brooklyn. The lines gather together higher on the map, then spread out again. There is no blue line down here, but there is blue above us, and brown, and gray. And purple. Along a line near to us, but not this line, there are evenly spaced stops, Avenue H, Avenue J, then Avenue M. I run through the alphabet in my head, ask, "Is there an Avenue I? K? L? A? B? C?"

"All the letters, H through Z, except Avenue Q is Quentin. All the letters, but it starts at H. So no ABCDEFG." There are a few white lines on the map, the most important roads are drawn in, but the map doesn't show the complete grid above our heads. I think I would like to see it. "Can I take a bus?" I ask. I would like to look out a window while being driven down streets, not tunnels, seeing with my eyes all that this map portrays as ribbons.

He thinks for a minute. "No. I am sorry. Sometimes, the subway is better. Sometimes, a bus. Here." He points at the map, at the tangle of lines above the tangle of lines that represents where we stand. "If you want to go from this part of Brooklyn, to our part"—he points to two parts not very far from each other—"by subway you have to go all the way into Manhattan, change trains, come all the way back out again. A bus, it is much better. But for you, no. Buses don't like to cross bridges. You will have to go back under the water."

"Okay," I say. I want to gather all the colored threads in my hand, pull them together, change their shape underground, hold them.

"This is how you go home," he says. He traces the route on the map with a pen as he speaks, drawing up the wall of glass, leaving a line over a line, evidence of his instruction. He uses a pink highlighter. None of the subway lines are pink. He must do this on purpose. "You will take the Five, this train, all the way to Grand Central Station. The Five is express, so it will skip all these stops," he says as he draws over them. "The stop right before yours will be Wall Street. Watch for it, to warn you it is almost time to get off the train." He goes back and circles Wall Street. He puts two circles around Grand Central Station. "You get off here. Then you will take the S to Times Square. The S goes back and forth between the two stations, so get on the train with open doors, and it will go the right direction. At Times Square, you will follow signs to the One Uptown. There are lots of trains at that station, so there are lots of signs. If the signs are confusing, you can ask someone for help, even if they aren't an employee." He is telling me directions the way I would tell them to myself. He draws a line all the way up to 168th Street, circles that stop, and puts a star by it. "And then you know where you are, yes?" he asks.

"Yes," I say. "I know how to get home on my own from there."

And Yet It Moves

He traces the entire line again with his finger, runs his fingertip over the pink line that starts where we are and travels to where I live. "Does this make sense?" he asks me.

"Yes," I say. I run my fingertip over the paper, tracing the route after him. "It does."

"Good," he says. "I am glad. It will take you about an hour to get home. Maybe more. Sometimes you will have to wait a long time for a train. But one will come. Do you need more food, to last you?"

"No. Thank you. The orange was delicious. And I have a good meal at home I can heat up, a filling meal. Pasta, homemade lasagna."

"Good," he says. Then, "There is one more thing." He taps his stop, the place where we are. "You want the Five train going the other direction. Toward Manhattan. Not deeper into Brooklyn, like the trains that drive on this track go. There are no crossovers here. We are one of few stations where you cannot get to one track from the other underground, you can only get to each from aboveground. It's why they have me here, to help people figure that out. You will have to walk up the stairs, leave the station, cross the street, and enter into the other station. You will have to pay another fare at a turnstile."

Getting here, by accident, was easy. Getting home, on purpose, is going to be hard.

A loudness cracks through the air. I startle, my hands jumping off the surface of the map. Another rap on glass, and I worry the window may shatter. The man sighs, lifts the map from the pane and folds it the way it was first folded, revealing an impatient gentleman standing on the other side. He checks his watch to signal his annoyance. The man next to me says into the microphone, "One moment please." He turns to me. "You will be okay now?" The man outside mutters something about there being two of us, one should be able to help him.

I feel a bit rushed. I think I understand. I nod, say, "I'm fine. I know how to get home now. Thank you."

He hands me the perfectly folded map and says, "There is no way for you to see the whole route without unfolding the whole map. Unfold it anytime you need to check. You do not have to memorize it."

I thank him again. My fingers are sticky. He opens the door to his booth and points to the stairs with a smile. I step out, then he closes it and leans in to the microphone, speaks. I cannot hear what he says, what the other man answers. I have no idea what the young man needs or wants.

My hands smell like oranges. It looks like I have two flights of stairs to climb. I will go up, then I will come down. I will see for just a few moments what the map shows. As I step up, my body feels heavy, but not too heavy for me to lift.

And Yet It Moves

Credits

Some of these stories have been previously published in the following literary journals and anthologies, sometimes with slightly different titles or content:

"Gravity," *Kenyon Review Online*; "In the Heart of the Heart of the Empire," *The Kenyon Review*; "With Strangers," H_NGM_N; "Ghost Writer," *The Tusculum Review*; "Ochre Is the Color of Deserts and Dried Blood," *Menacing Hedge*; "Brightest Corners," *The Sun*; "Why Things Fall: Newton," *[PANK]* and *Novembre* (Switzerland); "Why Things Fall: Einstein," *Hobart* and *The Narrow Chimney Reader: Volume 1*; and "Why Things Fall: Galileo, Hawking, Rabinowitz," *The Massachusetts Review*.

Book Club Guide

1. What threads do you see weaving through these stories, tying them together? What's being explored in this book?

2. The author says that the stories in this collection seek to examine both figurative and literal gravity, the ways in which our bodies and minds can be weighted and freed. How do you see that idea recurring, and varying, throughout the book?

3. Nearly every character in the collection has a unique profession: postcolonial theorist, hired mourner, prostitute, ghostwriter for suicide notes, ex-priest, chemist, phlebotomist, physicist, elevator operator. Which jobs were most interesting to you and why?

4. Physics and metaphysics interlace throughout the collection. How do you see the spiritual and the scientific intertwining? Are the two systems of thought ever at odds with each other?

5. These stories range from nonnarrative realism to narrative irrealism, and include science fiction, fairy tales, retold histories, monologues, mosaics, and stories that borrow the form of letters and anonymous internet entries, as well as stories that are gothic, absurdist, and magical. Many inhabit the space between reality and unreality, and explore things that aren't impossible, but that don't happen in current US

culture: keening, sky burial, ghostwriting suicide notes, etc. How do the less realistic stories comment on reality? Critique it? Does straddling realism and irrealism, and moving between narrative and nonnarrative modes, test your ability to believe these stories, or stretch it?

6. If you could ask one of the characters a question, what would you ask her or him?

7. Characters often seek to aid other characters, but usually through complicated means. How do people help and hurt each other in these stories?

8. Many actual people are given voice in the book, but Stalcup alters their realities: Albert Einstein writes to a daughter that did exist, but that history has no record of after two years old; Isaac Newton runs away to join the circus; Stephen Hawking drinks beer in a bar; Galileo Galilei receives a katsina from the US Southwest, and admits in his journals (which don't exist) that he did in fact tell the Inquisition that the earth does move. Yet Nikola Tesla's character only says things that are true. How do you respond to this version of historical fiction, which privileges fiction over fact, yet is rooted in truth?

9. The historical physicists Stalcup portrays are all male, but she ends the collection with two invented female perspectives: MIT PhD student in physics Elizabeth Rabinowitz, who is trying to find the Theory of Everything; and Cerise, a woman who didn't graduate high school and now operates an elevator in Washington Heights. What do these perspectives add to the collection?

10. Stories aren't essays, but some of these stories are essayistic. Are any of these stories making arguments?

11. If you know the story by William H. Gass "In the Heart of the Heart of the Country," how is Stalcup responding to, updating, or altering it in her story "In the Heart of the Heart of the Empire"?

12. What do you notice about the structure of the collection as a whole, and how readers move from story to story? The author thinks of the movement as a repeating structure: science fiction ("Gravity"), mosaic tribute to New York City ("In the Heart of the Heart of the Empire"), then a tetraptych investigating work, as well as helping, hurting, and healing ("Keen," "With Strangers," "Ghost Writer," and "Not Long for this World"); then the pattern duplicates, almost: a fairy tale ("Ochre Is the Color of Deserts and Dried Blood"), a mosaic tribute to New York City ("Brightest Corners"), then a tetraptych investigating science and faith, history and fiction (the four "Why Things Fall" stories); then the collection ends with a new form, a novella. These stories weren't written to conform to this pattern, but after they all had been written, they were arranged in this design. Does thinking about the formal echoes in the collection (beyond the content echoes throughout) change your reading of the stories?

And Yet It Moves is **Erin Stalcup's** debut story collection. Her fiction has appeared in *The Kenyon Review, Kenyon Review Online, The Sun,* H_NGM_N, *Hobart,* [PANK], and elsewhere. Erin studied English and physics at Northern Arizona University, where she joined the faculty after spending nearly a decade teaching in a community college, a large state university, a small liberal arts school, a religious institution, and prisons in New York City, North Carolina, and Texas. Erin holds an MFA from Warren Wilson College's Program for Writers, and she co-founded and co-edits the literary magazine *Waxwing* (http://www.waxwingmag.org). Erin is currently working on a pre-apocalyptic novel and a hybrid memoir that combines her teaching experiences with an investigation into the current state of higher education. She is married to the writer Justin Bigos and lives with him and her daughter, Thalia Estelle, in her hometown of Flagstaff, Arizona.